## TOO CLOSE FOR COMFORT

Jerry grabbed Cat's arm and spun her around. "Hey, one lousy drink won't kill you."

"Call me tomorrow," she said.

"Hey, I saw how you took down that guy in there, so don't play genteel widow. S'anything I can spot, it's a gal likes to play rough. Well, I can do rough, too."

"Play the perfect murder and do dead."

She hadn't meant it. Not literally. But the resounding crack came right on cue and Cat was thrown to the ground, her head striking the Maxima's rear bumper, then asphalt. Jerry's weight bore down on her. She rose unsteadily.

One eye, gun-metal blue, stared back at her, the other jutted over his cheekbone. A wet blackness crept from beneath the matted hair, one slick tendril snaked toward her right pump.

"It's not a game, it's real," she gasped aloud, and fell on top of him, face forward, unconscious.

# DEATH OF A DJ

A  MYSTERY  BY

**JANE RUBINO**

Harper Paperbacks
*A Division of HarperCollinsPublishers*

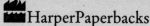
# HarperPaperbacks
*A Division of* HarperCollins*Publishers*
10 East 53rd Street, New York, N.Y. 10022-5299

This is a work of fiction. The characters, incidents, and dialogues are products of the author's imagination and are not to be construed as real. Any resemblance to actual events or persons, living or dead, is entirely coincidental.

Copyright © 1994 by Jane Rubino
All rights reserved. No part of this book may be used or reproduced in any manner whatsoever without written permission of the publisher, except in the case of brief quotations embodied in critical articles and reviews. For information address Write Way Publishing, 3806 S. Fraser, Aurora, CO. 80014.

A hardcover edition of this book was published in 1994 by Write Way Publishing.

ISBN 0-06-104433-4

HarperCollins®, ®, and HarperPaperbacks™ are trademarks of HarperCollins*Publishers*, Inc.

Cover illustration by Alexander Domek

First HarperPaperbacks printing: February 1997

Printed in the United States of America

Visit HarperPaperbacks on the World Wide Web at
http://www.harpercollins.com/paperbacks

10 9 8 7 6 5 4 3 2 1

"Birth and good manners are essential; but a little learning is by no means a dangerous thing in good company"—Jane Austen, *Persuasion*

For my company:
Bill
Bronwyn
Caitlen
Nicholas

# PROLOGUE

The gun had looked so real.

Cat, mentally chiding herself for the inept interview, had been asking Tom if she could give him a ring later in the week, flesh out the cursory bio sheets the station had given her. The door whacked the Red Hot Chili Peppers poster on the back wall and Jerry sprang across the threshold, revolver in hand. Cat saw only the blue band of fluorescent light reflected along the barrel, like a lethal beam aimed at her heart. Her pulse lurched and she thought: Chris.

"Hey, what'd you think, it's real?" Jerry fired off a few caps, laughed when Cat flinched. She wouldn't even let Mats have toy guns now. "They just videoed the promo, me like this—" he aimed the barrel at his temple. "—for the new promotional gigs. We're callin' it 'The Perfect Murder'."

Cat exhaled, considered jabbing the 'record' button on her tape recorder. " 'Is that anything like 'Dead or Alive'?" 'Dead or Alive' was a popular radio call-in game. The caller had to guess whether the celebrity named by the host was indeed alive or dead. The Six

A.M. Circus version targeted those known to be endstage, cancer or AIDS.

"Nah, everybody's doin' 'Dead or Alive' now, takes the fun out of it. This isn't over the air, anyway; it's a new way of handlin' the promotional stuff." Jerry twirled the toy gun on his index finger. "You know, we do an hour at a car dealership, over at the mall? So now, instead of shakin' hands, I'm layin' there dead, see? Makeup guy upstairs at NewsLineNinety'll do the fake blood. People come in, I'm a corpse, they get clues, they gotta guess whodunit. Get it? First one guesses right, they get a mug or something."

Cat assembled her wits. "So you're slated for some PR at the local deli. I walk in for lunch and the first thing I lay eyes on is your bloody corpse sprawled across the Congoleum, is that right?"

"Is that great or what?"

"Like one of those mystery weekend things?"

"But a lot sicker!" Jerry gloated.

"And I have to guess who wanted to kill you?"

"You got it."

"I should think it would be easier to guess who didn't."

Jerry cackled. "That's what makes it so great! Everyone I put it to on the air's gonna wanna come out to see me whacked!"

Cat did not dispute it.

"S'why we're not lettin' Tommy here play the vic. Nobody'd buy it, but there's gotta be, what, thousands out there wanna see me dead, right?"

"At least," Cat concurred, politely. Many days later, she would wish she had switched on her tape recorder.

Tom gave her a nudge. "My idea, incidentally."

"I hope it catches on with the public."

And Tom had replied, "Everybody loves a mystery."

# **CHAPTER**

## O N E

"**M**om! Come look!"

Cat Austen snapped a thin gold bangle onto her wrist below her Bulova, punched the tape recorder's PLAY button.

("Where would you like to start?") Her voice, shaky.

("Whatever's good for you, babe.") He had smelled inexperience, meant to give Cat a hard time.

Babe, Cat mouthed, then pursed away the frown as she applied lipstick. Carlo and Vinnie still called her that sometimes, but without Jerry Dudek's obscene inflection. Damn it! She had told Ritchie Landis: films, plays, concerts, casino reviews, the occasional club opening, but absolutely no interviews. They were not her forte. Ritchie had accepted her terms and lined up Ron Spivak for the Tom and Jerry profile, but when Spivak had lost his nose, the assignment reverted to Cat. "You're my entertainment girl," Ritchie had whined. "A couple dumb deejays, how rough can it be?"

"Entertainment *writer*," Cat had corrected, made him repeat it before she consented. Tonight she was inclined to believe she had let Ritchie off too easily.

"Mommmmm!" Jane. Jane Austen.

Cat's principles favored the retention of one's surname after marriage, but the oppressive fame of her father, and her six brothers had so defined her as someone's daughter, someone's sister, that she was not reluctant to resign "Fortunati" for "Austen." And when her firstborn was a girl, how could Cat—who had read *Pride and Prejudice* two hundred twenty-six times between the ages of twelve and thirty-seven—resist? Nine-year-old Jane Cassandra Austen did not appreciate the distinction. The Popular Girls had names like Ashley or Marla or Jillian; had pierced ears, fathers.

(Cat: "You two paired up in Baltimore, right?")

(Jerry: "I'm gettin' deejay vous here.")

(Cat: "I know you may have covered some of this with Ron Spivak, but I haven't touched base with him yet and your bio sheets are somewhat cursory.")

(Tom: "Spivak?")

(Jerry: "No-nose. I talked to him a while back. Let's just say I'm the Jersey Devil.")

A muted shriek and Tom's muffled "Cut it out." Cat frowned at her reflection, recalled how Jerry had actually made a grab for her, tried to bite her neck.

Cat Austen was the youngest of seven, the lone daughter. A gene pool that had discharged one Y chromosome after another had begun to show signs of diminishing enthusiasm, for there was a decided reduction in height and breadth as Cat's brothers descended from Carlo to Alfredo (Freddy). A lover's moon and a bottle of Capo Bianco had foiled the established six-month *intermezzi* between childbirth and the resumption of marital relations. Disoriented gonads, lured into play mere weeks after Alfredo's arrival yielded at last the long-sequestered X chromosome and Cat had been born ten months after Freddy.

Cat surveyed the black leather skirt, the pale beaded sweater, skeptically. Both had been Ellice's idea and Ellice had prevailed, though Cat had protested they were too dressy for CV's, too much for a routine interview, and she would be—here she had caught Jane's eye and converted a 'damned' to a 'darned'—be darned if she was going to try to impress Tom Hopper, Jerry Dudek and that crowd at the club.

(Jerry: "What about you, Tommy, you think the fans wanna know where we came from? How far back you wanna go, babe?")

(Tom: "I didn't know this was such an in-depth piece.")

(Cat: "Just maybe some college, what you did before you two got together.") Amateur, Cat accused her reflection.

(Jerry: "Tommy here's Ivy League. Me, I'm a student of what makes people tick.")

(Cat: "Or ticks them off.")

(Jerry: "Yeah. I like that. Can I use it on the air? Maybe you an' I oughta do it over lunch sometime—")

Cat punched the OFF button. "Creep." She swept her chestnut hair against the nape of her neck, clipped it in place with a mother-of-pearl barrette. "When this is over," she informed her reflection, "I'm telling Ritchie no more interviews, *finale.*"

Cat descended the L-shaped staircase, followed TV noise to the den. Ellice was sitting on the couch with Jane on one knee, little Mats (Matthew Christopher) on the other. "There, *there!*" she pointed at the screen. Cat got a glimpse of Jerry Dudek in the parking lot outside KRZI/*NewsLine*90. ". . . to see if you can solve *the perfect murder,*" he smirked, then raised a toy revolver to his temple, fired, dropped to the ground.

Cat flinched.

"That," Ellice fired off an imaginary shot with her index finger, "is one butt-ugly white man."

"You *missed* it," Jane wailed. "You were on TV!"

Ellice grinned. "The first part of the promo, we caught you and that other guy, Tom, at the front window. They must have taped it the day you did the first interview."

"Oh God, and I was wearing my brown checked skirt, the one that puts my hips out to *here!*"

"Don't say 'God,' " Mats counseled, solemnly. "Uncle Dominic says it's a bad word."

"Next time, wear your brown checkered blouse," Ellice advised.

Cat made a face. "This one's not too short, is it?"

"The skirt? It's fine, honey. That slezoid Dudek won't be able to keep his hands off."

"I gotta go change."

"You gotta go to work." Ellice grabbed Cat by the shoulders, spun her around and gave her a gentle shove.

"Well, I won't be late. You're sure you and Freddy didn't have plans, I could always—"

"Could not."

"Well, don't let them con you into staying up. Nine-thirty," Cat reminded her daughter, firmly.

"But we don't have *school* tomorrow," pleaded Jane. "It's *teacher's* conference." The annual state conference was held in Atlantic City every November.

"Nine-thirty." Cat could italicize, too. She dumped wallet, comb, lipstick, notebook, pens into the black leather attaché Chris had given her five Christmases ago.

"No tape recorder?" An inner door of smoky leaded glass enclosed the tiled foyer. Ellice yanked hard; sea air had expanded the wood, gnawed at the brass fittings.

Cat checked her hair in the foyer's oval mirror. "I can't tape over the music in that place. Go back in, I'll lock the front door." She kissed the children, flipped on the porch light, hit the lock and descended the wide, wooden stairs to the sidewalk.

The house had been a bequest from her beloved Aunt Cat. It was a typical seashore home, ground floor apartment boosting two stories of house above the dune line, ocean views on the east side that were only slightly abridged by the Ufflanders' corner property. Beyond the Ufflanders', Morningside Road curved and merged with Beach Road, which was bordered on the beach side by six-foot dunes, parking meters planted at ten-foot intervals.

The apartment was vacant. Cat and Chris had toyed with the idea of fixing it up and renting it out for the summer months. Cat had even composed the ad in her mind: "Ocean City 2BR, 1 1/2 ba. apt., separate din. area, w/d, cable, steps to good beach." Decent summer rentals in Ocean City (which was both barrier island and municipality) commanded $1,500 per week in mid-summer, maybe $12,000 for the season. Then Chris had been killed and Cat let the matter drop. Not even the town's most aggressive realtors could persuade her to revive it.

Cat backed her blue Maxima out of the concrete drive and headed northward. Atlantic City was on Absecon Island. From Ocean City's northern tip, its neon was visible, though the network of drawbridges and causeways that linked island to island exaggerated the eight-mile distance between.

Cat had been born in Atlantic City, raised there. That Atlantic City was myth and memory. Landmarks had decayed beyond recognition or been swallowed by casino development. Cat lost her bearings and nearly missed Bel-Ave Parking on the corner of Belmont and Pacific. She hammered the brake, veered right, provoking an obscenity from the jitney driver on her tail, and slammed to a halt in front of the lot attendant's shed.

The attendant shuffled out, took Cat's five dollars, shoved a parking stub under her windshield wiper. "Pull it up to the boards an' don' back it in, okay?"

A wire fence separated the back of the lot from the five-foot dunes under the Boardwalk. Wind showered sand onto the hood of Cat's car. She locked the door, hopped the chipped stone wall that bordered the Belmont Place side of the lot. Belmont dead-ended at the boards. CV's was right across the street. Music from the club muscled onto the sidewalk: BumbaBUM, badaBOOM-BOOMBOOM, bumbaBUM, badaBOOMBOOMBOOM.

Rap, Cat sighed. Ritchie owes me.

Purple neon pulsated above the entrance. Cat hesitated, peered through the leaded glass door to check whether Jerry was playing Perfect Murder on the lobby carpet. Coast clear, she entered, hung her coat in the unattended coat room. Was she supposed to pay the cover to the girl at the gate or had Ritchie gotten KRZI to comp her? The soles of her pumps vibrated to the gentle litany of "PUMPitup, PUMPitup, PUMPitup, PUMP-ITUP!" (Or, quite possibly, BUMP-, JUMP-, or HUMPitup, Cat reflected and pondered a discreet exit.)

Too late. Tom Hopper charged into the lobby, heading for the pay phone. He saw Cat, stopped short, nudged his glasses into place with the knuckle of his index finger and coaxed his frown into an easygoing smile.

Tom and Jerry. Tom Hopper had been a third string DJ with a minor radio station in Baltimore when Jerry Dudek latched onto him and wouldn't let go. Jerry had come from nowhere and Tom seemed to be headed nowhere, but something clicked. Soon, Jerry talked Tom up to Camden, New Jersey, where they went mike to mike with the early morning competition from Philly. The Arbitrons were inching up when Jerry hustled them off once more, this time to KRZI on the Jersey Shore.

Soon, their *Six A.M. Circus* owned the early morning audience in four counties with each weekday serving up its own special madness along with the Top 40. Mondaymania, callers were challenged to offend a minimum of three minorities with a single joke, which made it hell for the *Newsline90* crews and the clerical people who had to run the gauntlet of picketers from the NAACP and NOW and PETA and the Knights of Columbus. On Target Tuesday, Tom would cold-call the subject of the morning paper's most outrageous news item. ("And just how long does it take to smuggle a live goat up seven flights of stairs?" he inquired of a surprisingly good-natured santero, who had been cited for a certain animal rights transgression. "Two *hours*, man. That goat, he *stubborn*, man.") Wild goose Wednesday was the weekly scavenger hunt, though a lawsuit nearly put an end to it when the owner of a pedigreed black Persian declared that his Inky had been done in by an overzealous participant who needed an I to complement the bat, newt, gull and opossum he'd rounded up playing Roadkill Bingo.

"Didn't think you'd show; I was sure Jerry'd scared you off!" Tom steered Cat toward a round table, pushed up a chair for her. His wire-rimmed glasses gave him a scholarly (Jane would have said "geeky") look that barely camouflaged an uncharacteristic distraction. His curly blond hair was disheveled and his tie—he had actually worn a coat and tie—was unknotted, the shirt open at the neck.

Cat pulled her attaché onto her lap, took out a notebook and pen. "Short of gunfire, I don't scare!" she hollered over the din. "How much of a crowd?"

"This bunch likes it loud!"

"No!" Cat leaned into his ear. "I said, how much of a crowd? How many?"

"Three hundred, maybe more!"

Cat scribbled, scanned the room. The music was boring into her eardrums, the lavender lights ricocheted erratically, playing havoc with her equilibrium. A small stage with a DJ manipulating the recorded music, a microphone link to KRZI, a five gallon fish tank crammed with paper currency. Far to the right, a narrow passage led to the restrooms and CV's oceanfront restaurant.

Cat tugged Tom's sleeve, nodded toward the cash. "What's the deal?"

"Concert tickets! Dinner, limo. Write your name on a twenty. Drawing's in about half an hour. Gonna take a shot?"

Cat shook her head. She caught sight of Jerry on the dance floor. His stringy dark hair flagellated the prominent forehead, the narrow grey-blue eyes were hooded by the bony crown, the fleshy lids. He pursed his lips, air-kissed Cat while he ground his pelvis into the vinyl skirt of a girl who had no hips.

A trim blonde in a dark suit stalked up to Jerry, snatched his arm. Cat squinted, trying to caption the familiar face. The blonde spat a few words into Jerry's ear; he elbowed her aside, continued dancing. She uttered one parting expletive, jabbing her fist into his shoulder for emphasis, stomped off. Jerry laughed, continued gyrating between two groupies who looked no older than sixteen.

Cat shifted her gaze. The lavender lighting made the crowd look . . . consumptive? No, too archaic, Cat decided and mentally tapped her store of adjectives while wondering how she must look under the purple glow that was eroding complexions fifteen years her junior. She saw Jane's second grade teacher dancing with a

Special Ed teacher, five PTA members and the president of the Ocean City school board. She scribbled a few idle observations, reminded herself to get the background on Tom and Jerry from Ron Spivak over the weekend. *I want to go home,* she wrote, scribbled it away hastily when Tom peered over her shoulder, asked her if she would like a drink.

"Diet Pepsi!"

Tom checked his watch with a frown, ordered Cat's drink. Cat smiled, sympathetically. Since it was Thursday night, he had been in the studio before six, stuck here until midnight, then back to KRZI by dawn for Frantic Friday.

Jerry sidled over, jerked his chin toward the dance floor. Cat took her Pepsi from the waitress, shook her head.

"So, y'ever been to one of these?" Jerry hooked a chair leg with his foot, kicked it beside Cat's, sat and took a sip of Tom's drink. "Little stiff for you, isn't it Tommy?" He grabbed a passing waitress. "Gimme what he's havin', babe. So," he asked Cat, "what you wanna talk about?"

"Well," Cat inhaled, spoke louder. "You're both so reluctant to discuss the past, let's discuss the future. What's next? I mean, you two have been the only game in town for the past, what almost two years? But the *Six A.M. Circus* has picked up a few imitators—"

"Send in the clones!" Jerry warbled.

Tom rolled his eyes, shook his head.

Cat scribbled the remark. "Some of the clones are pretty good. There's *Chuck and Didi* at WNTS, *Johnny O and Ray* at WNNB, *Tiger and Allison* doing that show from Pomona. How do you stay on top? Or isn't that what you want?"

"Why wouldn't it be?" Jerry asked.

Cat shrugged. Should she ask again about the offer from Philly 104? "Your contracts expire January one."

"Gal's done her homework," Tom said, soberly.

"You haven't re-signed."

"Ah, we're makin' 'em sweat. An' not just them. I got a couple ideas'll keep us numero uno."

8

"Such as?"

"Off the record?"

"Of course not."

"What the hell. Once a month, Target Tuesday becomes Tattletale Tuesday. Exposé. Prime stuff and all local."

Cat glanced at Tom uneasily. Tom shrugged. "News to me. You check this out with Barry?"

Jerry downed his bourbon. "Aw, Barry'll love it. We'll make it like twenny questions. I go, 'What ritzy boutique owner is stepping out with her husband's business partner? What local TV personality made an amateur porn flick in college? Who doctored the ballots in the Little Miss Cape May county pageant last year—?' "

Cat jotted, *boutique-adultery, celeb-porn, contest-fix. Blackmail?*

"—What well-known DJ is sleeping with his sister? What media honcho's been seen cruisin' the gay—"

"Forget the notes, Cat." Tom finished his drink, signaled for another. "I can guarantee this'll never get past Barry."

"Wanna bet?" Jerry demanded.

"What about slander?" Cat inquired.

"Slander's if you can't back the facts, babe."

A willowy white-blonde with hair that extended beyond the hem of her silk tunic slid an arm around Jerry's neck. Cat recognized her as the newly hired receptionist at KRZI. Dawn? Diane? "You remember Deanna," Jerry offered.

"Of course."

"Wow, I can't wait to see your story," Deanna purred, sliding the third finger of her left hand into Cat's line of vision. Cat saw the ring, appraised it at forty dollars, said nothing.

"Wow, it comes out, I'm gonna buy about a hundred copies of *South Jersey* and actually read every word."

"Even the ones with syllables?" Cat inquired, politely.

Tom snickered.

"Wow, I think it's the neatest thing, getting your name in print and stuff." The finger fluttered, conspicuously.

9

"Some people don't want to see their names in print." Cat took a sip of her Pepsi. "And stuff."

Deanna grappled silently with this improbability. Jerry nipped her upper arm with his teeth, his lips flattening in a serpentine leer, then signaled to Tom.

"Raffle time," Tom muttered.

Jerry grabbed Cat's sleeve. "C'mon up, we'll let you pick the winner, be a great angle for the piece."

"I prefer to be objective and inconspicuous, thanks."

Deanna pouted and strode off.

Cat tapped her pen against her notebook absently as Tom and Jerry took the mike and swung into a racy dialogue calculated to titillate KRZI's late night listeners. What time is it, Cat wondered. How much longer should I hang around here? *You can't be so laid back, you know what I mean, so omnipotent, you gotta dig a little more,"* Ritchie had coached.

*"I think you mean omniscient, or maybe Olympian."*

*"One of those O words, I forget. What I'm sayin' is, you gotta mix it up more, don't be so astute—"*

*"Aloof."*

*"They do some PR, that let's play murder thing, get over there, jump right in with both your eyes and ears."*

Well, she was seeing, hearing, but everything seemed to be spinning away from her. Nothing worth writing about was happening, was it? Ron wouldn't be having this problem. Maybe once she got his background stuff, she could flesh something out. Maybe he'd even help her if he felt up to it. After all, she wouldn't be stuck here right now if it weren't for Ron.

Ron Spivak was an avid freelancer who worked six or seven stories simultaneously. He had begun a background check on the Six AM Circus duo when he'd nailed a hard-to-get interview with incarcerated murderer Gaetano "The Walnut" Nucci. The cold premeditation with which The Walnut had dispatched his victims camouflaged a volatile disposition, one which Ron underestimated when he made a glib inquiry into the derivation of his subject's nom de guerre. The Walnut responded to Ron's levity by leaning

forward, waist-, wrist-, leg-irons notwithstanding, and biting off
Spivak's nose. He swallowed it, too, although the rumor prevailed
that it had not stayed down, but had been disgorged an hour later
into an anemic casserole, an act which was regarded as a protest
against the penitentiary's indifferent cuisine.

"Aren't you Mrs. Austen?"

Cat turned in her chair to face a startlingly pretty woman. Late
twenties, pixiish brunette coif, grey-blue eyes, tall and long-
legged. Dancer, Cat decided. Dancer or athlete. "I'm Cat Austen."

"The one writing the story on Tommy and Jerry?"

"That's right."

The girl was wringing her slender fingers. Her steel-blue eyes
darted toward the pair at the mike. She slipped into a chair, her
back to the stage. "I was wondering . . . what kind of story is it
going to be exactly? I mean, just like this kind of stuff?" she gestured vaguely around the room. "Or a real in-depth piece with
their childhoods and all that?"

"You know them?"

"Sort of."

"Well, the truth is, I haven't been able to plumb to any great
depth. Every time I try, Jerry muddies the waters. Maybe you
could help me out, Miss—"

". . . reporter from *South Jersey Magazine*, here doin' a piece on
me an' Tommy, so we're gonna let her come up and pick out the
winning entry!"

Panic cinched Cat's diaphragm. Damn Jerry Dudek! She didn't
want to get up in front of all these people! But Jerry was pointing her out, the lavender spots had locked in. Cat gritted her teeth
and rose. "Could you watch my things?" she asked the girl.

"Yeah, sure."

Cat made her way through the crowd. Why on earth was Tom
staring at her so oddly? No, staring past her. Cat swung her head,
saw the back of the dark-haired girl sitting where Cat had left her,
tapping her palm absently against Cat's attaché.

Cat was yanked between Tom and Jerry, instructed to close her

11

eyes and plunge her hand into the fishbowl. She drew out a bill which Jerry grabbed and read aloud, "Miss Jessica Zaccarillo!"

"EEEeeeEEEeeeEEE!" An object with a lavender-tinted mane, silver halter top, bare arms braceletted to the elbows, purple Spandex biker shorts galloped to the stage on five-inch heels. She stepped on Cat's foot, screamed something inarticulate to the crowd, grabbed the mike and shrieked, "I don' believe it! I don' belieeeeeeve it!" to KRZI's nine-to-midnighters. Jerry shut her up by kissing her long and loud.

Cat crept toward the rim of the stage.

Tom pried the mike from Miss Zaccarillo and recited routine thanks on behalf of CV's, KRZI and their sponsors, while Jerry and the winner broke into a spontaneous gyration that reminded Cat of something Ellice had quoted about dancing being a vertical expression of a horizontal desire.

Cat jumped down and headed for her table. The dark-haired girl was gone. Cat's attaché lay unattended; instinctively Cat checked the contents: wallet, notebook, pens, keys, everything checked out.

"Where'd she go!"

"What?" Cat turned to face Tom. "You mean that girl?"

Tom nodded, his face wan, desperate.

"Ladies' room maybe, she—"

Tom darted toward the corridor.

The music started up again. "Wanna dance?" Jerry.

Cat latched her brief. "No, thanks."

"Hey, don't take off so soon, party's just started. Y'seen Tommy?"

Cat jerked her chin toward the corridor. "He went after this girl I was talking to. Tall, short, dark hair . . ."

"Noreen."

Jerry was frowning. Cat realized that she had never seen him annoyed, angry, commissioned her memory to scan, lock in. "Noreen? You mean your sister Noreen?"

The corners of his mouth leveled in a reptilian smile. "Tune in to tomorrow's *Circus*, Cat Lady, a surprise—"

"Don't hit him in the mout'! Don' hit him in the mout'!" A shrieking Jessica Zaccarillo was born half-mast on a forearm the diameter of a utility pole, brandished by a paramour who, Cat concluded: a) did not believe all the negative press anabolic steroids were getting; b) was clearly not tonight's designated driver; and c) had not looked dispassionately on Jerry's public fondling of his fair Jess. A fist the size of a Jersey melon hurtled Catward; instinctively, she shoved Jerry aside, feinted left and hammered her own fist into the man's median nerve.

The massive forearm went limp. "Damn, bitch, I can't feel my hand!" he screamed, and followed up with a dozen or so obscenities, two of which Cat had never heard in the entire course of her life, despite the fact that five of her six brothers were cops.

A pair of bouncers bisected the crowd. A bar stool whizzed over Cat's head, a tumbler missed her cheek by inches and struck Deanna in the chest as she flew to Jerry's aid. "It's silk!" she cried, pinching the wet tunic away from her breasts. "It's silk."

Cat grabbed her attaché, dropped to the floor, scooted under tables on hands and knees, catapulted into the lobby, snatched her coat from its hanger and fled.

"Mrs. Cat Austen," she gasped, jogging across Belmont, "daughter of the late restauranteur, sister of former Chief of Police Carlo Fortunati, widow of slain state trooper Christopher Austen, was arrested last night for assault, battery, inciting to riot and criminal stupidity . . ." She clutched her coat over her chest, vaulted the stone wall and threw herself against her car, shaking with laughter. A few shivering prostitutes, huddled on the corner of Pacific and Belmont, nodded with weary sympathy.

The sight of them sobered Cat. There had been a time when Pacific Avenue had been a thoroughfare of modest and reputable prosperity. Now, there was casino glitter and decay. Cat's mother held onto her memories: how she had lived next door to Lou Costello when she was a girl ("*Who?*" Jane had demanded), allowed her adventurous sister Caterina to drag her to Club Harlem, strolled a Boardwalk lined with theaters, jewelry shops, auction houses. Cat, too, harbored memories, memories of watching the diving horse, getting Frankie Avalon's autograph at the Steel Pier ("*Who?*" Jane had demanded), waiting tables at Fortunati's in summer, the man in a silvery suit who had tipped her a hundred dollars because she had a pretty smile, her father's rare frown when he had taken the bill and handed it back.

Cat flexed her throbbing fingers. She had really nailed that barbarian, just like Marco had taught her. But what a mess she had made of the assignment! She tossed her attaché into the trunk of her car, decided to take a stroll on the boards to clear her head.

Footsteps clacked against the stone wall, scraped the gritty asphalt of the parking lot. Cat clenched her fists, backpedaled, turned.

It was only Jerry.

"Hey, Cat, whaddayou mad? Look, don't print that about that stuff in there, happens all the time. Look, what say we cut out together, go somewhere for a drink?"

"I thought you had to stick around."

"Station's only gonna cut in once or twice more; I left word for Tommy to handle it."

"Left word? What if he took off? He seemed rather anxious to connect with Noreen."

"Oh, he'll be back," Jerry replied, cryptically, then converted to the leer that worked on the groupies, Deanna.

(*Though not on that irritated blonde,* Cat reminded herself. *Who was she?*)

"Like I was telling you, I got a surprise announcement for tomorrow's show. I'm gonna spill Tommy's engagement on the air. Tommy'll freak."

"It'll be old news when my story hits the stands eight weeks from now. Didn't you say the wedding was around Christmas?"

Jerry smirked. "He hasn't even told the old man. Thought I'd send Big Tom a tape of tomorrow's show. But that's only for openers. Like Macbeth said, the play's the thing."

"Hamlet."

Jerry shrugged. "Anyway, the play's a shocker. Want the dish?"

"Call Ritchie Landis at the magazine." Cat sidestepped Jerry, reached in her pocket for her keys. "My plate's full."

Jerry grabbed her arm, spun her around. "Hey, one lousy drink won't kill you. I guarantee the goods. Long lost kin, kinky sex, dysfunctional families, you reporters get off on that stuff, right?"

"Call me tomorrow."

"No, now."

"Why now?"

" 'Cause, I gotta put it in someone's head, like for safekeeping." Jerry positioned himself between her and the car door, his back to the dunes.

Sand drizzled in Cat's eyes. "Dirt on errant wives and fixed kiddie pageants? Not my style."

"Hey, I saw how you took down that guy in there, so don't play genteel widow. S'anything I can spot, it's a gal likes to play rough. Well, I can do rough, too."

"Play the perfect murder and do dead."

She hadn't meant it. Not literally. But the resounding crack came right on cue and Cat was thrown to the ground, her head striking the Maxima's rear bumper, the asphalt.

Jerry's weight bore down on her and she almost said, "Cut it out," but she knew the sound had been the real thing. Dazed, Cat gripped the pavement that rotated slowly beneath her, listened hard to the wind rustling through the wire fence, half-expecting someone to spring at her from the dunes under the Broadwalk. Play dead, she whispered.

No, she wouldn't play dead, she would fight. Shoving Jerry aside, Cat struggled to her knees, listened to the sickening quiet. She rose, unsteadily. Her breasts were wet. Cat pressed her hand to the dark, gluey patch on the front of her sweater; the darkness clung to her fingertips. She looked past them to the ground. One eye, gun-metal blue, stared back at her, the other jutted over his cheekbone. A wet blackness crept from beneath the matted hair, one slick tendril snaked toward her right pump.

"It's not a game, it's real," she gasped aloud, and fell on top of him, face forward, unconscious.

# CHAPTER
## TWO

Lieutenant Victor Cardenas, homicide investigator with the Atlantic County Major Crimes Bureau, spat a mild (by police standards) obscenity and grabbed his car phone on the first ring.

"I'm sorry, sir." Jean Adane, one of his four man—four person—unit, his unofficial right arm.

"What and where?"

"A shooting at Circolo Venerdi. It's a dance club on Belmont Place between Pacific and the Boardwalk. City units have been dispatched, a Sergeant Barone is in charge at the scene, but Captain Loeper says—"

"I get it." 'It' meant he would have to extend his fifteen hour day, forget he was slated to have the next three off. "Has the—"

"The ME's been called, sir."

"Would you—"

"I took the liberty of telephoning Mr. Raab at home, sir."

"Go home, Adane. No reason we both have to pull a twenty-four hour tour."

Victor's tour had begun in Trenton, a breakfast meeting with assemblymen preparing a "hate crimes" bill. Down to Mays Landing for a half-hour with DA Raab to review Victor's testimony at an upcoming trial. Over to Shore Memorial Hospital in Somers Point to witness the autopsy of one Renay Harris, prostitute, nearly decapitated and dumped in an abandoned house where she had been discovered by two ten-year-old runaways. Interviewing the runaways with Detective Long and a social worker, the terrified kids baffled because the dead woman "don' look like on the TV." Back to the Bureau offices in Northfield, a forty-five minute phone conversation with Mrs. Viola Finkle regarding the disappearance of her husband, Em ("I know he's dead, I just know it!"), and Victor chivalrously refraining from reminding Mrs. Finkle that Mr. Finkle had passed away six years ago of a heart attack (for which Mrs. Finkle's cholesterol-laden menus bore no minor responsibility) and that his ashes were currently residing in a cloisonné vase on Mrs. Finkle's night table. He gave his "Fundamental's of Homicide Investigation" lecture to the rookie class, called his mother ("Victor, that younger sister of yours, you talk to that girl!"), then settled behind a nine-inch stack of paperwork (he actually borrowed Adane's ruler to measure it), stopped from seven to seven-fifteen for a sandwich and a lukewarm cup of coffee, worked on.

A shooting. Drugs or armed robbery. Carjacking. Grudge match. Don't guess, Victor reprimanded himself. No facts. If there had been, Adane would have communicated them. She had sounded characteristically detached; nothing rattled her. Still, the scene that greeted him at the corner of Pacific and Belmont was a tribute to Adane's equanimity.

Victor double-parked beside a patrol car, its flashing lights rebounding off phosphorescent hair, Spandex, cheap jewelry. Two dozen uniformed officers manned a yellow crime scene tape that corralled the site from onlookers. Two hundred, Victor calculated, staring through his windshield. Maybe two-fifty. Who the hell was it got shot?

Victor slid out of his car, held his shield up to a young officer who was fending off a blonde in a stained silk tunic. "He's not really dead!" she wailed, insistently. "It's just perfect murder! It's just the perfect murder!"

Victor logged her words, her face, in his brain, stepped over the tape, automatically checking his watch, the sky. Clear, decent visibility for a good shooter, wind kicking some sand off the beach. Parking lot's full. Beside a blue Maxima, the ME knelt over the corpse, two uniforms attending his running monologue.

Victor looked down. Male, twenty-seven or so, probably never handsome, not even when the head was intact. "Who is he?"

"Radio jock. Dudek. Jerry Dudek."

Victor had trained his features to remain impassive. The slight elevation of the dark brows indicated a significant degree of surprise. "Tom and Jerry? *The Morning Circus?*"

"*Six A.M. Circus,*" corrected the first officer. "They were hosting a raffle over CV's. Place was packed."

Victor squatted beside the medical examiner, careful not to disturb the body. He took a pen light from his shirt pocket, swept its narrow beam around the perimeter of the shattered head, traced the red spatterings on the left rear tire of the Maxima to a patch of creamy white on the ground. A barrette. Victor lifted it with the tip of his pen light, looked up at the officers, cocked an eyebrow.

"Girl at the gate says Dudek ran out with some woman or after some woman, around ten-thirty. Anonymous shots-fired called in around ten thirty-seven." He produced a paper sandwich bag from his back pocket.

"The woman?" Victor dropped the barrette into the bag.

"Took her over the med center, two of ours went with. Unconscious, not hit. Maybe just passed out."

"Pro?" Victor jerked his head toward Pacific Avenue.

The officer shrugged.

"What does the phrase 'the perfect murder' mean?"

The first officer spoke up. "You know how they make a promotional appearance somewhere? They got this new idea to set it up like one of those murder mystery parties. Dudek's the vic."

"Ask the owner of the club if that was on tonight's agenda. And run the plates on this car. Doctor?"

"We gotta stop meetin' like this, Cardenas, my significant

18

other's gettin' suspicious. First the headless hooker, now the mad man of morning radio."

Victor frowned and the ME got down to business.

"Problem is, you guys all switched to the nine millimeters is what the problem is."

"He was shot with a department weapon?"

"Depends on how far you go back. A thirty-eight's my guess."

"You'd go back several years," Victor replied, evenly.

" 'S what I'm tellin' you. You guys all switch to the nines, the old thirty-eights, they get dumped on the surplus market. All over the place. Nineteen-year-old nephew picks up a ten-year-old thirty-eight at a swap meet down Tallahassee, guess how much?"

"I prefer not to guess."

"One sixty-five. My money says the shooter came from over there—" the ME jerked a rubbed sheathed thumb toward the wire fence, the dunes. "The beach."

Victor glanced over his shoulder. Through a U-shaped depression, in the dunes beneath the Boardwalk, he could see a triangle of ocean, hear the surf.

"So, maybe the guy gets a little careless about the shells," the ME suggested. "Break out the metal detectors, maybe you'll get lucky. So what about it, Lieut," he deadpanned. "You feel lucky?"

The officers groaned.

A two man, one woman crime scene unit was hustled under the tape. Victor rose, saw the NewsLine90 van turn onto Belmont. "Where's the lot attendant?" he asked, abruptly.

"Shed's locked up when we got here. Lot's full, he probably takes off."

"Get me a name. Get everyone who was in the club back inside, start taking statements. Find out if Dudek's car's here. Where's the partner, Tom what's-his-name?"

"Hopper. In the john tossin' his dinner. He ID'd the stiff. Look, Lieutenant, lotta these people, they're gonna take off. Chances are . . ."

"Chances are the shooter already has," Victor finished.

The crime lab photographer bounded over the tape and

shrieked "Jerry Dudek!" The Newsline90 crew hit the lights and advanced. Victor gestured for them to be held back.

"No press," he ordered the senior officer. "Get a summary over to me by eight A.M. Find out about next of kin. Call Sergeant Rice from my unit, tell him he's on the post mortem. Start moving those people inside the club before the press gets to them, and cut off access to the beach." He turned to the crime lab trio. "Get metal detectors, sweep about a thirty foot arc behind those dunes."

"I like Stan Rice," said the ME.

The photographer began snapping, muttering, "Jeez, Jerry Dudek, jeez, jeez, Jerry Dudek, jeez."

"A guy who can sight through a two-foot depression in those dunes is smart enough to pick up his shells, Lieutenant," suggested the woman on the crime scene team.

"Perhaps. But if Dudek ran out after some woman, that suggests it was opportunistic. Not premeditated."

"Stan's a riot," the ME chortled.

"Unless she lured him out," offered the woman.

Victor nodded, soberly. "Do your best." He spotted a patrol sergeant he had known from his days on the Atlantic City force. The officer was questioning a girl with green and white hair.

"Call for backup?" Victor asked.

"How's it goin' Cardenas?" He gave Victor a check-this-out nod. "We got a couple more units on the way."

"Tell your people to try to keep the witnesses away from the press. I'd like them moved back inside the club."

"Gotcha."

As soon as Victor hopped the police tape, a microphone was shoved under his chin. "Lieutenant Cardenas, can you confirm that the victim is KRZI radio personality Jerry Dudek?"

Victor ducked his head away from the lights. "No comment."

"Do you feel the police response is adequate—"

"No comment."

He pushed past the reporter, got into his car and headed down Pacific toward the medical center. A woman. With, or pursued

by, Jerry Dudek. Or lured Dudek? Don't guess. A hooker, a
groupie, an accomplice? Don't guess.

"We don't gotta name. She's layin' on toppa him, keys in the coat
pocket, no ID, that's it."

"They're callin' for backup over CV's."

"Gotta wait for this guy Cardenas. Major Crimes hotshot."

"C'mon guys, take it outside." That voice was very close to
Cat's face. Consciousness was seeping back.

"My God! That's Cat Austen!" Jackie Wing's piercing soprano.
Jackie was a nurse, a friend of Cat's.

Am I in the hospital? Cat wondered.

"You know her?"

"Look, I said everyone back off," insisted the close-up voice.
The two baritones, Jackie's high-pitched dismay, receded.

Cat's right eye was pried open, a narrow beam probed the iris.
A blurred male head invaded her intimate space. Obligingly, Cat
opened the other eye.

"Miss Austen?"

Cat pushed feebly at the face. It backed up; neck, shoulders,
reddish beard; green scrubs and white lab coat. "Am I shot?"

"No. Head abrasion. Knocked out. I ordered a scan."

"Stitches?"

"Nope. Listen, I'll write a few orders and we'll move—"

"Where's my coat?"

"Over on that chair. We'll move you to a room—"

Cat turned her head. It hurt. "I heard other people . . ."

"The police are outside. They want to talk to you."

"Oh. Oh." Jerry Dudek. God.

Another nurse entered, a pretty diminutive woman in her late
forties. "Babe, are you all right? Jackie Wing just came on duty
and told me!" She grabbed Cat's hand and turned to the doctor.
"Mrs. Austen's my sister-in-law."

"Stay with her while I write the orders." The doctor backed

21

out of the cubicle, yanked the curtain shut. Cat heard muffled voices in the corridor, "Austen . . . sister-in-law . . . orders . . ."

"Annie, help me sit up."

"You don't want to do that."

"I do. I really do." Cat tried. Halfway up, it no longer seemed such a hot idea. "Annamarie, I have to get out of here. I have to go home."

"Who's with the kids? That girl lives with you?"

"Ellice. Her name is Ellice. Oh God, Jerry; I think he got shot."

"I know. He's dead, Cat." Annamarie laid a cool hand on Cat's forehead. "Listen, I called Carlo."

"Oh no!"

Carlo was the oldest of Cat's six brothers, her senior by seventeen years. Annamarie was his wife.

"That's just great!" Cat braced herself against the examining table, sat up, took inventory. Her stockings were torn at the knees, her skirt and sweater tacky with blood; her hands were dirty, the crystal on her watch was cracked, her barrette was missing, her head throbbed. Cat explored the rough patch of gauze at her temple with shaking fingers. "I have to get out of here. I have to go home," she repeated, thickly. She wondered if her car keys were still in her coat pocket, if she could get to her car, if she could even get to her feet.

Batting away Annamarie's hands, she tried; lurched to the chair where her coat lay and decided to sit down.

The curtain was pulled aside and the bearded doctor reentered, followed by another man, not a doctor. A cop, Cat guessed. Not in uniform, so that meant detective. Tall, good-looking, in a somber sort of way, with serious brown-black eyes and a dark mustache bridging his upper lip. *He doesn't smile much,* Cat's instincts whispered, *and you're not what he expected to find.*

The detective drew the curtain.

"Mrs. Austen, you shouldn't be up," the doctor insisted. "I'll have your sister-in-law get you into a gown—"

"No. I'm going home."

"Absolutely not. You have to remain here overnight at least. Head injuries should not be taken lightly."

Cat shook her head.

*Obstinate*, Victor concluded. "Miss Austen—"

"Mrs. Or Ms. Or whatever, but not Miss."

"Mrs. Austen, then. Can you answer a few questions?" The voice was courteous, monotonal.

"Now?"

"Yes. You're our only eyewitness to the shooting."

Cat shivered, drew her coat around her shoulders.

"Mrs. Austen," the doctor warned, "you may be experiencing some symptoms of shock, and I absolutely insist—"

"—then tell me where they put her Mother of God!" roared a familiar voice. "Or do I have to take apart the whole damned hospital!"

Cat groaned.

Carlo Fortunati, six-five, two hundred fifty pounds, barreled into the cubicle, elbowing aside the doctor.

Carlo Fortunati was a law enforcement celebrity throughout the tri-state area, thanks to tireless dedication, rigid ethics and a flamboyant personal style that made him a media joy.

After twenty-five years on the Atlantic City force, minus his eleven weeks at Quantico, an untimely demise catapulted Carlo to the office of Atlantic City's acting Chief of Police, with every expectation that the appointment would become permanent.

But Carlo saw no point in marking time until the civil service records were tallied in his favor. He immediately evicted twenty officers from desk jobs and mobile units and transferred them to foot and bicycle patrols. Part of every day was spent walking the streets, listening to the grievances of shop owners, senior citizens, even the kids. He beat the leaders of two rival gangs in a free throw match and exacted an amnesty that lasts to this day, rounded up truants, then followed their progress for the entire school year, bullied the rookies into righteousness, castigated politicians for wastefulness, harangued city council for their failure to provide the police department with decent quarters. His wrath was superseded only by his generosity and kindness; during his reign, no officer's birthday, marriage, newborn or promotion went unacknowledged, and at Christmas time, a great, bellowing Santa charged through the pediatric wards, laden with gifts.

Such outrageous displays of rectitude were naturally distressing to local politicians who preferred a more genteel and recessive candidate for permanent chief, and when credentials were evaluated, Carlo was replaced, deposed to his former rank of inspector. Two thirds of the department, including the three other Fortunatis on the force, handed in their resignations. Carlo called a press conference, ordered the cops back to work, announced his retirement and told the city what he thought of their demotion in such imaginative scatology that the riveted *NewsLine90* censor forgot to hit the delay button.

Cat observed that the detective would not be elbowed aside by her brother, stood his ground, watching, as Carlo strode over to her, leaned down to look into her face, kissed her forehead roughly.

"Ouch."

"So now somebody's gonna tell me what the hell's goin' on!" Even in ordinary conversation, Carlo tended to bellow, a bellow that had been imitated by every local nightclub comic and disc jockey in southern New Jersey. Even Jerry Dudek had done a wickedly acute rendering of Carlo's televised swan song, substituting ". . . our for-ni-ca-ting elected officials" for the other F word that was Carlo's very favorite adjective (verb, noun).

The detective said, "Mrs. Austen was a witness to a fatal shooting tonight."

"Why the hell didn't someone call me!"

"I called you," Annamarie reminded him. "An' this is a hospital, you watch your language." Her head barely grazed his clavicle; she was less than half his weight.

"I mean before," he muttered, chastened.

"Before Jerry got shot?" Cat felt a hysterical desire to laugh.

"Don't be funny."

24

"*Carino*, they brought Cat in unconscious, her purse was gone so—"

"Someone stole your purse?"

"I didn't have—"

"And so they couldn't identify her until Jackie—"

"She was mugged? My sister was mugged?"

"No, I wasn't mugged, just shot at, and no one stole my purse, my stuff's in the trunk of my car—"

"A blue Maxima?" the detective asked. His sister?

"Are they gonna tow my car?" Cat moaned.

"Where'd this happen? Where's your car now?" Carlo demanded.

"In the lot across from CV's at Belmont and Pacific."

"That's where the shooting occurred," interjected the detective. "And if Mrs. Austen's feeling up to answering—"

"She isn't," interrupted the doctor.

"I'll say whether I am or not!"

"Put your coat on, you're coming home with us."

"I am not."

"You are, too. An' gimme your car keys."

"We may have to tow the car," the detective said.

"My stuff is in there," Cat wailed. She rose, reconsidered, sat.

"You see!" the doctor gloated. "She's faint!"

Cat slipped her arms into her coat sleeves, buttoned the coat over her bloodied sweater. "This is ridiculous. I'm going."

"I'm sorry Mrs. Austen, but there are a few questions you'll have to answer first."

"Look, I think my sister's had all she can manage tonight—sergeant, is it?"

"Lieutenant. Victor Cardenas."

Carlo squinted. "Do I know you?"

"I've been working with a state task force for a couple years," Victor offered, wondering how good Fortunati's memory was.

"That hate crimes force?"

Victor nodded. "I was AC before that; Major Crimes for the past year and a half."

"That task force didn't do a bad job. You know Gino Forschetti? Manny Alvaro?"

"Yes."

Carlo's tone softened. "Look, my sister's hurt, she's confused, worried about her kids, anything she says tonight, what's it gonna be worth?"

"It could be vital."

"Maybe, maybe not. Her head's not so clear, tonight she tells you one thing, tomorrow something different, just wasting your time. Let her come home with me, get some sleep—"

"I'm not coming home with you, I said."

Carlo turned on Cat. "Babe, you let me handle this, we're gonna do it my way—"

"Carlo, don't be such a *cetriul'*!"

Annamarie aborted a laugh.

"You think my sister's funny?" Carlo demanded of her.

"I'll call a cab," Cat threatened.

"I'll arrange a ride for you as soon as we're finished here," the lieutenant offered.

Cat raised her chin, combatively. "We're finished. Now you take me home," she ordered Carlo, "or I'll go out there on Pacific Avenue, hitch up my hem line and take my chances!"

Annamarie cut off her husband's retort. "Look," she suggested, diplomatically. "Let's do this. We'll take Cat home an' I'll stay the night. I'm a nurse, I can look out for her, the kids don't have school tomorrow, right? She can sleep in. In the morning, we'll decide what to do next, *va bene*."

Clearly, it wasn't *va bene* with the lieutenant, but he stood aside resignedly, as Carlo helped Cat to her feet and led her away. Pity he didn't have Stan Rice's easygoing gallantry. Rice would have gotten something out of her, brother or no brother. "Cat"? he wondered. And what was that about kids? Her kids? Where was the husband?

Cat nodded politely to the detective—Cardenas, she remembered—and suppressed a sigh. Pity he didn't have some of Carlo's steamroller officiousness. It would have been fun to watch the two of them go at it. The lieutenant didn't look like a man who backed down.

Victor watched until they passed through the exit. Cat. Fortunati's kid sister. I'll be damned.

A young officer approached. "Do you know who that guy was?" he asked, awed.

"Yeah," Victor replied. *He's the reason I'm a cop.*

# CHAPTER
## THREE

The Major Crimes Bureau was located in a rambling edifice of crumbling brick and weather-beaten white trim in the Atlantic county community of Northfield. The building housed several of the county DA's law enforcement bureaus, the old police academy, the medical examiner's office and one or two charitable organizations.

Victor Cardenas had been assigned a ten-by-fifteen retreat with marbled, green-black linoleum, tan walls, one metal file cabinet, one metal bookcase, buckling now under his procedural tomes and a dozen fraying blue binders, a tan metal desk with a broad surface of scarred pine. To this, he had added a high-backed executive chair, two padded armchairs of burgundy leather that he had picked up at a discount office supply, a bulletin board, a metal coat rack and a calendar.

Victor arrived in his office shortly before eight Friday morning, asked Jean Adane to bring him the paperwork on the Dudek shooting, sifted through the notes on his desk, threw half in the recycling bin outside his door and requested that his unit assemble in five minutes for their informal muster.

Sergeant Stan Rice knocked on the frame of Victor's open door. Victor waved him in.

Rice was in his late thirties, medium height, medium build with a mop of prematurely graying hair and a devilish, dimpled smile. "So someone iced that sleazoid radio jock Dudek," he grinned. "I had some good money said he wouldn't last two years from when they signed with KRZI. Autopsy's not 'til nine-thirty, gives me time to get some breakfast."

Rice found the matter of people killing other people incomprehensibly fascinating. He had never imagined wanting to kill anyone, a deficit in character which Victor believed might prevent Rice from ascending in rank.

"Jeannie says you got an eyewitness."

"One. Couple hundred in the club, but only one sure thing. Woman named Austen."

"Not King Carlo's little sister! Cat Austen?"

Victor sat, immediately alert. "You know her?"

"Cat? Sure. Was she hurt?"

Victor filled him in briefly. "She local?"

"Ocean City," Stan told him. "Morningside Drive, north end, near the beach. I can get her number from my book; it's unlisted. You want me to go over and talk to her?"

Victor tried to analyze the concern. His book? He was on the verge of responding when he heard his name pronounced by a familiar voice, looked past Stan to see Jean Adane pointing his office out to Mrs. Austen herself.

Victor rose immediately, but Stan beat him to the door.

"Cat, you okay? I just heard about last night. What's that?" He brushed the patch of gauze taped to her temple.

"Nothing. I'm fine, Stanley. How does Major Crimes?"

"'S'okay. How's Joey doin' these days?"

"He's going to be a father, did you hear? You should have had children, Stan. They keep you human."

"I asked you honey, you turned me down."

"But Stan," Cat shook a reproving finger, her brown eyes sparkling. "You ask *everybody*."

"Hey. Only women. And you, I was serious."

"You're never serious. Shoo, I came to see your boss."

"You'll excuse us, Sergeant." Victor's hand was on the door-knob. Stan opened his mouth, closed it, shrugged and backed out the door. Victor closed it, firmly.

Cat slipped out of her coat and sat in the chair Victor held out for her.

Victor perched on the edge of his desk, appraising her. Rather pretty, now that she was cleaned up, more composed. Her dark, shoulder-length hair had an auburn aura, the long lashes, arched brows a shade darker. Brown eyes that were clear and direct, maybe a hint of devilment, a sweet mouth that could contract stubbornly when she was not to be messed with. She wore a sim-ple navy sweater dress that clung nicely to a good figure, a wrist-watch, a pair of thin gold rings on the third and fourth fingers of her right hand, no ring on the left.

"So the head's okay?"

"Yes."

"How'd you get here?"

"A cab." She smiled, archly. "Lieutenant, would you do me a favor?"

Victor's brows lifted, inquisitively. "If I can."

"Would you please sit behind your desk?"

He smiled faintly. "Why?"

"That's a cop's trick. Perhaps you're not even aware of it. Sit-ting above me like that is an unconscious demonstration of au-thority. I'm forced to look up, placed in a subordinate posture, which puts me at a disadvantage and also makes my neck hurt. Now, you wouldn't want to intimidate me, would you, unless you suspect me of something. Do you?"

"Perhaps of being overly analytical."

"I should think a cop would find an aptitude for analysis to be an asset."

Obligingly, he rose, sat behind his desk. "Better?"

"More equitable. I suppose I should begin by apologizing for

Carlo. He's a wonderful brother and he does mean well, but he can be an officious jerk at times."

"A 'cetriul'," Victor reminded her. "Translation?"

Cat blushed, amended her Sicilian pronunciation. "Cetriolo," she said. "Literally, it means 'cucumber.' Figuratively, it's an—" she hesitated. "It has anatomical associations."

The mustache twitched. "I see."

There was a knock on the door. Before Victor could rise, a dark, meticulously attired man in his late thirties bounded in. "Cat, Cat, you should know better than this."

The dark eyes flashed. "Did Carlo send you?"

"Annamarie told you to stay in bed," he responded. "She got up and found your note and called Carlo and—"

"And Carlo called you. I think I'm competent enough to answer a few of the lieutenant's questions and find out what they did with my car without the assistance of an attorney."

"I'll spring your car." The man leaned into the desk, extended his hand to Victor. "Steve Delareto. I'm Cat's lawyer. If she's going to make a statement, I think she should have someone present."

"I thought that was only if I were arrested. Do I need a lawyer, Lieutenant?"

"I don't object to his being here; it's up to you," Victor replied, calmly.

"If I thought I needed you," Cat decided, "I'm sure it would have occurred to me to call. I resent Carlo's interference, Steve, and I resent your running down here without even disputing his right to interfere."

"You're confusing interference with honest concern," Steve objected, mildly.

"I've had enough of the former to know the difference," Cat retorted. She fished her car keys out of her purse. "Since you're here, you can make some phone calls, you lawyers are good at that, and locate my car. And don't start billing me for your time until you leave." She slapped the keys into Delareto's outstretched palm.

Delareto shrugged. "You're lucky I was always a little in love with you, Cat. None of my other clients get this kind of service."

"None of them have Carlo Fortunati for a brother."

Delareto kissed her on the cheek, muttered, "Nice to meet you, Lieutenant," and strolled out.

Victor wondered what sort of relationship "a little in love" implied. "We expecting anyone else?"

The somber mouth gave nothing away, neither did the voice. Cat detected humor in the eyes, though, responded to it. "I think we're okay for another fifteen minutes or so."

Victor leaned back in his chair. "Your brother Carlo I know by reputation, of course. And there's Marco Fortunati, who teaches self-defense at the academy. Something of a marksman, too, I hear. And then a couple more?"

Cat nodded. "Marco's my third brother. Carlo's the oldest, then Vinnie, who's a captain—"

"AC Burglary."

"Right. And then Marco and then Dominic—"

"What's his rank?"

"Clerical. Dom's a priest. Then there's Giuseppe—that is, Joey—he's with Special Ops, or I suppose they're back to calling it 'vice' again, I can never keep track, and last and best is Freddy. He's a state cop."

Six brothers, five of them cops. "And you?"

"Oh, I married one. Can you imagine, with five cops in the family already. It was the one thing I swore I wouldn't do."

Victor cleared his throat. "Where was your husband last night?"

Cat started, studied the CrimeStoppers poster tacked to the bulletin board. "Aren't you going to take me into one of those hideous interrogation rooms, Lieutenant? The last time I saw one, it was, let me see, some indescribable shade of beige."

"Green now."

"That ugly green, like school hallways?"

"I'm afraid so."

"Let's stay here then. It's sufficiently impersonal. You don't

32

have pictures on the desk or a custom name plate or anything." Cat took a deep breath. "My husband died over two years ago. Everyone knows about it around here, but I guess you were with that task force at the time. Chris was a state cop, too."

Victor heard the wistful catch in her voice. He thought of Marisol, who had always expected to be the survivor, the one left behind.

"Tell me what you want to know about last night," Cat prodded quietly. "It will help me keep everything in order if you ask questions."

"What were you doing at CV's last night?"

"Working on a story. For *South Jersey Magazine*."

"You're a writer?"

Cat shrugged. "I'm supposed to be their entertainment writer. You know, movie reviews, casino shows, concerts. Tom and Jerry weren't my story originally, but the writer assigned to the piece had—had to go to the hospital, so I picked up where he left off. I taped an interview at the studio with them last week, and last night I went to watch them work a personal appearance."

"Who else did you talk to during that interview?"

"One of the receptionists, another one of the deejays, Barry Fried."

"Who's he?"

"The station manager at KRZI."

"Was he there last night?"

"No."

"Not there, or you didn't see him? Remember, there was quite a crowd."

Cat concentrated. "At one point Tom and Jerry were debating over a change in format. Tom said Barry wouldn't go for it, Jerry said he would. I'm sure if he were there, one of them would have called him over."

Victor took a notepad out of his top drawer, began scribbling as she spoke. "What time did you get there?"

"Oh, a little after nine. The place was packed."

"This personal appearance, who set that up?"

Cat shrugged. "The club, I suppose. Tom and Jerry are in demand for that sort of thing, you know, malls, restaurant openings, they shake hands, sign autographs . . ." Her gaze lowered, introspectively.

"What?" he prodded.

"They were going to begin a new promotional gimmick this week. When they made a personal appearance, it would be set up like one of those murder mystery scenarios. Jerry was going to play the victim."

"So I heard."

She had a trick of pushing her hair behind her right ear when she was nervous. Victor noted the triangular gold earrings, 14K, if he was any judge (though it had been years since he had bought jewelry for a woman, not counting his mother and sisters). The clinging knit with its prim cowl neckline, long sleeves, corroborated his impression of her: smart, unpretentious, reserved but not timid. Someone it would be interesting to know.

"But they weren't playing murder last night, were they?"

"No, they were just there to mingle and handle the drawing. There was a raffle for some concert tickets, dinner for two and a limo thrown in; KRZI ran a remote."

"How long were you at CV's before this raffle?"

"Forty minutes, maybe. Jerry made me draw the winner."

"You and Dudek were friendly, then?"

Cat blushed. "Not really."

Victor tried to read her expression. "Did you know him before you got the assignment?"

"Only from the radio show. We'd never met."

"But you two left the club together."

"Not exactly."

"Be exact. Please."

Cat wondered if he had heard about the brawl. "After the drawing, things sort of fell apart. Tom went one way, Jerry another. I didn't see much point in hanging around, so I decided to take off. Then Jerry got into an argument with a guy and it got a little out of hand. While the bouncers were breaking it up, I left. Jerry followed."

"How serious was this argument?"

"I haven't been engaged in so many barroom brawls that I can categorize them, Lieutenant."

Victor smiled. "A brawl, then. Who was the other guy?"

"I don't know. His girlfriend's name was Zaccarillo. Jennifer or Jessica, something like that. She won the raffle. Jerry made a pass at her and the boyfriend didn't like it."

Victor wrote. "Why did Jerry follow you out?"

"Oh dear. He had—" she gestured, uncomfortably.

"Made a pass at you?" Victor suggested.

Cat nodded, embarrassed. "He had tried to get me to dance, then, when he followed me, he kept pestering me to go have a drink with him. He kept trying to pitch some story idea."

"What sort of story idea?"

"He wasn't specific. He made it sound like something terribly lurid, but then Jerry had a penchant for hype."

"I believe lurid is in vogue. You're a reporter. Why not go for a drink and hear him out?"

"Lurid isn't my forte, Lieutenant. And, let's face it, I'm ten or twelve years older than Jerry and even if I weren't he's not my type, and even if he were my type, I don't . . ."

Victor waited.

"I don't date."

Never? "I see. So Jerry went after you with the intention of pitching his story even though he was scheduled to remain at CV's for another hour or so. Sounds like he had something important on his mind, Mrs. Austen."

"I know. But my ESP shorted out in the awful club and all I wanted was breathing room. I locked my attaché in the trunk of my car and decided to take a walk to clear my head—"

"Alone?"

"I've gotten quite good at being alone, Lieutenant," Cat replied quietly. "It's one of the few things I'm good at."

"I can't believe that. In any case, Dudek shows up and he's not gonna leave you alone. Go on."

"He became insistent. Aggravating. He grabbed my arm and I shoved him off and told him—" *Do dead.* Cat swallowed hard, pushed her hair behind her ear.

"Take your time."

"That's when I heard the shots."

"Shots? More than one?"

"Yes. Everything happened so fast, but when I play it back in my head, I keep hearing two shots. Jerry fell against me. I hit my head on the bumper and I thought for a minute—"

"That it was this murder game."

Cat nodded. "Then I saw the blood on my—my clothes—and I wanted to scream, and then I saw Jerry's—his head—and I guess that's when I passed out, and came to in the ER."

"Mrs. Austen, would you like a glass of water?"

"No."

"Coffee?" He had risen, circled his desk, was leaning over her.

"No. No thank you." His head. Not even the mortician had been able to reconstruct Chris's shattered skull, and in the end, Carlo had made him close the casket.

"Mrs. Austen?"

His voice was urgent, alarmed. Cat pressed her hands to her cheeks, looked into his face. "I'm all right."

"You tell me if you feel ill. Want to take a break."

I must look awful, she thought. "I'm fine." She composed her voice and tried again. "I'm fine."

"Let's backtrack a little, shall we?"

Cat nodded, mutely.

"There was a parking lot attendant when you arrived?"

"Yes."

"But not when you got back to your car?"

"You pay when you enter. The lot was full when I came out of CV's. Once it's full, the attendant probably doesn't have to stick around."

"Someone might leave, free up a few spaces."

Cat shook her head. "People who come and go use the casino lots. People who put down five, six dollars are there for the duration."

Good point, Victor conceded, stroking his mustache, absently. Those brothers must have taught her a thing or two. He began to pace. "About the shots, now. Two, you said. You're certain the second one wasn't an echo, a car backfiring, a door—"

"I know what a gunshot sounds like, Lieutenant."

"Of course. And there was no one around?"

"A few members of the Pacific Avenue sorority."

He cocked an eyebrow, amused. "Which direction were you facing when you were fending off Dudek?"

"Toward my car door. Jerry was a little to my left, his back to that fence under the Boardwalk."

"The dunes underneath don't touch the boards. You could see past Dudek to the beach."

"The wind was coming from that direction. I was getting sand in my eyes. Of course," she added, slowly, "someone could have been watching us from the beach, his back to the wind."

"Not the easiest of targets."

"There was enough light for a good shooter."

"Possibly. Now Mrs. Austen—"

"Cat. Everybody just calls me Cat."

"Short for Catherine?"

"Just Cat."

She could smile like La Gioconda, quite unconsciously. "Cat, then. You got to know Dudek, you'd already conducted an interview with him, what about his personal life? Anything in his past? Enemies?"

"Actually, Jerry tended to sidestep personal questions. I got the feeling he was trying to invent himself. Ron Spivak—he was the first writer assigned to the story—began a background check before he was hospitalized. If I get anything from him that seems relevant, I'll let you know. Jerry riled people, certainly. If you've ever heard the show, you know that much. But a specific enemy?"

*Do dead.* Cat shuddered. Remorse, horror blurred the details of the preceding night. *Do dead.*

Victor tracked the flush that rose from her throat to her cheeks. Something's thrown her off. He could pressure her or he could postpone. Sometimes it took two, three interviews to get the whole picture. And he wouldn't mind seeing her again.

"I'm sorry, Lieutenant, where were we?"

"Look, let's wrap this up for now. Leave your address and phone with whoever's at the desk. The DA's office will call you about a formal statement." Victor opened the door. "Sergeant Rice, come in here."

Stan materialized, instantly.

"After the post mortem, check with AC, see if they spoke to the lot attendant yet. Then go over to KRZI and have a talk with the station manager—Fried, was it?" He looked to Cat for confirmation.

"Yes, Barry Fried." Not a bad idea, Cat thought. Fried had brought Tom and Jerry to KRZI. How was he taking this?

"Hopper's phone's been on the machine. If he's at the station, tell him to get over here to make a statement. I know KRZI shares building space with *NewsLineNinety*, so keep a low profile. Raab wants to hold off on the press."

"Excuse me, Lieutenant?"

"Mrs. Austen?"

"The receptionist at KRZI, Deanna something? Maybe Stan ought to talk to her, too."

"Why?"

"She was there last night, hung around our table. She seemed to imply that she was Jerry's girlfriend."

"How did Dudek act toward her?"

Cat shrugged. "Like Jerry acted around all women. Do straighten your tie, Stanley. She's quite young and very pretty and no doubt feeling particularly—receptive."

"Oh yeah?"

Cat threw her coat over her arm and extended her hand to Victor. She had a firm handshake.

"I'll walk you out, Cat. What was her name, Deanna?"

Stan returned several minutes past the requirements of simple courtesy.

"How well do you know her?" Victor asked.

"I played some ball with Joey Fortunati, he introduced us. You meet the King?"

"Last night." *And twenty-six years ago.* "'Cat'?"

Stan shrugged. "Whole family calls her that."

"Did you know the husband?"

"I met him once. I know what happened."

"What happened?"

"He's a state cop; one of the brothers introduced the two of 'em. He's coming off his shift, car's stalled near the Somers Point exit on the parkway, pregnant woman in labor. He runs her over to Shore Memorial, it's the day before Easter, ER's a zoo. Guy walks in, his arm in a sling, shoves past the security guard, pulls out a thirty-eight, gets off three, four rounds, first one gets Austen right here—" He leaned into Victor, aimed his forefinger at Victor's right temple, cocked his thumb. "Bada boom. Point blank, then he hits an ER doctor, and a patient, before the security guard and two nurses take him down. But he's still got the gun, see, and he jams it right here—" Stan punched the center of his chest, emphatically. "Baboom. What a mess. He was a stand-up guy, Austen. Damn shame."

Victor recalled Cat's pallor when she had described Jerry's injuries. No wonder.

"Lives in that place her aunt left her, got a couple kids, been doing some writing, she's pretty good, too. Smart. No social life, though."

"Really?" Victor hoped his tone sounded impersonal. "What about that lawyer, Delareto?"

Stan shook his head. "Him, she's known from way back. That's strictly business, at least on her part. Me, I asked her out a couple times, she turned me down. Joey says they tried to fix her up, she's not interested. Why? You wanna give it a shot? I got fifty bucks says you strike out. I know a safe bet when I see one."

Victor's expression relaxed in a cool, impassive frown. "How long have you worked in this area, Rice?"

"Atlantic City eleven years, almost two here, you know that. Why?"

"That's long enough to have learned the cardinal rule of the gaming industry."

"Which is?"

"There's no such thing as a safe bet."

# CHAPTER

## FOUR

Steve Delareto was as good as his word; better. He'd had time to run Cat's Maxima through a car wash in case bits of Jerry Dudek had clung and had it waiting on Dolphin Avenue when Stan Rice escorted her to the door.

He handed Cat the keys, brushed off her "Send me the bill," insisted, "You need anything, you call me," as he helped her behind the wheel. She flashed the same sweet-stubborn smile she'd worn since they were kids and he knew she wouldn't call. Cat Austen seemed to be working hard at needing nothing, no one. Except her kids, and a little freelancing on the side.

Cat turned south on Shore Road, which linked the "offshore" communities of run-down Pleasantville, commercial Northfield, upscale Linwood, blue collar Somers Point. The colloquialism distinguished these from the barrier islands, which were "on-shore," "down the shore," or simply "the shore."

KRZI/Newsline90 was based in two stories of whitewashed concrete and smoked glass on a scrap of bay front in Somers Point, overlooking the Somers Point-Ocean City bridge. Cat pulled up beside the NewsLine90 van, with its red and blue logo declaring "News You Can Be SHORE Of!" Her impulsiveness ebbed. What if Stan had beaten her over and wanted to know why she was there? What if she ran into someone from the news who'd heard she was an eyewitness? It's the "what-ifs" that'll kill you she told the scairdy Cat, and set her chin, firmly. You're a reporter. Sort of. Until Ritchie tells you he's decided to kill the piece, you may as well stick with it.

Deanna was not at KRZI's general reception desk. The three offices shared by the twelve on-air personalities were silent. Faint music drifted from the control room at the end of the hall, and a little to the left, a lone secretary sat guard at the station manager's office.

The girl was in her early twenties, plain, lanky with a corona of reddish hair, round hazel eyes, milky skin dappled with rusty freckles. As Cat approached, she saw that the girl's eyes were swollen, the too-black mascara smeared, the foundation layered over the freckles rubbed clean at the nose, the freckles beneath abraded, dark red. Cat had met the girl when she had interviewed Tom and Jerry at the station; the poor thing had been pathetically eager to be of use to Cat, hopelessly infatuated with Jerry. Cat's eyes darted to the nameplate: Sondra Du Bois. Cat remembered that the girl had pronounced it "Duboice."

"How can I help you?" The inquiry was punctuated with sobs; the girl dredged the bottom of a Kleenex box as she spoke.

"I was wondering if Mr. Fried was in."

"Oh (sob) yeah. You're the writer, Mrs. Austen, right? You're doin' a article on Jerry an' Tom." She jabbed the intercom with mascara-stained fingers. "Mr. (sob) Fried?"

"Sandy, I said no calls. No calls means no calls."

"Mrs. (sob) Austen the writer is here to see you."

"Oh." Pause. "Okay."

Barry Fried was a small man. The lifts in his shoes put him eye level with Cat (who was five-seven) but only when he sustained exemplary posture and she was wearing flats. Today, Fried looked deflated. His shoulders slumped, his jaw sagged, his head lolled mournfully to one side; limp brown hair sprouted errantly around the bald spot he had been too distracted to camouflage. He waved Cat toward a chair.

"So whaddamy gonna do? Siddown. Landis over the magazine calls, guy sounds happy as a pig in turpentine. What is he, crazy, what? He wants pixtures of Jerry's office, I said no pixtures 'cause the cops, they call, they wanna go over it with a nine-tooth comb."

"Oh? When?"

Fried shrugged. "Whenever. Jesuey. You know what I hadda do get Tom an' Jerry to come down here from Camden? Camden wannid to get 'em back, offered 'em some good money, but the boys, they're loyal to KRZI, say what you want."

"Really?" Jerry hadn't impressed her as someone who would place loyalty over personal advantage. Tom might. "Was it Camden that made them an offer, then? I heard it was Philly One Oh Four, and that they were considering it."

"Ah, prob'ly something Jerry made up to jack up their price when it came time to re-sign. No truth to it."

So much for loyalty. Cat changed the subject. "Have you talked to Tom?"

"Yeah, he's in his office. He's a mess."

"He came in today?"

"Where's he gonna go? He said he's just gonna go through some of their stuff, keep himself busy so he don't have to think. I think he's in waddayoucall, shock. I mean, they been together what, six years? Hell, marriages today, they don't last that long, my marriages didn't didn't last that long. Losin' Jerry's like him losin' a brother, a husband, you know what I mean?"

"Yes," Cat replied, quietly. "I know what you mean."

"I mean, he's not on the air. We're just runnin' music this morning, you know, respec'ful kinda music, Phil Collins, Judy Collins, Simon an' that other guy he was with."

"Garfunkel."

"Whatever."

A shudder ascended from Cat's stomach to her throat, threatening to emerge as laughter. She coughed away the impulse.

"So what's gonna happen with the piece? Landis, he still sounds gung ho, sounds like a cannibal in Calcutta."

Cat coughed. "I'm not sure."

"Tell him he should make it like a tribute. Like a euphemy. You got a cold?"

Cat shook her head. "You mean eulogy?"

"Whatever. Like what we're gonna do on the air next week. I already got it figured out. We'll use somma Tom an' Jerry's old tapes, give Tommy a break, time to pull himself together, then maybe we could team him up with Andy Bowker, you know, Andy the Count, does nine to midnight? Whaddayou think?"

"I—you were saying about filling in with some of their old material next week?"

"Yeah, like I was sayin', we'll play somma their old stuff, call it 'The Best of Tom an' Jerry,' fill in with somma Jerry's favorite music, you know, like the Stones, an' Metallica an' Guns an', you know."

"Roses."

"Whatever. Arrowsmith, Red Hot Chili Peckers, stuff like that. An' put in somma those ads Jerry would screw up on purpose. He was too much that sonofabitch! Didja ever hear somma that stuff?"

"I don't think the Bayside Restaurant appreciated the salmonella Newburg remark, or the Ringside was particularly pleased when he referred to their 'Out of this World' party as an 'Out of the Closet' party."

"It was a joke."

"The Gay and Lesbian Task Force didn't quite see the humor in it, as I recall."

"Aaahhh, whadda they know?" Fried chuckled. "The Bayside, they're gonna sue us, right? Then business picks up an' they realize gettin' worked over by Jerry's 's good as an ad in The Press! It was gettin' to where Tom an' Jerry could make or break a place! Four delis named hoagies after them, f'crissakes!"

Cat thought for a moment. "Can you think of any place they did break? Or anyone?"

"Nahhh! Everybody loved 'em! I mean, they hated Jerry, but they really loved him, you know what I mean?"

"Someone didn't."

Fried wagged his head in bewilderment. "Look, everybody wannid to kill that sonofabitch once in a while, me included, it was what made him so great. He could get on your nerves like beach sand in the CheezWhiz. He could make you mad as a yellow jacket in a kite shop. But what the hell? We're a point and a half from the number one slot. You wanna see the Arbitrons?" He seized a hefty, soft-bound book from the shelf, plopped it on his desk. "I mean, you really wanna see 'em?"

Miss Du Bois-pronounced-Duboice had finished off the dainty pop-up Kleenexes and was working her way through a wad of generic paper towels snatched from the ladies' room. The freckles had gone two shades darker.

"Where's the receptionist?" Cat asked, casually. "Deanna what's-her-name?"

"Hal-(sob)-prin. Called in sick. Says she's too traumatized to work! What about me? I'm four times as traumatized, but I know someone's gotta keep things running, 'cause that's what Jerry would've wanted."

"Well, I suppose, she being Jerry's girlfriend—"

"*Deanna!* Did she tell you that? Like she wants you to put it in your article? That—"

"She didn't say a thing," Cat soothed. "It's just an impression I got."

"Well, take a look at this!" The girl jabbed her left hand into Cat's face, flashed a ring identical to the one Deanna had flaunted the night before. Had Jerry passed them out like party favors?

"We were keeping our engage-(sob)-ment a secret 'til Jerry an' Tom signed the new contracts after Christmas. Jerry said they were gonna get a big raise, an' then I could get rid of my apartment and we'd look for a hou-oowse!" The girl burst into tears and sprinted for the ladies' room.

Fried was wrong, Cat concluded. Not everyone hated Jerry. She passed Tom's door, paused, knocked softly.

"Yeah. I'm here."

Cat slipped into the room. Tom Hopper was slumped over a desk littered with cassette tapes, magazine clippings, notepads, stacks of *Rolling Stone* and *Spin*, that morning's *Press* on the floor, the headline—"Local Celebrity Slain in Parking Lot"—staring up at Cat, boldly.

Tom stumbled to his feet, offered Cat the only chair, shoved a folder into a drawer, spilled a mug of pencils, snatched the newspaper and tossed it headline-down on the desk. "Gimme your— let me take your coat," he offered.

Cat gently pushed Tom back into the chair, closed the door and tossed her coat over the litter on the desk. Tom was wearing the same clothes he'd worn the night before, Cat observed. He hadn't shaved and his blue eyes were underscored with dark crescents. Without his glasses, the eyes looked naked, haunted. "Tom, you shouldn't be here."

"What does it matter where I am? Maybe nobody'll look for me here. Jesus, someone came into the club, pulled me out and made me identify him. I thought it was a joke at first. I mean, Jerry could—Jerry really knew how to put one over on you."

"What about Noreen?"

Tom looked up, blearily. "Huh?"

"She's his sister. Why didn't they ask her to identify the— him?" Cat tried to imagine losing one of her brothers; couldn't.

"No one there knew who she was."

"You did."

"I told her to take off. I heard some commotion in CV's, I didn't want her mixed up in anything. When I went back in, someone told me Jerry got into it with some drunk."

"What did you do then?"

Tom shrugged. "I looked around for Jerry. I never thought he'd take off; we were supposed to hang around for at least another hour. Why? You tell the cops about Noreen?"

"You know, I never even thought to mention her. I guess I assumed they knew. How is she taking it?"

"I don't know. She—I haven't seen her since last night."

"Were she and Jerry close?" Since last night before or after the murder, Cat wondered?

Tom's blue eyes filled with tears. He blotted them with the palms of his hands. "Sorry. This hasn't all sunk in yet."

"Tom, you ought to go home and get some sleep."

"I can't sleep."

"When's the funeral, has she decided?"

"She?"

"Noreen. She's his only family, isn't she?"

"I, uh, guess it'll be around Monday, Tuesday—today's Friday, right?"

"Right."

Tom groped for his glasses under Cat's coat, shoved them in front of his eyes. "What about you? They took you away in an ambulance. Someone told me you were shot, too. I couldn't believe it."

Cat tapped the gauze at her temple. "Just this. Lucky."

"Guess it goes with the name. Fortunati, right?"

"What? Oh, right, it means 'lucky.' "

"So I guess this kills your story. Or is that a rotten thing to think about at a time like this?"

"No. But it changes everything. Ritchie may want to give it back to Ron Spivak. He's more experienced, and he'd already done some of the background."

"I thought Spivak was out of commission."

"He should be out of the hospital by the weekend. I guess I'll just stick with it until I get pulled off."

"Or scared off?" he suggested pointedly.

*"Short of gunfire, I don't scare,"* she had quipped. Cat shuddered. "Maybe the Fortunati luck will hold. Tell me something: were Jerry and Mr. Fried's secretary really engaged?"

Tom emitted a snort of mirthless laughter. "I guess there's no harm in letting her think so now."

"And Deanna Halprin?"

The corners of Tom's mouth dropped, coldly. "Jerry had a lot of women. A lot of women," he repeated in a low voice. "They were a game."

"Not a very nice game."

"Jerry didn't like nice games. The nastier the better."

"Nasty as in blackmail?"

"Huh?"

"Last night. Stuff he was handing me. This one's sleeping with that one, somebody's fixed a beauty pageant . . ."

"He was just playing with your head, Cat. Having fun with the small-time freelancer."

"Thanks."

"No offense. Look, Jerry pulled a lot of stunts, on the air and off, some of them not so nice. But blackmail?" Tom shook his head. "I mean, I'm not saying he didn't make enemies. He even got a couple death threats. Crackpots. He got a kick out of it, said he loved feeling all that animosity, said hate was a better high than sex. Enmity was his orgasm. That's why he worked so hard at cultivating it."

"And you're certain he wasn't turning it into a cash crop?"

"You just don't get it, Cat. Alienating people was what Jerry did because he was good at it. Not for money, though God knows there wasn't anything he wouldn't do for money, but because he loved it. That wild, take-no-prisoners persona he created, he stepped right into it and never looked back. Or looked around to see who was getting hurt."

"Or getting fed up. Or worse."

Tom nodded grimly. "God, I don't envy the cops."

"Why?"

"I mean, how are they going to figure out who killed a guy that almost everyone who owns a radio wanted to kill?"

# **CHAPTER**

## FIVE

Little Miss Du Bois jogged across the parking lot, her short, coiled mane ballooning around her splotched face. "Mrs. Austen! Mrs. Austen!"

Cat turned.

Miss Du Bois extended her hand. "Did you drop these?" She held out a key ring suspended by a pitted brass tab engraved with Cat's initials, A F A.

"Must have dropped out of my pocket, thanks." Cat unlocked her car door.

"Look, there's anything you want to know about Jerry, I'm the one to ask, I was closer to him even than Tom or Mr. Fried."

"Closer than family?" Cat baited.

"Jerry didn't have no family. He was a orphan. He said we were each other's family. I gotta run."

She doesn't know about Noreen. Or she's the next Sarah Bernhardt. Cat opted for the former.

Ellice was draped over a chair reading Marcus Aurelius when Cat walked in at eleven-fifteen. "Annamarie gone?"

"Yeah. She wasn't thrilled at you sneakin' out, either."

"The only way I could get past her was to sneak." Cat hung her coat in the closet under the stairs, went to the kitchen, knocked on the back door window and waved to Jane and Mats in the yard below, grabbed a Diet Pepsi and rejoined Ellice.

"'Consider that everything which happens happens justly and if thou observest carefully, thou wilt find it to be so,'" Ellice greeted.

"'Pepsi's the taste for a new generation,'" Cat replied, popping the lid.

"Honey, you look beat."

"What'd Annie tell the kids?"

"She said you bumped your head last night and needed a ride home, so you went to get your car this morning."

"Steve got it. Annie called Carlo and Carlo sent Steve to run interference." Cat drank. "Any messages?"

"Freddy called right after you left."

"Called for *me?*" Cat teased. Freddy Fortunati was infatuated with Ellice.

Ellice grinned, wryly. "Ritchie Landis called twice. Call him back, call him back. Some secretary from the DA's office called, she'll call *you* back. Whitney Rocap called—"

"Who?"

"You know. The weather gal on *NewsLineNinety?*"

Cat's mind locked onto the sprayed-to-immobility coif, the hazel-green eyes, but the expression was not camera coy, it was pale, vicious. Cat realized it had been Whitney Rocap who had quarreled with Jerry on the dance floor, stalked off.

"She seemed real annoyed you weren't around. I didn't know you knew her. Oh, and that cop called."

"Stan Rice?"

"No, the lieutenant. Cardenas."

"I just came from there. Well, actually, I made a detour."

"This was about fifteen minutes ago."

"Does he want me to call him back?"

"Yeah. So where were you?"

"At KRZI."

"And your mom called."

"Does she know anything about last night?"

Ellice shook her head. "Relax. She just wanted to remind you about Sunday. Your name wasn't in *The Press*, I guess you can thank *fratelli* Fortunati for that."

Cat stretched an arm for the phone on the end table, dialed *The South Jersey Magazine* and asked for Ritchie Landis.

"Are you all right?" shrieked Ritchie's secretary.

"My name wasn't in the paper."

"Ritchie finds out everything, you know that. God, the people he hangs out with, he oughta. He's goin' crazy here! I'll put you through."

"He's goin' crazy there," Cat informed Ellice.

"Cat! Cat!" Ritchie spoke too fast, too loudly. "I'm goin' crazy here! When I heard it, I'm thinkin', we're already two steps ahead of the game, 'cause of our piece an' here Dudek goes an' gets himself whacked, my entertainment girl's an eyewitness, an' I'm thinkin', if I hadn't gone sending you out there last night, I'm thinkin'—"

"Preterite," Cat interrupted. "You ought to be using the preterite tense, Ritchie, or at very least past progressive. Present progressive's all wrong. You're an editor."

"Who the hell's thinking verbs! We're standin' here with a major story dropped into our lap—"

"When you're standing you don't have any lap."

Ritchie ignored it. "You tell me how many editors get this lucky, get one of their girls right next to a hit?"

"Writers," Cat corrected. "Not 'girls.' "

"Yeah, yeah. You talk to the cops?"

"Just now."

"You feel 'em out? They got any leads?"

"Let me get this straight, Ritchie. You're not dropping this or giving it back to Ron? Green light?"

"Show me how good you are."

"I'm good enough to have overheard some very revealing

conversations last night, not to mention the tape of their interview last week and a private exchange with Tom Hopper this morning."

"I'm lovin' this! I'm lovin' it! I'm goin' crazy—"

Cat held up the receiver for Ellice's benefit, put it back to her ear. "So let's talk."

"We're talkin'."

"I meant money."

"Caaaaat. We talked money."

"For an interview that was half Ron's, not for a major crime story dropped in my lap." She winked at Ellice.

"You show me yours first."

"I get the background Ron dug up, what I got last night, talk to a few people, see what I can pry out of the cops, it's your March cover."

"The cops get the shooter, February. You got some connections at ACPD, right?"

"They have a couple detectives on it, but it's Major Crimes' ball game. A lieutenant named Cardenas."

"So what, you're sayin' you're not sure you can deliver?"

"I can deliver, but not for free." Cat hardly recognized her own voice. She had always been too unsure of her ability to be anything but accommodating with Ritchie. Confrontation was a luxury of the pros, like Ron Spivak.

"I gotta know what you got first."

"I got in the line of fire last night, that's what I got!"

"Look, fax me a draft—"

"Fax you, I can't even afford a PC."

"Okay, ballpark."

"Fifteen hundred."

Ellice tossed her book in the air.

"Plus a roll in the sheets, you got a deal."

"Twelve."

"High opinion of yourself, Austen. Seven-fifty."

"Twelve."

"Eight-fifty, and maybe some expense money."

"A thousand and some expense money."

"Get lost."

Cat drew the phone away from her mouth, said to the room at large, "*Who* called from *The Press*? And he wants me to get back to him *today*?"

"All *right!* A thousand plus. Bitch."

"I'm getting there."

"You better be worth it." He slammed down the phone.

Cat swallowed a wave of panic. She had to be worth it. This wasn't a column and a half on the local flower show. Could she deliver?

"Getting where?" Ellice asked.

"Bitchhood."

"It's about time, don't you think?"

Cat nodded, dialed Major Crimes, asked for Lieutenant Cardenas, was put on hold, listened to a couple bars of "Feelings." "Did he say what he wanted?"

Ellice shook her head.

"Mrs. Austen?"

"You need to upgrade your Musak, Lieutenant. People who are compelled to listen to 'Feelings' can become downright felonious. I'm sure there must be statistics to back me on that."

"I'll make a note of it. You didn't go straight home."

"Is that what you forgot to ask me?"

"No. I forgot to ask you to have dinner with me tonight."

Cat dropped the phone into her lap.

"What?" Ellice whispered. "Are you under arrest?"

"Worse." Cat slipped her hand over the mouthpiece. "He asked me to dinner!"

"What's he look like?"

Cat lifted her brows expressively, put the receiver back to her ear. "Lieutenant, I'm not really—"

"He's not married, is he?" asked Ellice.

"Shhh!"

"I can watch the kids. But not if he's married."

"What, you want me to ask him if he's married?"

"I beg your pardon?" asked the phone.

"I'm sorry, Lieutenant, I have someone here."

The inflection of his "Oh?" requested particulars. Cat wondered if he were wondering if she meant a man. "Lieuten—"

"Victor."

"Yes, of course. You see, I don't—"

"Date."

"Date."

"You're depriving yourself."

Vain, Cat smiled. "I'm depriving you," she countered, archly. That would have gotten a laugh from Steve or Stan Rice, but the phone was silent, waiting. Cat shot Ellice a what-should-I-tell-him? look.

Ellice jammed Marcus Aurelius under a cushion, stalked to the phone and yanked the receiver from Cat's hand. "Lieutenant, this is Ms. Watson, Mrs. Austen's social secretary. I see here in her engagement book, if we re-schedule the laundry for Saturday afternoon and bump the grocery shopping ahead to this afternoon, we should be able to free her up for a couple hours this evening. Can I pencil you in for seven o'clock?"

Cat choked on a swallow of Pepsi, grabbed back the phone. "Lieutenant," she coughed, "I'm sorry. Ms. Watson is our resident lunatic. We generally keep her locked in the attic. I can't for the life of me imagine how she got out."

"It happens. Seven sounds fine, though."

"I'm not sure it's a good idea."

"Well, there are, of course, the financial inducements."

"Sorry?"

"Sergeant Rice has offered fifty dollars to anyone who gets you to go out. Come to dinner with me and I'll cut you in for twenty percent."

"You've underestimated me, Lieutenant," Cat replied coolly. "I couldn't possibly agree to less than twenty-five."

This time she heard a smile. "Very well. Twenty-five it is. I'll pick you up at seven." He hung up.

"There!" Cat accused Ellice. "See what you made me do!"

Ellice perched next to Cat, put an arm around her. "Honey, what's bothering you? I mean, he's not a—what did Jane call that kid in her music class?—a total dweeb, is he? Not into heavy metal or golf or any revolting thing like that?"

"I don't think so. He seems almost normal for a cop."

"Good-looking?"

"In a kind of dark, Latin, serious kind of way."

"I give extra credit for dark."

"You're too late. I've passed the and-what-did-you-major-in-in-college? stage."

"No sweat. Ask him about his job. Better yet, ask him about his *car*. You won't have to do any of the talkin' then, believe you *me*. Dinner, straight home, had a lovely time, kiss, kiss, good-night."

Cat bit her lip. "Back in the dark ages, before I got married, it was: you don't kiss on the first date."

"Hey, he met Carlo last night, that oughta be enough to keep him in line. Weren't you just tellin' Landis you could deliver on Dudek's shooting? Dinner with the lieutenant in charge gives you the inside track. Use it."

The phone rang. Cat reached for it.

"Mrs. Austen?"

"Yes?"

"You know who this is?"

A woman. A TV voice, but harsher. "Miss Rocap?"

"Do you have it?"

"I beg your pardon?"

"Look, let's cut to the chase. You got it, I want it. So what do you want? It's your move."

"I'd like to hang up and take a nap."

"You do that. Just remember, Jerry screwed someone like you're doing to me right now; look what it got him. Think it over."

The line went dead.

# CHAPTER
## SIX

Five years before, a state task force had been organized to investigate a series of links connecting a white supremacist cult known as The Order, arms smuggling and racially motivated crimes. Victor had been pulled from the Atlantic City force for a year's work undercover. The year had become three, and he returned to AC to find many of his former colleagues promoted or burnt out. His reputation as a patient, tenacious investigator, and his twelve months at the FBI Academy put him on the track that often led to an assignment with one of the county prosecutor's investigative units: racketeering, narcotics, arson, major crimes. Victor had been with the latter for eighteen months.

He took an apartment on Delancy Place, a quiet, beach block street near the boundary dividing AC from middle-class Ventnor. The commute offshore was tedious, but Victor had lived in Atlantic City as a boy, after the move from San Juan and before his father's death, then again when he joined the department, married. He felt something for the town, some residual affection that in his cynical moments he felt the place little deserved.

Two- and three-story houses flanked his dead end street. Victor's apartment was the second floor of the only subdivided residence. He liked the location; three houses from a non-commercial strip of Boardwalk and beach. Mornings, he could have his swim, his occasional jog, ignored by the handful of year-round neighbors who looked down on Mrs. DiLorenzo for taking in a tenant.

Mrs. DiLorenzo, Victor's landlady, lived in the apartment beneath his. She had made it clear to Victor that she didn't need the income and wouldn't rent to "just anybody," then turned around and bragged to her cronies that Lieutenant Cardenas paid his rent on time, kept to himself, didn't smoke or play loud music or run around with women, had shoveled and salted the walk last winter, was exceptionally well-mannered, good-looking ("for a Portorikkan," she was wont to add), and it couldn't hurt to have a policeman living right there in the neighborhood. Besides, who was it climbed on the roof to get poor Nero last summer when she had called the fire department and they told her no way?

Nero was a Mexican boa constrictor that Mrs. DiLorenzo cultivated "for protection." She had absentmindedly pushed the air-conditioning to sixty-four one scorching July afternoon; Nero became disoriented, heaved aside the screen on his tank, beat a path through the oven vent and scuttled three stories in quest of an ambient eighty-five degrees. Coiled upon the north slope of his owner's slate roof, the obstinate snake could not be persuaded to descend, not even when his desperate owner stood upwind and swung a live mouse by the tail.

Victor chivalrously ascended the ancient fire stairs and hoisted the torpid animal onto his shoulders, thanking God the whole time that his kid sister Remy wasn't there to see it, he would never have heard the end of it.

In time, Mrs. DiLorenzo's neighbors conceded that Lieutenant Cardenas seemed a decent enough man, perhaps even handsome ("for a Portorikkan"), though somewhat grim.

Romantically, Victor had not progressed beyond the casual and temporary, though he was once again receptive to serious involvement, often longed for it. There had been a vibrant nurse who manned a casino medical station, but Victor had been one of many, and she opted, eventually, for a high-roller from Long Island. There had been a shrewd, redheaded bartender who frankly wanted little more than sex, which had surprised Victor, though not unpleasantly. A pair of former husbands had been Victor's rivals for the attentions of a bewitching caterer, and after losing out to bachelor number two, Victor decided three strikes, out.

Of course, Marisol's death hit him hard. Then, too, there were lines he was reluctant to cross, impediments of conscience that his colleagues bridged quite guiltlessly: never a married woman, never a co-worker, never a suspect. Not even a woman tangentially connected with a case. Until this Friday in November when he found himself at Cat Fortunati Austen's front door.

Victor surveyed 1043 Morningside Drive: off-street parking, well-kept, prime location, even a bit of yard in the back. What had Rice said? That she'd inherited it? You're off duty, he reminded himself. It's none of your business.

He rang the bell, peered through a border of glass block. An inner door opened, a silhouette of someone adult and female, not Cat. The door was opened by one of the loveliest women Victor had ever seen.

She was somewhat taller than Cat, skin the color of expensive chocolate, matching eyes alight with wry curiosity, maybe a dash of suspicion. The glossy black hair was cut low on the forehead, short on the sides. The cheekbones were slanting and prominent, the lips a full, perfect bow and the figure was outstanding.

"Victor, right?" The voice was throaty, sensual, with an amused lilt.

He recognized it. "The social secretary."

"And resident lunatic. Ellice Watson." She shook hands and waved Victor through the tiny foyer to the center hall. "Sorry about that business on the phone. But then, 'no excellent soul is exempt from a mixture of madness,' after all."

"Aristotle?"

The lips pursed in appreciation. "Make yourself comfortable, Lieutenant. I'm gonna go hurry Cat along."

The open hallway extended to an L-shaped stair. A den around back, he gathered, from the sound of TV laughter. Dining room to the left, a picture window with a good ocean view, living room to the right.

He stepped into the living room and looked around. Furniture upholstered in dark, Victorian florals, carpet a warm rose, oak mantle over the fireplace, a wall of bookshelves filled with classics, bios, reference works, a few novels, plays. Someone read philosophy and someone fancied Jane Austen, Oscar Wilde, Edith Wharton, Shakespeare. He turned to the photos on the mantle, black-and-whites of a middle-aged couple posed beneath a restaurant awning, two young men in state police uniforms (was one the husband?), school pictures of a little girl, younger boy, grinning self-consciously into the lens.

He felt them, turned. They had their mother's large, solemn eyes, and the girl at least had her resolute mouth. She was about nine, the boy four or five.

"Are you a real cop?" the boy asked.

"Yes."

"You know karate?"

"A little."

"You got a gun?"

"I do."

"Right now?"

Victor nodded.

"Guns kill people," declared the girl, her eyes wise and wary. She would be old enough to remember her father's death, Victor thought, and had no intention of allowing another man into her life.

"C'mon Mats, I'll read to you." She grabbed her brother's hand and led him away.

Ellice refused to go downstairs and tell Lieutenant Cardenas that Cat had taken sick. "What's wrong with him?" she demanded as she rummaged through Cat's closet. "He knows Aristotle."

"Cops meet the damnedest people."

Ellice emerged with a droll smile and a hanger draped with black velvet.

"That's too dressy. Black silk pants and a blouse?"

Ellice threw the dress at her. "Okay, so he's a little somber, maybe he'll lighten up. What was that line? 'I am the somber one, the un-consoled widower, the Prince of Aquitaine, whose tower was destroyed, my only star is dead,' duh da duh da, I forget the rest. Put on the dress."

Cat stood, resignedly, yanked the garment over her silk teddy, adjusted the wide, square neckline. "It is a pretty dress," she conceded, smoothing the princess seams. "I bought it four years ago to celebrate getting my figure back after Mats was born." She poked gold and onyx ovals into her ears, put on the gold chain with the floating heart the children had given her last Mother's Day. "Go tell him I'll be down in a minute."

"An' don't go locking yourself in here, 'cause I'll break the door down," was Ellice's parting comment.

"Okay," Cat addressed her reflection, "you're stuck, so make it work. Some general conversation first. What a nice car! Good God. So do you live in Atlantic City? How about those—what is it, football season? Segue, segue, how's the investigation going, anything turn up?" She prodded her reflection in the chest. "You told Ritchie you could do this, Lois Lane. Think of the money." She pinned her hair behind her ears with gold and enamel combs, gave a thumbs-up to the Cat in the mirror.

Victor's somber expression did not change perceptibly when Cat appeared, but she could read approval in his eyes. Ellice hustled the children away from the television.

"Are you going to be as late as last night?" demanded the daughter.

Cat took a white wool coat from the stair closet. "Not too late. You'll be in bed when I get home, but I'll come to check on you. Victor, this is Jane, that one's Mats."

"We've met."

"You gonna leave a number?" Ellice asked.

Victor scribbled the restaurant's number, his cellular, the Major

Crimes switchboard on a pad beside the phone, nearly wrote his home number as well, but decided not to take too much for granted. Cat kissed the children goodnight.

She was relieved to see that his Jaguar was new, coddled; it allowed her to open with, "Nice car." But the lieutenant simply replied, "Oh, thanks" and did not plunge into a monologue about pistons and horsepower and torque as her brother Joey would have done. Cat sighed and fell silent, considering her next gambit.

Victor tried to analyze the sigh, wondered if her head still hurt, if she had been thinking about Dudek's murder, maybe remembered something more. He glanced at her periodically, saw minute shifts in expression, a fluctuating light in her eye that suggested a vibrant mind beneath the reserved exterior. He fumbled in his coat pocket, came up with a penny, tossed it on the dashboard in front of her.

Cat pushed it aside delicately, with a quiet shake of her head. "No. I think I'd sell anything I own before—" she tapped her forehead. "Certainly not so cheap." Again, the Mona Lisa smile.

This was no common woman. "Have you ever been to Giacinto?" he asked.

"No, never. I don't really go out."

Victor had been lucky to get a reservation. Giacinto, wedged between an Atlantic City doughnut shop and a pharmacy, had no sign, no parking lot, no listing in the Yellow Pages. The phone number circulated by word of mouth among the privileged, and the owner was wont to inquire, when the phone line opened at two P.M., "Are you one of our regulars?" Tables for the evening were booked by three. The cleverer patrons had put Giacinto's number on speed dial.

Victor owed tonight's good fortune to the heart attack and subsequent cancellation of an Atlantic county freeholder and a reliable endorsement from Paulie "The Apron" Forgione. Paulie the Apron was an executioner by trade, renowned for his obsessive tidiness and keen eye for detail. Upon Paulie's arrest, Victor had arranged for Mrs. The Apron to procure some toiletries and a few linen handkerchiefs for her husband before he was dispatched to a federal penitentiary in Texas. Never one to forget a favor (and facing exile from Giacinto for some twenty-five to life), Apron passed the coveted phone number to Victor. "They give you any trouble, you tell Pasquale you're a friend of mine. Not once did I have to put on the apron in his place and he knows how to return a favor." Victor had received the last table due to the aforementioned heart attack and so was spared the necessity of invoking The Apron's name.

They were ushered to a black lacquered table set among textured walls, Georgia O'Keefe prints, mauve and white dinner service, handed a menu by a pretty girl with a dimpled chin and a Catanese accent who recited the specials, offered Victor the wine list and departed.

Cat smoothed her napkin on her lap, looked around. "It's lovely. However did you hear about this place?" She wondered if anyone had reviewed it. She wouldn't mind putting together four, five hundred words if the food was good.

Impulsively, Victor told her about Paulie the Apron, rendering The Apron's Jersey Sicilian dialect with such wicked accuracy that Cat laughed aloud, lilting, spontaneous laughter that flattered Victor.

"I have a peculiar sense of humor," she apologized. "My family says it borders on perversion."

He found that rather promising.

A waiter came to take their orders. Victor was amused by her transition to hard-boiled connoisseur. Did they use fresh basil? Imported *parma reggiano*? Some pesto over ricotta gnocchi if it wasn't the pre-frozen kind, no salt. Swordfish *salmoriglio* after, perhaps a little steamed spinach on the side, the salad after that with no onions or radishes or croutons out of a box and she would dress it herself at the table. "Can you make *bagna cauda* for an appetizer?" she challenged.

"*Si, signora.*"

"*Grazie, bene.*"

"For two." Victor handed his menu to the waiter.

"Will you be ordering wine?"

Victor cocked an eyebrow in Cat's direction.

"Greco di Tufo if it's not too fresh, and chill the glasses, please."

The waiter retreated.

Victor's dark eyes shone with reminiscence. "I remember Fortunati's. Down Pacific Avenue, past the old Convention Center. Big awning out front, red, white, green stripes."

"My dad. I waited tables there when I was a kid. He was thinking about retirement, gambling made it through the state house. He got a great deal on the property. It's gone now," she added with a sigh.

"You grew up here, then?"

"Over Richmond Avenue."

He tapped his tie pin. "Euclid Avenue."

"Not really!"

"After we moved here from San Juan. My dad had a bodega near Rhode Island Avenue. After he died, my mother and sisters and I moved in to Vineland." He paused, studying her expression to see if anything registered, if Carlo perhaps had remembered anything, told her.

But she only asked, "How old were you then?"

"Fourteen."

"Too young to lose your father."

"It is." Was she thinking about her own kids?

The waiter placed individual chafing dishes beside them, slid a tray of raw vegetables and *foccacia* between.

Cat took a fondue fork, speared a mushroom. "We used to make this Sunday evenings. When the vegetables were gone, Mama would scramble eggs in the leftover oil. This—" she raised her fork, "is a concession to *garbo*—"

"Greta?"

"It means good manners. *Bagna cauda* is usually eaten with the hands." She held a slice of bread under the dripping mushroom, nibbled.

Okay, they were talking. All she had to do was get from menus to murder. Should have made your move when he told you that Apron story, perfect opening, you dropped the ball, Cat reprimanded herself. But that story had been so funny!

Victor tried a chunk of broccoli. "What is it?"

"Olive oil, butter, fresh garlic, anchovy."

Okay, she sounded relaxed. Should have made your move when she was talking about her father's restaurant, it wasn't five blocks from where Dudek was shot. Perfect opening, you blew it, he told himself. Tell me about your family, what'd they say about last night, tell me about yourself Mrs. Cat Short-for-something Austen. "Your friend Ellice," he said abruptly. "What's her story?"

He liked the way she looked at him, grave, wary, not trusting him right off, too smart for that.

But she told him about Ellice.

# **CHAPTER**
## SEVEN

Chris had been dead more than a year.

One September afternoon, Cat had gone to the hospital to visit her sister-in-law Lorraine Fortunati, who was married to Cat's second brother, Vinnie.

Lorraine was in her mid-forties, a large, querulous hostage to fad diets and relentless hypochondria. No one in the hearty Fortunati clan could comprehend a preoccupation with skinniness and poor health, but Lorraine's husband and three sons attended to her with a genuine, if patronizing, devotion that nearly killed her off.

Attempting to minister to what they insisted was simple indigestion, Vinnie and the boys coddled Lorraine too long with bed rest, warm milk and Motrin until her outraged gall bladder campaigned for immediate extraction. Of course, something rare and unpronounceable would have been more gratifying than mundane gall bladder surgery, but Lorraine took what she could get and contemplated her remaining disposable parts— spleen, adenoids, appendix—like a winning hand waiting to be played.

Lorraine was not in her room when Cat arrived. The roommate lay aside her book and invited Cat to wait. "She's havin' some tests run and lovin' every minute of it."

The woman's perceptiveness made Cat smile.

"Ellice Watson," the woman said.

Ellice Watson appeared to be in her early thirties. In a state of good health, her beauty would have been extraordinary, but she was not in good health now. There was a sickly grayish caste to her brown complexion, a bonyness that suggested poor nutrition, a rasp underscoring the contralto lilt.

"Pneumonia," she offered. "But it's not the catchin' kind, so don't panic. Sit down."

Cat, having nothing better to do, sat.

Ellice nodded toward the balloon bouquets, floral arrangements, candy boxes, trays of dried fruit, cluttering Lorraine's side of the room. "You're visitor number eight, not counting the encores. You her sister?"

"In-law. She's my brother's wife." There was not so much as a card on Ellice's nightstand, Cat noticed. Nothing but a few well-worn paperbacks. "And you're right. She loves being a patient. I couldn't stand it."

" 'How sickness enlarges the dimension of a man's self to himself.' Or a woman's self, in this case." She broke off, coughed heavily.

"Charles Lamb, isn't it?"

"You *read?*" Ellice asked, with mock incredulity.

Cat grinned. "That's me. I'm the one."

"It's no joke, honey. We're pterodactyls."

Cat moved her chair closer to Ellice's bed. "So what are the extinct reading these days?"

"Tacitus. Thomas Mann. Wilkie Collins."

"I loved *The Woman in White,* better than *The Moonstone.*"

So had Ellice; moreover, they agreed that Marian's gumption was admirable and Laura's frailty was a drag, compared notes on *No Name* and *Blind Love,* talked Shakespeare and Jane Austen and E.M. Forester as well, in a bonding ritual peculiar to the extinct. In an hour, they were fast friends.

When Lorraine was discharged, Cat continued visiting Ellice. "Don't you have any family, Ellice?"

"A brother in California. We stopped keeping in touch."

"Friends?"

"Can't afford them."

"Where do you work? Where do you live?"

Ellice worked in a coffee shop on Pacific, rented a room on dingy Connecticut Avenue. Cat saw, of course, that Ellice's style was not coffee shop/boarding house; she offered to run errands, pick up Ellice's mail in order to satisfy her curiosity and Ellice accepted with a reluctance that conveyed a distrust of unconditional kindnesses.

Ellice's correspondence, which she calmly related to Cat, stated that her off-the-books job had been given away, that her rent, her share of the utilities were overdue, her medication was going to cost and how did she plan to pay her hospital bill?

Now, Cat was a Fortunati, and the Fortunatis personified the fundamental contradiction in the Sicilian character: abundant generosity in conflict with the tenet that first, you take care of your own. But Cat had always been minion to impulses unrelated to nurture or indoctrination instincts that seemed almost prescient in their unfathomable origins, their fortunate results. She offered to put Ellice up and Ellice refused, but Cat had the Sicilian stubbornness, too, and finally Ellice broke down and told her that she could cause Cat trouble.

Cat's brothers, and Chris, had swapped stories about such things, obsessions that were relentless, often fatal; none of the stories had been real to Cat. The one time she had run from trouble, it was back to her family, then marriage. Ellice had abandoned everything, submerged, only begun a tenuous ascent when she met Cat. "You have kids," Ellice pleaded. "If he finds me—"

"If he finds you, I'll sick Carlo and Vinnie on him!" Cat replied, obstinately.

Carlo and Vinnie. She thought they gave her a hard time when she decided to marry a Protestant, but that was nothing. "You lost your friggin' marbles, baby girl?" Carlo thundered over the phone the day Ellice moved in. "What about the kids?"

"They like her. Mats calls her Auntie Ellice."

"Oh yeah? You won't like it so much Auntie Ellice goes does something to one of those kids. What if she got AIDS or something catching the kids pick up—"

"She's got brains. It might do the kids good to know someone who talks something besides the almighty department and ESPN!" That wasn't fair, but she wasn't going to back down now. "You know what's really bothering you, Carlo? I made up my own mind for once. I didn't come to you first and ask 'may I?' "

"Okay, fine. But I'm gonna check her out, she doesn't have a record as long as King Kong's co—"

"Coccyx," Cat inserted, hastily.

"—I'll eat my badge."

When Freddy, who backed Cat in everything, called and asked, "Are you sure you know what you're doing?" Cat knew they'd put him up to it. She just laughed and said, "Et tu, Alfredo?" and hung up.

A week passed before a decidedly chastened Carlo called back. "So what'd she tell you about herself, anyway?"

"Buon' appetito."

"Shut up. She's a Ph.D. summa cum laude up Princeton. Philosophy and European Literature! Who the hell studies philosophy anymore? She taught Columbia, got a fellowship with some think tank up New Brunswick then, boom, drops outta sight. What's the story?"

"NOYB," Cat replied, hung up and dialed a chocolate shop in Linwood that made candy molded to order. Of course they could do a policeman's badge, and if Mrs. Austen wanted one that big, they would be happy to deliver it, too.


"A Ph.D.?" Victor asked.

Cat had omitted the part about Ellice's lover. She nodded and turned to thank the busboy who refilled their water glasses.

Victor was impressed by her unconscious courtesy. His own good-natured parents had been tyrannical on the subject of one's manners.

"And friend, of course," Victor continued. "I suspect a kindred spirit."

"She's the best person I know."

"So, does she work?"

"She just got her certification, literature, history, social studies, French. It's getting her back on her feet financially. Just substitute teaching, but maybe she'll go back to full time. I hope not soon, though."

"Why?"

"Because I'm selfish. She's been great about helping out with the kids and they're nuts about her."

"I imagine her availability was particularly welcome this morning. When you decided to detour over to KRZI instead of going straight home."

Cat eyed him gravely. "Has it come time for me to sing for my supper, Lieutenant?"

Victor shrugged. "Fried told Sergeant Rice you'd been there. Okay, look. I got hold of some of your writing and you're not bad. Pretty observant. And I'd really like an independent opinion. You're the only person I know of who's spent time with Hopper and Dudek lately, outside of people at the station. I'd really appreciate an objective point of view, that's all."

Cat sipped her wine, warily. She distrusted flattery. "Ron Spivak did a lot of background and I haven't talked to him yet. He's still in the hospital in Philly. What can I say? I didn't like Jerry, I did like Tom. Jerry was too high on . . ." *Hate,* Tom had said. *Enmity. A better high than sex.*

"Power?"

"Well, shock power. With everybody unfair game. Paramedics, female impersonators, the homeless, Catholics, Gamblers' Anonymous, cops." She smiled, disarmingly. "If it was in poor taste or socially taboo, Jerry would do it on the air. You remember the Rhinebeck murders in Philadelphia?"

Victor nodded. "Two years ago? Rhinebeck and an accomplice lured five or six young people into a row house, down the basement and . . ." he hesitated.

"And ate them," Cat finished, serenely. "Three of them, and I think a little bit of the fourth. It became a running gag on the *Six A.M. Circus*, all through the trial. The USDA jokes, the steak sauce jokes, the scrapple jokes. The Midwest Beef Council pulled their ads after Jerry did a parody of one."

"I recall being surprised that something like that got on the air. Why didn't Fried put a stop to it?"

"Well, I'm sure if you asked him, he'd embrace the First Amendment, but the reality is, two years ago, KRZI was number four in the area, behind easy listening and *country*. Six months into the *Six A.M. Circus* they were number two and closing. Barry Fried takes all the credit for the ratings boost, but it was Tom and Jerry who pulled in the listeners. I'm not sure what that says about the public consciousness. Or conscience."

"The Rhinebeck stuff, the parodies, that was all Dudek?"

"Oh, no. Tom could be wickedly funny. But Jerry was more—more out there, on the edge—"

"Pushing the envelope?" Victor suggested.

"Dear God, have we sunk to clichés so soon? In that case, I'll respond by saying Jerry loved going for the jugular and the audience couldn't get enough."

"Save the possessor of the jugular."

"Yes." Cat took the last bite of her swordfish. "I'm sure the possessor of the jugular probably wanted to kill him."

"Well, that narrows the field of suspects to a few thousand, wouldn't you say?"

Cat reached over, patted his hand, lightly. She pulled away hastily when the waiter came to remove their plates, silently dressed the salad he laid before her.

"Are you a good cook?" Victor smiled, watching her.

"Oh, yes. Italians. It's in our DNA."

"So, go on about Dudek. You were right when you said no one knows much about him. I checked with his former bosses;

Stan Rice talked to Fried, to Hopper, they don't even know if he went to college, where he was born. A mystery. Maybe a deliberate one."

"Maybe," Cat sighed. So he's interrogating you, she berated herself, so what? Weren't you planning to do the same to him? He was faster on the—beat you to the—he's got you so addled you're even thinking in clichés!

"Sorry," Victor apologized. "Cop talk must bore you."

Cat shook her head. "Carlo says all you have to do is fill in what happened twenty-four hours before a murder and be very observant for twenty-four hours after and it solves itself."

Victor shrugged. "Okay. Before? He worked that morning, left KRZI around ten-fifteen A.M., showed up at CV's at eight. Between? Not with the Halprin girl, she worked until five-thirty. Possibly with Whitney Rocap. One of the sound men said he's heard they were—"

Cat clapped her hands to her cheeks. "Oh, dear God!"

"What?"

"I forgot! I know people tell cops that all the time, that they forgot something important, but I really did."

"Forgot what?"

"Whitney Rocap. She was there last night. At CV's. And she and Jerry had words, right on the dance floor. You couldn't hear what they were saying, but she was angry. He brushed her off, kept on dancing, and she stormed out. That was before the raffle. I knew her face was vaguely familiar, but I didn't place it until Ellice told me that Whitney Rocap called while I was out this morning. That's when it clicked. Before I could get back to her, she called again."

"Before or after you called me?"

"After. She said, 'Do you have it,' something like that. I didn't know what 'it' was and she didn't say, she just told me that I'd better look out because Jerry—do you want this verbatim?"

"Please."

"Jerry screwed someone like I was doing to her and look where it got him. Then she hung up."

"You should have called me right back."

"I haven't a whole lot of experience as a murder witness, Lieutenant."

"No matter. That story he was trying to pitch in the parking lot, could it have had something to do with Rocap?"

"I don't know. I wonder if she did the weather last night?"

"She did. I checked that out as soon as her name came up. Dudek was shot around ten-thirty, she's in the studio for the eleven o'clock news, punched in at ten fifty-seven."

"I can get from Ocean City to CV's in eighteen minutes."

"And deliver the weather half an hour after killing your paramour? That's pretty cold-blooded."

"Precisely."

"I like your mind, Mrs. Austen. Could Rocap have been angry with Dudek for being there with the Halprin girl? If he was coming on to them both, we have jealousy as a possible motive."

"He wasn't dancing with Deanna at the time. And I'd find it hard to imagine anyone killing Jerry out of jealousy."

"Perhaps he had attractions you were in no position to appreciate."

Cat blushed.

"Can you give me an idea of who he was dancing with?" Victor asked hastily, afraid he'd offended her. "Maybe she overheard something that might have made its way into one of the police reports."

"No. They were groupies. Minors. And minors take off at the first hint of trouble. I'll wager they weren't even there when the police arrived."

Victor frowned.

"Come on," Cat prompted. "Try another motive."

"Money."

"I got the impression Jerry liked it. He was making it for KRZI, hamburger humor notwithstanding. Their contracts were up for renewal in January and Jerry had said something about getting a raise."

"He'd need one. Checking account was pretty thin. Evidently

72

he believed in pumping it back into the economy. Racing bike, clothes, CD player, laptop in his efficiency, all top of the line. Add to that the cost of entertaining a couple girlfriends."

"Expensive stuff and no money in the bank. I've heard radio's not very lucrative. Expenses like that would put him in the red, unless he had another source of income."

"Such as?"

"Blackmail. Or selling highly classified government secrets. Personally, I'd vote for the first. By the way, did Jerry leave a will?"

Victor smiled. She was interrogating him now. "Is this for the record?"

"Turnabout's fair play, no?"

"Yes. No will that we know of, no life insurance, couple hundred in the bank. He was generating money for the station. Dudek was worth more alive than dead."

"Then money wasn't the motive. What else?"

Victor propped his elbows on the table, clasped his hands. "Mistaken identity, vengeance, insanity, all of the above. Random, maybe. I hate admitting it, but these days, people kill for nothing. Just to kill."

Cat paled, looked down at her salad. "I know."

"Cat, I'm sorry—"

She excused herself and hurried to the ladies' room, paced, gave herself a pep talk. You're doing okay. You're making conversation, got a little information out of him. If he said something that hurt, it wasn't intentional, just cop talk. Forget it. Go back out there and get this date thing over with!

When she came out, they ordered coffee (for him) and cappuccino (for her), raspberries with *zabaglione* for dessert.

Victor was angry with himself. He didn't want the evening to end with her brooding about her late husband. "Let's go someplace for a drink," he suggested, remembered too late that Dudek had tried the same tactic with her the night before. Her "Okay" surprised them both.

The Boardwalk was two long blocks away and a stinging ocean breeze made a trek eastward uninviting. Victor helped Cat into his car, contemplated the obvious alternative to someplace loud and public. Something touched off a sixth sense, some current of movement in the silent November night that he knew, instinctively, was out of place.

"Victor?"

He got into the car, snapped on his seat belt, took off quickly.

Cat noted that he was glancing in his rear view mirror a bit more than caution warranted. "You're driving like you think we're being followed."

"Clever girl."

"Woman," Cat corrected. "My nine-year-old daughter's the girl."

"Woman. You're right. And I prefer women."

"Really? Most men like them excruciatingly young."

"I wouldn't have anything to talk about with someone excruciatingly young," he replied with a faint smile.

"Most men wouldn't consider that an obstacle. Where are we going?"

"Someplace quiet. Tell me, who knew where we were going tonight?"

"No one. Except you left the number with Ellice."

"Would she mention it to one of your brothers?"

"Maybe, if they called the house." She saw his eyes flick toward the mirror again. "Victor, you don't think one of them would follow us!"

Victor turned left on Delancy, coasted to a stop in front of his apartment, got out of the car and looked back toward the intersection. Traffic up and down Atlantic Avenue. Maybe it had been his imagination. He opened Cat's door, held out his hand.

Cat ignored the assistance. "Where are we?"

"I said I'd buy you a drink. Come on."

Too late. He was leading her up the splintered wooden steps to the second floor landing, to a weathered door inset with an old-fashioned, stained glass sunburst.

His apartment was small, very neat, less impersonal than his office. Bright Mexican throw rugs livened the beige and mocha furniture. There was an antique oak coat rack beside the front door, a wicker basket where he tossed his junk mail. Framed prints, Zubaran and Murillo, a heap of magazines stacked beside the couch, the July *South Jersey* on top, the one with her article about the summer underground work force. A hallway to the left leading to the bedroom, a dining area converted to a study, a small bachelor's kitchen, counter and bar stools, but no table, an uncurtained window facing the rear alley.

Victor helped Cat out of her coat, hung it on the rack by the door, did the same with his own. "What are you drinking?"

"Club soda."

"That's it?"

"I'm not much of a drinker." It was true. The glass and a third of wine had given her a perceptible buzz. Cat slung her purse over her coat, watched as Victor tossed his jacket on the counter, got out glasses, ice, a lime. Her eyes dropped to the gun in his waistband.

"What's wrong?" Victor handed her a tall glass, a quarter of lime floating at the rim.

"You're always armed, even when you're off duty?"

"Habit."

"It can't be comfortable."

"You get used to it. Does it bother you?"

"Oh no. Well, yes."

Victor set his drink on a coaster, snapped the gun into a shoulder holster hanging on the coat rack. "Better?"

Cat smiled weakly. What on earth were they going to talk about now?

He retrieved his drink, tapped his glass against hers. "*Salud.* Sit down."

Cat sat.

Victor dropped into a chair opposite, studied her. Sitting like a schoolgirl, knees pressed together, nothing straight-laced about that black velvet, though. A widow, what, two years now? Married twelve, fifteen years before that, married young and no man before the husband, nice Catholic Italian girl. Correction: woman. And definitely no man since his death.

"Do you do this a lot?" Cat asked, faintly.

"What?"

"Bring women here?"

"Three or four times a week."

"Touché," Cat smiled. "What do you talk about with those three or four?"

"Whatever interests them."

"Because you have ulterior motives, or because you want to know what they think?"

"I'd like to know what you're thinking, Cat Austen. I'd like it very much."

It startled him that the remark provoked tears. Cat blinked determinedly. "Oh, I don't think I'm nearly as interesting a person as I used to be. Or could have been."

Victor got up, fiddled with the radio-cassette player on the floor next to his desk. "Let's try this." He got some music, something slow, rhythmic. "You dance?"

"I used to."

Victor took the glass from her hand, pulled her to her feet. "There's no 'used to.' It's like falling off a bike, or a horse. You get back on."

"I think I fell off my life."

Victor guided her around the small living room, holding her a bit too close. Cat remembered how she had loved to dance, how she and Freddy had executed a wild merengue at Marco's wedding, how Chris had secretly practiced with Arthur Murray videos to surprise her on their tenth anniversary. She could tell by the way Victor moved that he had liked to dance, too, and that, like her, he was a little rusty. She wondered if he had fallen away from life as well, was trying to get back on track. "Have you ever been married, Victor?"

His lips brushed her temple, descended toward her mouth. He nudged her chin up, angling her lips toward his.

Cat felt a rush of panic, shook her head. "Don't. I can't do this. I'm sorry."

"Do what?"

"This! This! I must be out of my mind!"

"Cat, let's sit down and—"

"Please take me home."

"Cat, I'm not—"

"Look," Cat tried to control the tremor in her voice. "I've just about got my life back to where I want it. This isn't in the plan, okay? It's just not part of the plan."

"Plans change."

"I've worked too hard on this one. I had no business letting myself get talked into this, story or no story."

"Mrs. Austen. Do you mean to say you've been using me?"

Cat suppressed a laugh. He had a sense of humor, though you wouldn't think so to look at him.

"Okay, I'll take you home. But I feel obligated to inform you that you had a good ten, fifteen minutes before I made a serious move."

This time she did laugh.

He bussed the glasses to the kitchen. "We're gonna do this again, though next time we'll keep the whole evening on neutral ground."

*Not likely,* Cat resolved, reaching for her purse. The strap slipped from her hands. Nerves, she thought, annoyed at letting him think he'd rattled her. But then, it was nerves that saved her.

The glass sunburst in the front door exploded. The bullet sheared past Cat's bowed back, shot across the counter, grazed Victor's left sleeve and slammed into the wooden windowsill above the sink.

# **CHAPTER**
## E I G H T

"Get down!"

Victor vaulted the counter, pitched into Cat, dropping them both to the carpet. "Keep your head down!" he ordered. He extended one hand toward the hem of her coat, yanked the rack to the floor, snatched his holster.

In the street, an engine revved.

Victor unsnapped the holster. "Get in the bedroom."

Cat struggled to her knees, hesitated.

Victor backed up to the wall, his 9MM cradled in both hands. He slid one hand toward the doorknob.

Cat saw the jagged tear in his sleeve. "Victor—"

"Go, dammit, and call it in!"

Cat fled.

Victor threw the door open, counted three, inched around the broken glass toward the threshold. He jerked his head out, in, one thumb on the safety. Silence. Another swift glance into the street.

Across the street, someone pulled drapes apart, then shut, a porch light came on. Another.

A car coasted to a halt in front of Victor's house, swung wide and inched backward onto the narrow driveway. Victor could hear Cat's shaky inflections as she spoke to the dispatcher.

Mrs. DiLorenzo, her coat hunched high on her shoulders, stepped out of her car. Nero's nose poked out from her collar, put the Fahrenheit somewhere in the forties and retreated to the 98.6 emanating from the maternal bosom.

"Don't shoot!" Mrs. DiLorenzo caught sight of Victor, threw her hands, clutching paper cups laden with coinage, into the air. One Friday a month, Victor's landlady hit one or two of the casinos, recycled quarters for a few hours, dragging Nero along to ward off the carjackers. ("They see him on the dash, they think twice," she had told Victor.)

"It's all right, Mrs. DiLorenzo." Victor rose, tried to ease the nauseating tightness in his belly. "Go inside and lock your door please. I'll be down to explain in a while."

The woman scuttled inside. Victor heard her throw half a dozen locks.

The first siren's whine was audible now, distant but coming on fast. Victor went inside, side-stepping the shards of glass, and headed for the bedroom. Cat was sitting on the bed, the phone on her lap, shaking visibly.

Victor sat beside her, put an arm around her shoulders.

"Dating sure isn't what it used to be," she stuttered.

The siren was plural now, tires screeched against asphalt. Someone hollered Victor's name. "Let me handle this," he told Cat, rose and went to meet the officers.

Cat leaned forward to peek down the hall. She saw two uniformed cops, saw her brother Vinnie. She'd said "Austen," but the dispatcher must have made her. Well, it wasn't Carlo at least. She heard Vinnie demand, "So where's my sister?" groaned when Victor replied, "In the bedroom." She got up and joined them.

Vinnie put his arm around her, gave her a fierce hug. "So you okay, or what?"

"I'm okay."

"You wanna tell me what you're doin' here?"

"Drinking soda and getting shot at. Every night it's the same old thing."

One of the uniforms choked down a laugh.

Vincenzo Fortunati was a slightly scaled down version of Carlo; two years younger, a shade shorter and many pounds lighter. A faint sprinkling of pock marks on the slanting cheekbones, a little less grey in the hair and mustache, but otherwise a pretty good copy. Before the emphatic alterations of puberty, Carlo and Vinnie had often passed themselves off as twins, gotten away with it.

"Go get in my car, Cat. I wanna talk to the lieutenant here, then I'll take you home."

Victor spoke up. "I think she'd better stay inside for now. And when it's time to take her home, I'll take her home." His tone was ominously quiet, scrupulously polite.

Vinnie looked from Victor to Cat. "So, you two seein' each other, or what?"

"Far be it from me to correct you in matters of police procedure, but I believe a bullet fired into someone's home takes precedence over inquiries into my social life."

"You're my kid sister, I'm only askin'."

"Look," Victor interrupted coolly, "Why don't we do this: I'll fix you up with my kid sister, we're even. Then maybe we can get down to business."

Vinnie scowled. "Look, Cat's my only sister, she's a nice girl, got two nice kids, the family looks out for her."

"Whether I ask them to or not," Cat shot back.

"Lieutenant," asked one of the uniforms, "you're sleeve's torn. You hit?"

Victor shook his head. "Close call."

Nausea convulsed Cat. "I feel sick."

"Through the bedroom," said Victor.

Cat grabbed her purse and dashed into the bathroom. The nausea ebbed, replaced by a chill that sent tremors along her thighs. She leaned over the sink, splashed water on her face, blotted it dry, took a deep breath; another.

There was a knock on the door. "Babe, you need me?"

"No."

"I asked Freddy to run over your place, check on the kids."

"Thanks." Why? He didn't think the bullet had been intended for her, did he? That someone might try to get to her through— No! No.

When Cat emerged, Victor was relating the incident to a third uniform, who was taking rapid notes. Vinnie was conferring with a crime scene officer who was patiently digging at the round embedded in the windowsill.

Cat sat down and answered her share of the questions. Had she been standing close enough to the glass to be visible from the street? Had she heard anything right before the shot? Who knew where she'd gone tonight? Had she seen anyone familiar at the restaurant?

A fourth uniform poked his head through the shattered door to report that a woman across the street had seen a white car, or maybe it was ivory or beige, sometimes it's hard to tell, stopped in front of Victor's place around the time the shot had been fired. It had definitely been a foreign car, but possibly it could have been American, sometimes it's hard to tell, and she only saw a person at the wheel, but maybe someone else was in the car, it was dark and sometimes it's hard to tell and the person at the wheel was either a man or a woman.

"Sometimes," Cat concluded wryly, "it's hard to tell."

"Need a place to stay tonight, Lieutenant?" asked the guy carving into the windowsill. "I got an efficiency down by Lincoln Avenue, you're welcome to the couch. My people gotta go over here and your front door's shot, anyway."

"You could stay at my place." The words beat it out of Cat's mouth before her brain had time to run interference. *Are you out of your mind?* the brain demanded, but, "I've got a spare room," emerged from the lips.

Victor frowned and the room went dead quiet.

Victor knew that he ought to refuse, but he would be damned if he was going to back off so Fortunati could save face. Still, he was influenced by something more than machismo. He knew that

Cat's backlit figure must have been visible to the shooter. That morning, she had insisted that Jerry's killer had fired more than one shot. He had doubted it then. But someone who could sight and hit Dudek from thirty feet in only fair light hadn't needed a second shot.

Unless he had a second target.

Cat.

Why?

They drove down well-lit Atlantic Avenue, through Ventnor, Margate, Longport, hit the causeway that forked inland to Somers Point or over a narrow drawbridge to Ocean City. It distressed Cat to watch Victor grip the wheel, check the rear view mirror every five seconds, his gun tucked next to his thigh. She looked away, let her gaze idle on the shivering fishermen hugging the bridge railing, their lines drifting in the bay.

Victor checked his watch when they reached the toll booth at the northern entrance to Ocean City. Twenty minutes. Cat had said she could make it from CV's to Somers Point in eighteen. Close enough. First thing when he got to Cat's, he'd check KRZI, see if Whitney Rocap had punched in.

Morningside Drive had its somnolent winter aspect. Only three houses were occupied year round, the rest were summer homes, shuttered and dark. Cat wondered if her neighbors, Mr. and Mrs. Seldom-Seen Ufflander and the elderly Misses No-Relation-to-Richard Nixon had noticed the patrol car idling conspicuously across the street from her house.

A dark Jeep Cherokee was parked in Cat's driveway, bumper to bumper with her Maxima. "Freddy's car," she said.

Victor grabbed his overnight bag from the back seat. "You go up," he told Cat, watched as she scurried up the porch steps, slipped a key into the lock.

Ellice and Freddy Fortunati were sitting on the living room floor, playing Scrabble, Ellice contemplating her tiles with a wicked grin.

Freddy was willing to like this Ellice if Cat told him to, discovered their mutual obsession with games and fell into a competitive accord that progressed to interest, infatuation, love. He had been in love only once before, suffered a bitter rejection, and was pretty much set against falling in love again, but Ellice had his heart before he knew it was gone. Her heart was not so easily secured. Freddy saw that she was hurt and badly frightened, suspected it had something to do with a man, but Cat would tell him nothing. He tried Jane next—she had a decided knack for getting the goods—but all she could come up with was, "Sometimes she has bad dreams." Cat made Jane give back the five dollars and told Freddy off.

A couple of his brothers gave him a hard time when he and Ellice started dating, but Freddy had always been attracted to clever women. Ellice had a combination of intellect, wry humor and serene good sense that captivated him and he was vain enough to feel flattered when they went out and Ellice's beauty turned heads. She tried to straighten him out. "It's just the black and white thing," she insisted, but he didn't believe her.

"No rate, what is that, that's two words!" he challenged.

"No, you semi-literate, it's 'norate'," Ellice informed him. "It means to spread news over a distance. I've got an old Webster's up in my room if you wanna look it up."

Cat dropped a kiss on Freddy's hair.

"I'm changin' the rules. Only words from dictionaries published in this century."

Victor entered, closed and locked the door.

"Fredo, I'd like you to meet someone. Victor, this is my brother Freddy. Freddy, Victor Cardenas."

Freddy looked over his shoulder. "I got a Q, two U's, two N's, a D and an I. Any suggestions?"

Victor scrutinized the board. "The seven spaces in front of that C. Quidnunc." He spelled it.

"What the hell is that?"

"A man after my own heart," Ellice grinned.

"It means busybody," Cat informed him. "As in, 'I have six older quidnuncs.' "

Freddy threw one hand over his head, pushed tiles onto the board with the other.

Victor shook the extended hand, waited for the who-is this-guy?, the you-two-seein'-each-other?

"So how far behind am I now?" Freddy asked.

Ellice pushed seven tiles onto the board. "Don't even ask."

"Xiphoid! What the hell is a xiphoid!"

Cat gave Victor an apologetic shrug. "Kids get to bed okay?"

"Yeah fine. Is that like a noun, or what?"

Cat nudged Victor, nodded toward the stairs. Victor picked up his bag and followed.

A corridor extended from Cat's front bedroom to the spare room overlooking the backyard. There were three more down one side of the hallway, a bathroom and a laundry along the other. Cat switched on the bathroom light.

It was larger than Victor's bedroom, turquoise and ivory tile, patterned paper, marbled countertops, double sink, seashells etched on the glass shower doors.

"There are plenty of towels in the linen closet. Plenty of every-thing. My nieces and nephews come to the beach a lot in sum-mer, so I'm usually well-stocked."

She left the light on and checked the opposite bedroom. Jane was in a deep slumber, one long leg thrown on top of the eyelet spread, her face pushed into the pillow. Cat eased her under the covers, gave her a gentle kiss.

In the next bedroom, Mats was hunched under the covers, a ragged plush bunny lodged under his tummy. Cat detached it.

"Mommy . . ." Mats moaned, sleepily.

"I'm here. Mommy's here." She laid a hand on his unruly hair, felt tears swell under her eyelids.

Victor came up behind her, put an arm around her. "It's okay now, Cat. Everything's going to be all right."

Cat wiped her eyes. "I'm tired. Come on."

She led him to the back bedroom, turned on the light. It was small, neat, looked rarely used. Dark furniture, double bed, one curtained window facing back.

Cat knelt and opened the floor vents. "It'll warm up in a minute. No one uses this room much. All this was my furniture when I was a kid."

"It's fine." Victor threw his bag on a chair. "Let's go down, I need to make a call and I want to talk to your brother."

Freddy was on the phone, hung up hastily when Cat and Victor appeared. Victor observed that he wasn't as tall as Carlo and Vinnie, a shade shorter than Ellice. He was pleasant-looking rather than handsome, had Cat's dark oval eyes and long lashes, seemed close to her in age.

"Who's on the phone?" Cat demanded.

"Our oldest quidnunc."

"Any other calls?"

"Some woman," Ellice said. "Real soon after you left. Wouldn't give her name, but it sounded like that weather girl again."

"Anyone else?" asked Victor.

"Right after that Ritchie Landis called, said he had something to tell you right away, urgent."

"And you gave him the number of the restaurant?"

"Did I do something wrong?"

Freddy glanced at Victor, shrugged.

"Somebody gonna tell me what's goin' on around here?"

"C'mon upstairs," Cat said. "Help me get out of this dress." She kissed her brother and said a polite good-night to Victor.

In her bedroom, Cat kicked off her shoes, snapped on the small TV, praying the night's adventure hadn't made the eleven o'clock news.

"So what's up?" Ellice dropped down beside her. "You don't look so hot."

Cat told her what had happened.

Ellice's eyes widened, impressed. "He got you over to his place? First time out?"

Cat smacked her with a pillow.

They had missed the update on the Dudek shooting. Roland Atkinson, at the anchor desk, was congratulating Whitney Rocap on her promotion to the six P.M. anchor slot. Whitney smiled her flirtatious weather girl smile, thanked Roland and segued into the weather, looking not in the least like Jerry's—one of Jerry's—heartbroken paramours.

"So you think they hired a replacement?" Ellice quipped. "Maybe I could lean on their minority hiring practices, finesse my way into an affirmative action weather girl gig."

"Weather *woman*," Cat corrected, giggling.

"That has to be the cake job of all time. You think I got potential as a local TV personality?"

Cat's grin slackened. (*"What local TV personality made a porn flick in college?"*)

The slender arm flourished a pointer. The seductive green-tea eyes flirted with the camera.

Cat grabbed the remote, hit the mute button, told Ellice to shush. She lifted the phone off the hook and heard an unfamiliar voice speaking to someone on the extension.

". . . because she's on the air right now, Lieutenant."

"If you would just check the sign-in sheet."

"Got it. She clocked in at ten fifty-five."

Which had been more than an hour after the shot was fired through Victor's front door.

# CHAPTER
## NINE

Victor woke at eight, lay still for a moment, reflecting on the previous night, then rolled down onto the braided rug, did seventy-five push-ups, grabbed his overnight bag and headed for the bathroom. A child's laugh drifted from below, some TV prattle. Saturday morning, he and Milly and Remy used to sit in front of the old black and white until their mother shooed them outside.

Victor closed the door, turned on the hot water. There was a vinyl-coated rack over the COLD knob with three kinds of soap, shampoo, conditioner, a loofah and two rubber squeeze toys. Victor stepped under the hot spray, opted for plain old Ivory and let his mind slide into a review of the Dudek murder.

Jerry Dudek. Had Cat been a target Thursday night, or just a bystander? Both possibly. And what about last night? Freddy hadn't pressed him for details. His concern for Cat had been heartfelt, not overbearing. Victor had liked him.

Jerry Dudek, Cat Austen. Relationship: reporter and subject. Had Dudek said something relevant, something that lay filed in Cat's notes, Cat's mind? ("*He made it sound like something terribly lurid.*") Blackmail? Vengeance? What? Don't guess. Victor groaned, dropped his head forward, sending a scalding rivulet over his shoulders and back.

He shaved by instinct in front of the fogged mirror, carefully preserving the crescent curves of his mustache, pulled on khakis, a white cable knit sweater, tan Rockports, eased his 9MM into his waistband. He opened the bathroom door and smelled coffee. Someone other than the kids was up.

Ellice was reading the morning paper at the small booth-style table in the kitchen. She wore a robe of orchid satin, her short hair was brushed behind her ears, no makeup, stunning. Freddy had good taste.

The kitchen was a large rectangle with a narrow corridor projecting toward the back door. Black and white checkered linoleum, glass-paned cabinets, granite-like countertops, crocheted valances at the windows. A half dozen cast iron skillets hung on the wall next to the stove, an Ansel Adams calendar above the table with notations scribbled into most of the dates, shopping lists and children's artwork tacked to the refrigerator with magnets shaped like cartoon characters, fruit.

Ellice looked up from *The Press*. "Well, you didn't make the papers. Coffee's in the pot over there, sugar's on the table, cream in the fridge."

Victor took a white china mug from the drain board, poured coffee from the electric pot. "Cat still in bed?"

Ellice tossed *The Press*, switched to *The Wall Street Journal*. "Out runnin'."

Victor set his mug down, slowly. "I beg your pardon?"

"She runs. You know, runnin'?" Ellice lay down her paper, jogged her arms.

"I know running. Alone?"

"Uh huh. She goes out before I'm up. What is it, eight-thirty, eight forty-five? She'll be in soon."

A swift, light step ascended the outside back stairs. There was a scratching at the door, a muffled exclamation, a frustrated knock. "Ellice!"

Ellice strode to the back door, turned the bolt. "Forget your key?"

"It must have fallen off my key ring. God, I hope I didn't lose it on the boards. Joel Kaminsky was out, raced me the last mile."

"How'd you do?" Ellice resumed her seat at the table.

"Beat him by half a block." Cat entered, carrying her grey running shoes. She was wearing a navy hooded sweatshirt, the hood pushed back and a cap with JERSEY DEVIL embroidered on the brim covering her hair, navy shorts with a magenta stripe, gloves, white socks. "It's cold! I should have worn tights. You sleep okay?" she asked Victor as she tugged off the sweatshirt to reveal a grey T-shirt that clung to her in wet patches between her shoulder blades, her breasts.

"What were you thinking of, going out alone?" Victor's voice was ominously quiet.

Cat raised her chin. "I run. It's no big deal."

"You have a dangerously short memory, Mrs. Austen."

"So you gonna put me under house arrest?"

"If I have to," Victor replied calmly, wondered who the hell Joel Kaminsky was.

Cat, accustomed to her tumultuous brothers, found Victor's restraint unnerving. She turned her back, got a Diet Pepsi from the refrigerator, popped the lid, drank.

Mats shuffled in, his hair every which-way, his Superman pajamas sleep-wrinkled. "We got any Cheerios?"

"Sure, baby." Cat busied herself with a bowl, spoon, cereal. "You want milk on this?"

"No, regular. An' apple juice please."

"What about Sister?"

"She's watchin' mermaids. Can I have this in the TV room?"

"If you get Jane to set you up a tray."

"You wanna know what Uncle Freddy showed me las' night?"

"What?"

"You see this hole in front of my pajamas? That's so if I need to go potty, I can just get my penis out an' I don't hafta take my whole pants down."

Cat's mouth twitched, her eyes took on a merry glow. "Uncle Freddy learned that in the state police academy."

"See?" Mats fished out the miniature appendage to demonstrate his newly acquired skill.

Jane entered, shot a what's-he-doing-here glare at Victor, turned on Mats. "Will you stop taking your penis out! It's disgusting! Do we have any doughnuts?" she demanded of her mother.

"No." Cat tried a sober expression, but her eyes were dancing. "What about cereal?"

"No. What's he doing here in the morning?"

Mats adjusted himself, took his cereal and cup. "Mom says you hafta set me up a tray."

"Do not. I'm not your slave."

"You may say Lieutenant Cardenas or you may say Victor, but I don't want to hear 'he' in that tone of voice again." Cat's rebuke was quiet but firm. "And you're not anybody's slave, but it would help me out if you could set up a tray for your brother."

Jane grabbed a bunch of bananas from the counter, yanked one free and stalked out, pointedly ignoring Victor.

"Saturday mornings aren't very structured," Cat apologized. "If you can wait 'til I get a shower, I'll fix you breakfast."

"I'll fix you breakfast," Victor countered.

Ellice licked her index finger, gave Victor a "score one" in mid-air.

"You're on," said Cat.

Victor watched her bound out of the room, appraised the shapely calves, the clinging shorts and wondered again who the hell Joel Kaminsky was.

"Cat's a good person."

Victor turned. Ellice's dark, sloe eyes met his. "I can see that," he said.

"I've been here over a year. First date she's had and she could have had her share."

"Really? So you're saying she's not over her husband?"

"No. Oh, I know it was rough when he died, but it's more than that. Cat's the type of woman who's always been someone's daughter or someone's sister, someone's wife. Now she's on her own, gotta take care of herself, her kids, and she's finding out she can do it. If she's careful."

"Careful not to get involved?"

"Careful not to slip back into being too dependent. Not to count on someone who's here today to be here tomorrow. Cat's got a real independent streak, but it's taken a beating. I know about that, and I know it takes a while to heal up."

"GB Shaw said independence is middle-class blasphemy, that every soul on earth is dependent upon another."

"Yeah, an' about six years later, he said that all great truths begin as blasphemies. Go figure. But, hell, you quote Shaw, that's good for another point. And one for Cat for finding herself a guy who reads." Her laugh was ungrudging. She folded the papers and got up from the table. "You really gonna cook for her?"

"I am."

"You got a brother?"

"What about Freddy?"

"Freddy's too good for me," she replied gently.

"I don't believe it."

Ellice shrugged, smiled, and left him alone.

Victor took a faded apron from a peg beside the refrigerator, tied it around his waist. He rummaged in the fridge for celery, an onion, a few plum tomatoes, a large yellow pepper, butter, eggs, lifted the largest of the black skillets from the wall, scouted for a spatula, knife, cutting board. By the time Cat came down, he had the vegetables meticulously diced, butter sizzling in the pan.

"What're we having?" Cat had dressed in jeans, a navy and white turtleneck sweater, sneakers, pulled her wet hair into a French braid. Her mouth dropped open.

"Spanish omelets. What's wrong?"

"I've just realized that even at my age there are a few things I haven't seen or imagined."

"Such as?"

"A Latino in an apron."

Victor grinned, the first genuine smile she had seen from him. She realized that she had not heard him laugh. "I'm secure in my manhood Mrs. Austen. And I think you're a woman of limited experience."

"I applaud the sense of security, Lieutenant. A Fortunati upbringing has exposed me to a lifetime of machismo, thank you very much. But you're hardly in a position to evaluate my range of experience. Can I do anything in my own kitchen?"

"Toast."

Victor slid the vegetables into the skillet, sautéed them expertly, lowered the heat to simmer off the liquid, broke eggs into a bowl while Cat hunted up some whole wheat bread and plugged in the toaster. Victor put two stoneware plates into the oven to warm, slid the eggs into the skillet. "You asked me last night if I had been married," he said abruptly. "I was. For five years. Her name was Marisol. She died eight years ago."

Cat set two plates at the table, refilled Victor's mug.

"She was a city clerk. Very pretty. She began having trouble typing, numbness in her hands, then blurred vision." He cleared his throat. "It was a brain tumor. She died four months after the diagnosis."

"That's not—" Cat's voice faltered, "that's not a lot of time to get ready."

"You're never ready."

"I'm so sorry, Victor."

"So am I. But life went on. It was the biggest surprise of my life when I realized that. How stubborn life can be."

Cat nodded. "How old was she?"

"When she died? Twenty-nine. I was thirty-two." He took the warm plates from the oven, halved the omelet, waited for Cat to sit before he took his place opposite her. "So now it's your turn. You tell me something about yourself."

Cat tilted her chin, inquisitively.

"Start with the name. Catherine, yes?"

Cat tasted her omelet. "Not bad."

"You think Italians are the only ones who can cook?"

"Yes. Don't you have computers over at Major Crimes, Lieutenant? You can find out anything about me you want to know."

"All right, Cheshire Cat. Tell me something I don't know, then."

"We're going to talk about Jerry again, aren't we?"

Victor nodded. "Your story. Is it still on?"

"Yes. And accelerated. Ritchie wants it to be the March cover."

"Good for you. When you interviewed Tom and Jerry at the station, did you take notes?"

"Some. I taped it, too."

"Can I see your stuff?"

"Now?"

"Yes."

Cat lowered her coffee cup. "You think that what went on last night was connected to Jerry's murder?"

"Don't you?"

"I'm trying not to think about it at all."

The phone rang. Cat reached up to the wall unit behind her, propped the receiver against her ear with her shoulder. "Hello? . . . Si, Mama . . . No, I didn't forget . . . Yes, Ellice is gonna stall Freddy . . . Did Annamarie order the cake?" There was a long pause. Cat smiled at Victor, slipped a hand over the receiver. "You working tomorrow?"

"I've always got some paperwork. Why?"

"Would you like to come to a birthday dinner?"

"Where?"

"Here. Freddy's birthday. It's a surprise."

Victor opened his mouth to refuse, then reconsidered. His presence would bug the hell out of brother Vinnie. "Love to."

"Mama?" Cat spoke into the phone. "I invited someone else, so we'll be . . . No, a man . . . No, not Stan . . . He is not . . . No, not him either . . . I thought Kevin was coming with Dominic . . . Yes, I saw Steve yesterday . . ." Cat switched to rapid Italian.

Victor felt his jaw tighten. For a woman of limited experience, Cat had a few too many he's and Joels and Stans and Kevins in her conversation to suit him.

Cat hung up. "Sunday dinner was always a big deal. Now it's hard to get everyone together. Freddy's birthday was actually the fifth; he thinks we all forgot."

Mats came in, set his empty bowl on the counter, peered at Victor's plate. "What's that stuff?"

"Eggs and vegetables."

"Jane says eggs are yuck. Mom, do you know how we choose our food?"

"Choose our food? Why, we go to the grocery store, try to pick out things that are nutritious, some snacks—"

"No," Mats interrupted, shaking his head. "We choose our food with our *mouths closed*. They said so in school." He departed.

Cat smiled, briefly, rose and fished a key ring from her pocket. "I keep my office in there," she gestured toward a door in the kitchen corridor. "It was a pantry."

"You keep it locked?"

"The kids got in there and spilled Hi-C down my typewriter once." She went in, emerged with her tape recorder and the battered attaché she had carried Thursday night. "I haven't looked at this stuff yet. You really think there may be something in my notebook that's relevant?" She slid into her seat, pushed a cassette into the tape recorder.

"Or in your head."

(*" 'Cause I gotta put it in someone's head, like for safekeeping."*)

Cat's elbow jerked, knocked her coffee mug to the floor. "Oh, dear God." She grabbed a handful of paper napkins, dropped to the linoleum and began blotting up the spilled coffee.

Victor got down to help her, alarmed by the expression on her face. "What is it, Cat? What's the matter?"

Cat scooped up the sopping wad, dumped it into the trash, rinsed her hands. "I remembered something Jerry said."

"Come sit down, Cat." Victor eased her back into her seat, poured her another cup of coffee. "Now, what did you remember?"

"I told you Jerry was pitching some story idea to me in the parking lot? A real shocker, he said, something about kinky sex or something. I told him to call Ritchie, he kept at me, so I said 'Call me tomorrow' and he said it had to be now. I asked him why and he said, 'Cause I gotta put it in someone's head, like for safekeeping.' That was a minute before he got shot. I mean, *one minute*."

Victor stroked his lower lip with his thumb, absently. "All

right. All right. That sounds like he suspected he might have been in danger."

"It does, doesn't it? But you wouldn't have known it by the way he was acting in the club, dancing, life of the party. Just that brush with Whitney Rocap, that's all." Cat nibbled her toast. "She said, 'Do you have it?' on the phone, like she was afraid I'd been told something or given something she didn't want me to have."

"She punched in at—"

"Ten fifty-five last night. I know."

"Ah, then, it was you eavesdropping. My place was hit around nine-fifty."

"I turned on the news last night. Whitney's being promoted to anchor. What if Jerry had something on her that she wouldn't want made public now that her career's on the rise?"

"Such as what?"

Cat shrugged, helplessly. "Like maybe she's an ex-porno queen. Would someone kill to hush that up?"

"People have killed for much less."

Cat shuddered.

"Let's play some of this tape first," Victor suggested. "Then we can go back to last night."

Cat checked the recorder. "This was more than a week ago. It was the day Jerry was taping that promo for 'The Perfect Murder.' Tom was doing a voice-over, so I grabbed Jerry before he had to shoot the video, tried to get some background, but with Jerry, it was like pulling teeth—too trite, delete that. He wouldn't even tell me where he went to high school. I'm counting on Ron Spivak for that stuff."

"What about Hopper?"

"I know he's from a well-to-do family somewhere in North Carolina; his mother died; I think they were close. He never settled into any one job, drifted, worked several radio stations, wrote copy, did voice-overs, sales, stuff like that, until he and Jerry paired up."

"How did that come about?"

"Fried told me that Tom said once he had been filling in for a vacationing DJ in Baltimore and Jerry came out of the blue, talked his way into a part-time job, the two of them just hit it off. They took slots no one wanted, Friday nights, Saturday afternoons, when no one much is listening, and worked up a following. Jerry sent a demo to WSLM in Camden and got them a solid weekday morning slot."

"Camden would seem like a comedown after Baltimore."

Cat shook her head. "In Camden, they started calling the shots, siphoned off some of the Philadelphia audience. They got noticed by KRZI, accepted an offer." She fiddled with the tape, pushed the PLAY button. "This is when Tom came in and before Jerry ran out, when I had them both together."

(Cat: "—how Tom Hopper from—where is it?—Raleigh, North Carolina and Jerry Dudek from parts unknown became the ringleaders of the Six A.M. Circus?")

(Tom: "He told you about Baltimore? He blows in, no references, no resume, nothing, literally talks his way into a job, next thing I know, we're a couple.")

(Jerry: "A couple of what?")

(Tom: "Jerry sends a tape, we take the Camden spot, he sends one to Barry Fried, we get the offer from KRZI.")

(Cat: "Fried claims he found you.")

(Tom: "No, it was Jerry. I thought we'd have a better shot at getting noticed by Philly if we stayed in Camden, but Jerry kept pushing the move to the shore. It was like an obsession.")

(Cat: "Why?")

(Tom: "He said we had to take on a really weak market, build it up, if we ever wanted any real muscle when contract time rolled around. Radio, it's not real secure, you gotta prove you can bring in the audience.")

(Cat: "Under the circumstances, I should think his instincts were correct.")

(Tom: "The move down here never would have occurred to me, but you're right. Six to ten was KRZI's weakest spot, now we're virtually tied for number one.")

(Cat: "I meant correct about getting Philly to sit up and take notice. My editor said he heard a rumor that Philly One Oh Four actually made you an offer, is that true?")

(Jerry: "Where'd he hear that?")

(Cat: "And that it was only for one of you, a solo act.")

(Tom: "I don't know where Landis came up with that.")

(Cat: "Hypothetically, what would make either of you go it alone? More exposure? Money?")

(Jerry: "Landis is off base. We're a team. What would Tommy do without me? Exposure? Only reason Tommy's stuck with radio so long's 'cause it's so anonymous, and he's got the Hopper inheritance to fall back on so he doesn't need the bucks. Why else would I fix him up with my sister?")

Victor jammed down the STOP button. "Dudek has a sister?" he demanded.

"Yes—"

"You knew about her?"

"Didn't you?"

"And Hopper's been seeing her?"

"I think they're engaged," Cat replied. "Victor, what's wrong? You have people on the Dudek case, I assumed—"

"You never assume. You *never* assume." He rose from the table, paced, frowning deeply. "You didn't mention her yesterday."

"I was so shaky, I don't remember what I said and what I may have left out."

"All right. Tell me about her now."

"She's a dancer, works at the casinos. Jerry made a big deal about introducing them. They've been together awhile, there's been talk of a wedding. Her name's Noreen."

"Noreen Dudek?"

"Dunn. Sort of a stage name, I guess."

"Don't guess. Damn. *Damn.* Rice went over there, he interviewed Fried, Hopper, that Halprin woman, some secretary, there's no mention of this sister in his report."

"Well, Deanna might not know about her; I don't know about the secretary, and Tom? Maybe he's trying to protect her. You know, Stan doesn't ask, so Tom doesn't volunteer."

He felt unreasonably irritated that Cat hastened to Stan's defense. "You think to ask about the damn next of kin! You asked, didn't you, when you ran over to the station yesterday?"

"I just sort of—wondered—why they asked Tom to identify the body and not Jerry's sister."

"Oh, this is beautiful," Victor muttered, coldly. "She was there at the club Thursday night."

Cat bit her lower lip, nodded.

"With Hopper?"

Cat shook her head. "More like she was avoiding him. She came up to me before the raffle, asked if I was doing the article on Tom and Jerry, we chatted a few minutes. After the raffle, she disappeared. Tom went looking for her."

"She's avoiding him, why does she show up where she knows he's going to be?"

"Maybe she wanted to talk to Jerry. Got wind he was going to announce their engagement on the air the next day and wanted to talk him out of it."

"Why?"

"I don't know."

"Theorize."

"You mean guess," she teased. "The relationship seemed hush-hush. Tom hadn't even told his family yet, according to Jerry. And I know Tom didn't want me to mention it in the article."

"Will the tape back that?"

Cat nodded, fast-forwarded several times. "Here."

(Cat: "*—that seems to be working out to everyone's advantage. Will being related affect the partnership?*")

(Jerry: "*Hasn't so far. I mean, I love Tommy like a brother already.*")

(Tom: "*I love you, too, you moron.*")

(Jerry: "*So how's about a little kiss?*")

(Tom: "*Keep those lips to yourself. God only knows where they've been.*")

(Jerry: "*How about you, babe?*")

(Cat: "*I never kiss on the first interview.*")

(Jerry: "*Not even a little peck?*")

(Cat: "*No, thanks. God only knows where your little peck has been.*")

Cat blushed. She had forgotten that exchange.

"You do all right, Austen," Victor grinned.

Cat raised her chin. "I had six brothers."

(Cat: "*And Jerry was the one who introduced you?*")

(Tom: "Look, you weren't planning to mention Noreen in this article, were you?")

(Cat: "Is there some reason I shouldn't? Will the impending marriage turn off the female eighteen to twenty-fives?")

(Tom: "I'd like to check it out with Noreen first. I'm not sure she wants it known she's got you-know-who for a brother.")

(Jerry: "You can say that again.")

(Tom: "I'm serious. It oughta be Noreen's call.")

(Cat: "Maybe you could arrange for her to talk to me.")

(Tom: "I'll ask. Let me get back to you.")

Victor pushed the STOP button again. "Did he?"

"No."

"Then that's not why she approached you Thursday night?"

"She never introduced herself, just asked what I was putting in the piece. I thought she was another one of Jerry's groupies."

"She didn't come to give you an interview, didn't let on who she was, didn't want to see Tom. So why was she there?"

Cat dropped her forehead into her hand, fingered the abrasion on her temple, thoughtfully. "Jerry was full of energy—"

"High?"

"Alcohol. But it wasn't a chemical high, he was wound up, before and after he had words with Whitney Rocap. Then he finds out Noreen's been around and all of a sudden there's something he wants to put in my head."

"Something lurid," Victor recalled. "Involving Noreen possibly?"

Cat concentrated. "You know, before Noreen showed up, Jerry was talking about some change in format he had in the works. Tattletale Tuesday, he called it. Some local dirt he was going to air."

"What sort of dirt?"

"Wait, I think I took some notes while he was talking." Cat rummaged through her attaché, pulled out a notebook, flipped through the pages, backtracked, ran her hand along the inside of the brief.

"What's the matter?" Victor asked; knew.

"My notes! They're gone!"

# CHAPTER

## TEN

"Noreen!"

Victor reached for the attaché, probed the inside pockets. "Why Noreen?"

"She was sitting with me right before the raffle. Jerry called me up to draw the winner; it took me by surprise. I asked her to watch my things. When I got back to the table, she was gone."

"Just the notes from Thursday night?"

Cat scoured the notebook, blinking back tears. "Some of the stuff from last week, too. Three or four pages."

"Do you remember what you'd written?" Victor took her hand. He knew it took two, three, four interviews to piece together a witness' impression of a crime. Trauma could cloud details for days.

"Some of the bio stuff is gone, and what Jerry was talking about Thursday night."

"Tattletale Tuesday."

Cat nodded. "I was asking them if they had anything new in the works now that the *Six A.M. Circus* had so many imitators. The stuff Jerry came up with sounded like on-the-air blackmail. It made me a little uncomfortable."

"How did Hopper and the Halprin girl react?"

"It all went over Deanna's head. A Rhodes scholar she isn't. Tom said it wouldn't get past Fried."

"But Fried wasn't much of a censor from what I've gathered. Did Dudek say anything specific? Name names?"

Cat summoned Jerry's words. "A boutique owner who was having an affair with her husband's business partner, a TV personality who made a porn flick in college—"

"Rocap?"

"That's what I was wondering. Something about doctored ballots in a kiddie pageant, a media bigwig who was cruising gay bars, a disc jockey sleeping with his sister, I think that was all he said before the raffle intervened."

"Did you see Jerry talking to Noreen at all?"

"No. He seemed surprised when I told him she was there. Annoyed, like she was blowing something for him."

"What?"

"I don't know."

"Could he or Hopper have gotten into your notebook?"

"Anyone could have."

"You never checked the contents until now?"

"No. I was going to do some work this morning."

"But someone might assume you'd go over the material as soon as you got home from CV's Thursday night."

"So they rip off a few notes? It was fresh in my mind, I'd still have what's in—" Cat tapped her forehead. "Oh. I see."

Victor nodded, grimly. "Noreen takes off, Hopper went after her, you said. Did he catch up with her?"

"He said he did, but he heard the fight inside the club so he told her to take off. Didn't want her involved."

"Then he can't give her an alibi for the time of the murder. Got Hopper's phone there by any chance?"

Cat drew out a folder, handed Victor a scrap of paper. Victor reached for the receiver, dialed. "This Margate?"

"That new beachfront condo on Atlantic, Brisas de Mar."

"Answering machine," Victor frowned, hung up. "I'm going to have to go. I want you to—"

Mats skipped in. "Can I get dressed and go outside?"

"Better stick close to home," Victor murmured.

Cat rose, swung Mats into her arms, looked at Victor over her son's tousled head.

"Are you going home?" Mats asked, as the three of them mounted the stairs.

"No, to work."

"It's Saturday."

"Sometimes cops have to work Saturdays."

"I know. We got lotsa cops in our family an' I'm gonna be a cop, too, when I grow up."

"No you're not," Cat said. She set him down and sent him off to get his clothes.

Victor retrieved his things from the back bedroom, made the bed hastily. He approached Cat's room. The door was ajar. Mats was trampolining on the bed, chanting a song about caterpillars, which he pronounced "callapitters." Cat snared him with an undershirt; the two of them tumbled onto the bed, laughing.

The room had been turned out with a designer's eye. Thick green carpet, textured wallpaper; the draperies at the window matched the upholstery on the window seat. A working fireplace, flanked by book shelves, TV, VCR, pictures; a wedding picture in an antique frame, Cat and a tall, sandy-haired man, her veil falling over his sleeve, arms laden with red and white roses.

"Why's there a cop car outside our house?" Mats asked, kneeling on the window seat. "Are we under arrested?"

Cat's smile vanished. "Go downstairs and tell Jane to come up and get dressed."

"They're just going to drive by once in a while," Victor assured her. "Try to stick close to home, okay?"

Cat led him down the stairs. "I don't want the kids to think anything's wrong."

"Just take a few precautions. No solitary morning runs, for example."

*I'm getting my life back on track,* Cat thought, stubbornly. *I won't let anything change that.* "Look, you don't have to come by tomorrow if you don't want to, I mean. Carlo and Vinnie . . ."

"I want to. Freddy seems like a nice guy." He picked up a pad by the living room phone, began to write. "Here's my office, car, home. Call me if you remember anything, need anything, just want to talk, okay? I'll call you later today." He slipped into his battered leather jacket, glanced around quickly, drew Cat close.

"Are you guys kissing? That's disgusting!"

Cat pushed Victor away. "Jane, go upstairs and get dressed."

"I'm still hungry."

"Then go into the kitchen and get something to eat."

"Can I make a grilled *cheese?*"

"For heaven's sake. Oh, go ahead."

"Is *he* going?"

"He is," Victor replied, waited for her to leave.

Jane held her ground and Victor repressed a smile. Stubborn. Like her mother.

Cat watched as Victor crossed the street and said a few words to the patrolman idling opposite her house. Then he tossed his overnight bag onto the passenger seat of his car, looked up and made a lock-your-door gesture to Cat. She smiled and waved, watched him drive away and locked the door.

Margate was a well-to-do "downbeach" community, that is, a few miles below—downbeach from—Atlantic City. Tom Hopper's condominium was a six-story oceanfront complex and Tom's unit, number 606, had locked in the prime southeast corner. His parking spaces were vacant.

The uniformed security guard had the bulk, the impassive glare, the parlor tan of a bouncer at a trendy club. He hunkered behind a console of screens, their bluish images relaying the activity within the elevators, corridors above.

Victor produced his shield and asked if Tom Hopper was in.

The man gave Victor a faintly hostile once-over. "He went out."

"When?"

"Early."

"Say when he'd be back?"

"Didn't ask."

"Guess."

"Sooner or later."

"He live alone?"

"His name's the only one on the lease."

"That's not what I asked."

"He's a popular guy."

"That's not what I asked."

The man shrugged.

"Girlfriend?"

The man shrugged.

"Look," Victor said patiently. "I'm gonna find out what I want to know, we both understand that much. Do you really need for me to demonstrate what a hard time I can give you—" Victor's gaze dropped from the unblinking stare to the name tag clipped to the blue shirt. "—Mr. Borch? Or should I just discuss your attitude problem with your parole officer?"

The leaden gaze flickered.

"You tell me I'm wrong, I'll run a check. Take me thirty seconds."

The man blinked. "I'm straight; I'm gonna stay straight."

Victor politely refrained from expressing his doubt.

"Place like this, people're payin' for privacy, you know what I mean?"

"Yes. Did you work yesterday?"

"Yesterday, day before, day before that."

"See Hopper around?"

"I get on at eight. Weekdays, he's outta here before I start my shift. Usually gets in around ten-thirty, eleven A.M."

"Were the past few days usual?"

"No. His girlfriend. She split. Same day as Hopper's partner got whacked. Moved out, suitcase, the whole bit."

"How long has she been living here?"

"I been here three months. She's got her own key; first I thought they were married or something."

"Name?"

"I think I heard Hopper call her Nadine, Noreen, something like that. Great-lookin' broad. Five-ten, five-eleven, legs like a Rockette, don't talk much, crazy about him, or so I thought."

"What changed your mind?"

"Tuesday, everything's fine. Wednesday morning, it's like, ten-fifteen, she comes down here, pacin' like she's waitin' for someone, he pulls up, she runs out the door, grabs him, they go up to the boards, I can see down that hall to the beach entrance, them talkin', she's walkin' up and down, wavin' her arms, and he's holdin' some paper up, laughin'—"

"Why didn't she and Hopper just go upstairs?"

"It wasn't Hopper, man, it was the partner, Dudek. Anyways, this goes on maybe twenty minutes, she looks like she's yellin' an' cryin', he's laughin', folds this paper, stuffs it down her shirt, real arrogant. Then he takes off. She walks down to the beach. Fifteen minutes later, Hopper gets in, I wonder should I say anything, I figure it's none of my business. Goes upstairs. A few minutes later, she comes in, looks like she cried herself out. Goes up, fifteen minutes later, she comes down, takes off in Hopper's car. She don't have a car."

"Did she come back?"

"Yeah, 'round the end of my shift, five. Hopper, he'd went out, some PR gig, took a cab. When she comes in, she don't even go upstairs, tells me give Hopper the car keys, calls a cab from the lobby, takes off again."

It hadn't been the threat to call the parole officer, Victor knew. People just loved to talk. Given time, they would reveal anything. It was a source of continual amazement to one of Victor's rather taciturn disposition. "What time did she come back Wednesday?"

"I don't think she did. Like I said, it's the end of my shift, an' I'm not here when Hopper leaves for the station Thursday morning. But around ten A.M., she shows up, wearing the same clothes she had on the night before, looks shell-shocked. Tells the cab to wait, goes up, comes down in ten minutes with her suitcase and takes off. Haven't seen her since. She musta left a note, 'cause when Hopper comes in, he's down here in five minutes pumpin' me for information. Did she say anything? What'd she act like? Hopper, he's a generous guy, you know what I mean, but I couldn't tell him more'n that I'm tellin' you, 'cept the name of the cab."

Victor ignored the hint. "What was it?"

"JJ's Tri-County Cab Company."

Victor took out his card, scribbled his office extension, his home number. "The girl shows up, Hopper gets in, I want to know."

The attention of the skeleton staff was palpable from the moment Victor stepped into the Northfield complex. The ruptured conversations, the sidelong glances, the wake of whispers, trailed him to his unit. It was a slow Saturday and the business had been hushed up, but everyone down to the custodians knew that Lieutenant Cardenas' apartment had been the target of a sniper and that he had been entertaining Cat Fortunati Austen at the time of the hit, King Carlo's kid sister. As gossip went, it had Captain Loeper's fourth divorce beat, hands down. Those who had worked with the undemonstrative lieutenant longest and could identify tones and inflections, decoded the quiet request that Jean Adane get Sergeant Rice on the phone immediately: Stan Rice screwed up. They were bitterly disappointed when Victor retreated to his office and closed the door.

Rice sounded groggy. Victor checked his watch. Eleven-thirty. There was a sleepily irritated, distinctly feminine moan underlying Stan's muffled "Hello." Stan was divorced.

"Cardenas," Victor greeted.

"Yessir."

"Jerry Dudek has a sister."

"Huh?" Befuddlement yielded to apprehension. "Sister?"

"A sister. Calls herself Noreen Dunn."

"His resume says no next of kin. Fried showed it to me."

"When was the last time you saw an honest resume?"

"Not since yours."

Victor sighed. "She's engaged to Tom Hopper."

"What!"

Victor heard an impatient "Staaaaan" in the background. "She's been living with Hopper for several months. Wednesday, she has words with Dudek outside of Hopper's condo, takes off overnight, runs in Thursday to pick up her things, takes off again. Looks like she's leaving Hopper. But she shows up at CV's that night. Cat Austen saw her there."

"Jesus Christ."

"Hopper's not home. Find him. I want his version by the end of today." He hung up, punched the intercom. "Adane, please come in here."

When Jean Adane had been plucked from the Academy two weeks before graduation, she was flattered, assumed that the prosecutor's office had identified her as investigator material. Alas, the transfer had been prompted by budgetary concerns. A routine check revealed that the Academy's number one recruit had maintained an A+ average in English composition, communications and computer science in college, possessed a MENSA-class IQ, a phenomenal memory and a mechanical aptitude that had allowed her to master the operation and repair of every known make and model of office machinery. She could type one hundred eight words a minute without a single error, accurately record, file, compute and retrieve any item of information from the simple to the complex. She had replaced three full time office staff, and a part-timer in maintenance and become Victor's unofficial aide de camp.

Three women in her Academy class; now Sherilyn was on Boardwalk patrol, Ernestine was a vice decoy and she, Jean was marking time as Northfield's Jill-of-all-trades. Ernie and Sheri scorned her infrequent griping. Okay, so Cardenas wasn't a laugh a minute like Stan Rice, but he was good-looking and unmarried and straight A real gentleman, too. What was Jean's problem?

Jean conceded that Victor was an excellent boss; intelligent, fair, good-looking, if you liked the type, but frankly she found his courtesy a little unnerving. His habitual "please's" and "thank-you's," the standing whenever she entered a room and opening doors were unnatural for a seasoned cop. He never told risqué jokes or bragged about his sexual conquests or raised his voice or used profanity and he never laughed, not ever, and it just didn't seem right.

Jean entered Victor's office. Victor rose to his feet. "The preliminary autopsy report?"

"It's just been sent over, sir."

"I'm going to want the phone records from Dudek's apartment. Hopper's, too."

"I'm already working on it, sir."

"Who's the city detective assigned to the case?"

"Detective Carbone, sir."

"Ask him if Dudek's apartment's been—"

"Sealed. It has."

"Find out if and when Dudek's body's been released, to who and where it goes."

Whom, Jean corrected mentally. "Yes, sir."

"Call JJ's Tri-County Cab, check their logs. A woman took a cab from Hopper's apartment Wednesday afternoon, the seventh, again Thursday morning, the eighth. Find out where she went."

"Yes, sir."

"That's it. Thanks. Please ask Detective Long to come in here."

Detective Philip Long was the most recent addition to Victor's unit. He was lean and black, with a smooth complexion, large dark eyes and fine-boned hands. As part of an Atlantic City vice unit, which was shy of eligible females, Long had been drafted to play decoy on several of the department's sporadic Pacific Avenue sweeps. Properly decked out, Long was a rather engaging street-walker, but he could do society matron, too, or grandmotherly slot addict, laden with winnings. Paired with Joey Fortunati (as "Joey G. and his number one lady, Phyllis") he'd helped bust a prostitution ring operated by a trio of entrepreneurial baccarat dealers, been egged on to a series of similar stings that became departmental lore.

The amazement and regret of the deceived johns, the never-ending calls from colleges wives requesting tips on skin care, depilation, did him in at last. Long campaigned for a transfer and Victor, who'd worked with him once or twice, promoted the move to Major Crimes. "That Long," they lamented to Ernestine Moore, the new girl on the streets, "he was one great-lookin' broad."

"You weren't assigned to the Dudek investigation." Victor gestured for Long to take a chair.

"No, sir, I been workin' the Harris girl. The hooker?"

"Talk to her pimp?"

"City vice did. He's got an airtight. Hate to say it, but that one's a shi—a dead end." Victor's unit reluctantly deferred to his unaccountable aversion to obscenities.

"Put Harris on hold for now. I want you to look for a girl named Dunn. First name, Noreen. I want her picked up for questioning."

Long took out a notepad, started writing. "She a suspect?"

Victor nodded. "And Dudek's sister."

Long drummed his pencil against his thigh. "I didn't know he had a sister."

"Neither did I until a couple hours ago. She's engaged to Tom Hopper. She was seen arguing with Dudek the day before the murder. Thursday night, she was seen at CV's, took off right before the shooting. Mrs. Austen and Hopper both spoke to her."

"Want me to yank Hopper?"

Victor shook his head. "Rice is on that. Dunn is, or was, a dancer, worked some of the casinos. The performers, they must have some kind of union keeps records."

"I guess."

"Don't guess. It's destructive to the logical faculty."

"Sherlock Holmes." Long smiled. It was one of the few personal facts they knew about their lieutenant, that he was a Holmes aficionado.

Victor smiled, briefly. "Dunn's about late twenties, brunette, tall, very attractive. See if you can get a line on a former address, people who worked with her, someone she might be staying with."

"Got it."

"One more thing. I want you to pick up Whitney Rocap and bring her in here for questioning."

"The weather girl?"

Victor nodded. "Adane can dig up the address. Tell her we'll get a warrant if she gives you a hard time." He stood. "That's it for now."

Long rose, opened the door. Adane poked her head in, handed over a folder. "Here's the autopsy report, firearms lab apologizes for the delay. They said the gun was an older Smith and Wesson Model Ten, standard police revolver, or at least it was."

Victor nodded. The ME had been right about the gun being a surplus weapon, it seemed.

"We haven't been able to trace ownership yet. The ME says Mr. Dudek has been released to the Wylie Funeral Home in Linwood. The funeral's scheduled for Monday morning, a memorial service at Wylie's, no church, then interment in Upper Township. Seaside Heights Cemetery."

"Who's picking up the tab?"

"Tom Hopper. He was out there this morning making the arrangements."

It made sense, Victor decided. Hopper had money; he was almost family. "I want the statements that were taken at the scene Thursday night. All of them, please."

Jean withdrew, returned with two canvas three-ring binders, thick with typed reports. She had punched holes with mathematical precision, affixed gummed reinforcers. Victor would be willing to bet—if he were a betting man—that not a word was misspelled.

He would be willing to wager, too, that of the two hundred seventy-nine (Adane had numbered the pages) bystanders who had hung around to talk to the cops, not one of them had anything relevant to say.

He thanked Adane, began shuffling through the testimony. Hopper said he had talked to Mrs. Austen and Jerry before the drawing, did not know that Jerry had left the club, no mention of Noreen Dunn. The club owner, a guy named Vitale, had witnessed an altercation between Jerry and some drunk, "the lady reporter nailed the drunk with some kind of karate chop" (Cat?) before he could send his guys in to break it up.

Victor kept scanning. Jerry had left the club with a group. With a girl. Alone. Ran after that reporter. Damn. *Wanted to put something inside Cat's head. Something the killer doesn't want known? Thinks Cat knows? Had last night been a warning or an attempt to silence her? Don't guess.*

Victor put the stack of papers in order, took it from the top. Abruzzi, Mary Ann. Adane had even alphabetized them, clever girl. No, woman. Woman.

# CHAPTER

## ELEVEN

Victor grabbed his phone on the first ring.

Detective Long. "I got Rocap. We'll be over in twenty; she's callin' her lawyer."

Then Stan Rice, contrite. "Hopper's in shock; Wylie wants to get this wrapped, wants to know should he go with the silver and blue stripe or the burgundy. Tie. With the dark suit. For the stiff. So he asks me, I told him to cremate the sonofabitch. Hopper wants to know can we let him into Dudek's place so he can pick up the clothes, get Wylie off his back."

"You go with him, make a note of everything he takes. What'd he say about Noreen Dunn?"

"He swears to God he hasn't seen her since Thursday night and it's makin' him nuts."

"He say what they argued about?"

"He says they didn't. Says she was kinda jittery Wednesday, borrowed his car to take a drive, she came in when he was out, they didn't connect 'cause she left, stayed out all night. Thursday, she comes back, she packs up and takes off, leaves a note. Says she needs time to think."

"What about her fight with Dudek?"

"Hopper says she never mentioned it, first he's heard of it."

"What'd they talk about Thursday night?"

"He said he never caught up with her Thursday night, he went out lookin' for her, hears a commotion in the club, runs back in, people start tellin' him Jerry and some guy got into it over a girl, he looks around for Jerry, next thing he knows, the cops drag him out to ID the stone."

That wasn't what Cat had said. She had said Tom had met up with Noreen, got her out of the way when he heard trouble inside CV's.

"Check the restaurant people, see if anyone saw the Dunn girl and Hopper, can put them together."

"Restaurant's only open weekends off season."

"Hopper have any idea where she might be?"

"He says no."

"What about the upcoming wedding, was there a wedding party, girlfriends she might be with?"

"Hopper said they were gonna tell his old man, invite him and the stepmother, few friends from the station, nothing formal."

"Hopper own a gun?"

"Nope. So he says."

"Noreen?"

"He says no."

"Check it out. And check the firearms report against lost or stolen."

Stan knew a punitive assignment when he heard it. "What do we got Adane for?"

"I didn't catch that."

"I said ten-four."

Whitney Rocap was pacing the interrogation room, raking her fingers through her trademark flip. Her attorney was sitting calmly in a scarred wooden chair, tapping her black, manicured fingers against a five hundred dollar briefcase.

"Hello, Lauren."

The attorney looked up. "Victor, dear, I have my modern dance class Saturday afternoons." Her ebony hair was slicked away from her face, pinned into a chignon at the nape of her neck. The straight black brows and penetrating amber eyes had a disconcerting effect upon juries; Victor had seen her work both to her clients' advantage more than once.

"Will you take a chair, Miss Rocap?"

Whitney looked at her lawyer, sat.

"Your client's been informed of her rights, I trust?"

"By that cute little Philip Long. You the one got him out of a dress? I'm beginning to see him in an entirely different light."

Lauren had once argued that in order to prove entrapment of her client, Detective Long would have to appear before the court in his working attire. The judge concurred. No one in the courtroom ever forgot it.

"Has your client signed a consent to be questioned?"

"Can we get on with this?" Whitney snapped.

Lauren tapped her palm on the table. "She has. If you're going to tape this, Victor dear, I want another tape recorder brought in to make a simultaneous recording."

"Lauren, I'm hurt."

"You'll get over it."

Victor sent for the second tape recorder and set it up. He pronounced the purpose of the meeting, the names of those present, the date into the recorders, replayed both to make certain they were copying.

"Miss Rocap, were you at the dance club Circolo Venerdi on the night of November eighth?"

"Yes." Whitney flicked a thumbnail against her front teeth, nervously.

"For how long?"

"I got there around eight forty-five, nine, stayed about an hour."

"Where was your car parked?"

"Across the street."

"What's that parking fee?"

114

"Jesus. Five dollars, okay?"

"Can we pick up the pace?" Lauren checked her hair in the wall mirror, waggled her fingers at whomever was behind the glass.

"Did you speak with Jerry Dudek at all?"

"Yes."

"What did you talk about?"

"You don't have to answer that," Lauren drawled.

"No," Victor said. "But that might slow down the pace considerably—"

"We had a fight, okay? I know people saw us. Jerry was coming on to anything with ovaries and I didn't like it."

"Why not?"

" 'Cause, we're engaged, that's why not!"

"I see. How long have you been engaged?"

"Three months. Jerry says he wants us to wait until he signs the new contract with the station, it's a three-year deal, he's getting a big raise, then we're gonna set the date—" She broke off, realized she was using the present tense. "That sonofabitch!" She began to sob. "That sonofabitch!"

Lauren scooted her chair closer to Whitney's. "We can do this another time."

"Let's get it over with," Whitney sniffled.

Lauren nodded to Victor; he resumed. "How long had you known Dudek?"

"Almost since they came to KRZI. I get a job in copy two months after they were hired. We got on together right off."

"You fight often?"

Lauren tensed, but her client responded, "Yeah, lotsa times. Jerry could be a real bastard. But he could be really funny, too. You know, wild."

"And you liked that? Wild?"

"Sometimes. Don't you?"

"Did he ever borrow money? Steal from you?"

The heart-shaped face hardened. "No."

*Lie number one*, Victor calculated. "Threaten you? Coerce you into doing anything you didn't want to do?"

"You mean illegal stuff?"

"Or personal."

"The lieutenant means sexually, dear. Don't you, Victor?"

"Yes."

"No, never. Well, maybe your run-of-the-mill kink sometimes, but no S and M."

Victor considered asking her to elaborate, saw Lauren's droll amber gaze fixed on him, changed tactics. "We've sealed Jerry's apartment of course, and there will be a thorough search of the place. Are there any of your possessions in there that we ought to know about?"

"How should I know?" She began gnawing at the thumbnail.

"Keepsakes? Letters or snapshots, anything like that?"

"Jerry lived in that dinky efficiency, we mostly went to my place," she feinted.

Victor saw the panic, changed course again. "What about his family. Did he ever mention them to you?"

"Jerry didn't have any family. He was an only child; his parents are dead."

"Where was home?"

"Around here, he said once. South Jersey, somewhere. Jerry didn't like to talk about his past much."

"Odd then that he should come back to a place that had so little meaning for him." On Cat's tape, Tom had said that Jerry was "obsessed" with grabbing KRZI's offer.

Whitney shrugged.

"What about friends?"

"Jerry made lots of friends. Everybody knew him."

"I mean particular friends, ones you socialized with."

"Nobody, really. I guess he was closest to Tom, but after work, they went their separate ways."

"And what about women?"

Whitney frowned. "Look, I know he'd been coming on to that new girl, Deanna, and yes, we had words over it. Don't you ever fight with your wife, Lieutenant? It doesn't mean you want her dead."

Lauren's gaze softened. She mouthed an "I'm sorry" to Victor.

"And that's what you were arguing about on the dance floor Thursday night? Other women?"

Whitney examined her fingernails. "Yeah, right."

*Lie number two.* "Then you walked out?"

"I had to get to the station by eleven."

"So you weren't around when the shooting occurred."

"No. No."

"Do you know Mrs. Austen, the magazine reporter?"

The hazel-green eyes narrowed. "Yeah. I've seen her."

"You called her."

Lauren looked from her client to Victor.

"I wanted to know what Jerry told her about me, okay? And I didn't want her to write about us fighting. I just got the six o'clock anchor slot and I don't need negative publicity."

"She says you threatened her."

"Look, I was upset. I don't want to be trashed, even in a local rag like *South Jersey.* Jerry just got killed; I was upset."

Victor's impassive expression masked his frustration. Her story hung together. Try to build a case on what she was withholding and Lauren Robinson would take him apart in court. "So you were upset when you spoke to Mrs. Austen solely because of Dudek's death, and not because he had been, say, blackmailing you?"

"Jesus!" Whitney shoved her chair away from the table. "Do I have to sit here and take this?" she demanded of Lauren.

"No, of course not." Lauren rose. "Always a pleasure, Lieutenant. We can find our way out."

"I'm not finished."

"Are you arresting my client?"

"Three more questions."

Lauren looked at Whitney; Whitney nodded, her jaw set.

"You own a gun?"

Whitney shook her head.

"The witness indicates the negative," Victor stated to the tape recorder. "Ever fire one?"

"No."

"Are you familiar with the name Noreen Dunn?"

"No, I never heard of her."

The response seemed genuine. "Tom or Jerry never mentioned the name? You're certain?"

"That's four questions, Victor," Lauren cautioned.

"Wait—" Whitney examined a ravaged thumbnail. "I think Tom was going with someone who might have been called Noreen."

"You ever meet her?"

"No. Like I said, Jerry and Tom didn't socialize."

"Can you think of anyone who would want to kill Dudek? Did he have enemies? Gamble? Owe money?"

Whitney tensed. "He spent a lot. He made enemies on the air. If you ask me, it was one of them, some obsessed fan, like the kid who shot John Lennon. Jerry attracted a lot of those."

"Thanks." Victor punched off both recorders and released one of the tapes, handed it to Lauren. When they left, he pocketed the other, rapped on the two-way glass and nodded toward the hallway.

Adane met him at the door.

"Analysis?" he asked.

"She's lying about something, probably about the blackmail. The nervous mannerisms exacerbated, she blinked twice as often and her voice rose in pitch, too. She'll refuse a lie detector if you ask. She's frightened, but not of the killer. She feels no need for personal protection. That could indicate that she is the killer, or that she's convinced Dudek's death is not connected to their relationship."

"Which?"

Adane concentrated. "The latter. She's not very bright. It appears that Dudek's killing was opportunistic. The murderer could not have foreseen that Dudek would follow Mrs. Austen to the parking lot, yet he was able to take advantage of it with little preparation and get away clean. That takes some presene of mind."

Victor nodded. "What have you got so far?"

Rice or Long would have pulled out a notebook. Adane spoke

from memory. "Tom Hopper made periodic calls to a North Carolina number, Thomas Hopper, Jr., his father. Local calls of course, a few to a Philadelphia radio station and three to Ancora Hospital. Those were unusual because they all took place within the past six months and always between nine and ten A.M."

"Ancora?" It was a state psychiatric facility, about a half-hour drive from Atlantic City. "Hopper's at the station until ten, ten-fifteen. Call Ancora and check—"

"I spoke to Records and Personnel. One maintenance worker named Dunn, but he's an elderly black male. No other Dunns, Dudeks or Hoppers."

"Okay, what about Dudek's calls?"

"Local only, apparently. No collect or long distance from his apartment. I took the liberty of checking out the pay phone in the lobby of Club Central, that's where he lived. He didn't receive any person-to-person calls there, nor did he make collect ones."

"The cab?"

Adane nodded. "Both pick-ups were dropped at a McDonald's down on Route Nine in Rio Grande. Thursday morning, it was round trip, McDonald's to Hoppers and back, with suitcases on the return trip. That cost her almost forty dollars. The driver remembered her. He said she seemed distraught. Perhaps we should circulate her picture; maybe someone down there saw who picked her up."

"I'll get one from Hopper." Victor thanked her and returned to his desk.

Long called in shortly after six. "Noreen Dunn used to live in Ocean City, place called Club Central, recognize it?"

"Dudek lived there."

"Converted motel, efficiencies, furnished, mail slots in the lobby, switchboard, though most of the tenants put in a phone line. Rents by the week or month, caters to a lot of casino help and the sunbirds, you know, folks run a seasonal business in summer, run down Florida come October. No off-street parking, but close to the bus line into AC. Motor V doesn't have a registration for Noreen Dunn, license gives the Club Central address,

119

she didn't bother to change it when she moved in with Hopper seven, eight months ago."

"Ask around about Dudek?"

"Uh huh. Desk clerk thought I was kiddin' I said Noreen Dunn was Dudek's sister. Dunn's place's been rented a few times since she left. Dudek's is sealed off. I took a look, got a partial inventory. Guy had a lot of top-of-the-line toys. Didn't think radio paid that well."

"The landlord understands that the room is not to be touched?"

"Uh huh. I checked out the performers' union, got a line on a few girls knew Noreen Dunn, got a picture, she's a looker all right.They all tell the same story: Noreen Dunn was a nice kid, kind of a loner, no runnin' around, no drugs, no going out for drinks with the crowd. One of them, a—lemme see—a Denise Santos, says Noreen was goin' with some guy a year or so ago, a Danny or Denny Somebody, they broke up and Noreen was real upset for a while, 'til she meets some new guy I guess is Hopper. Noreen and this Denise, they're in some show over the Showboat. 'Round last spring, Noreen starts flashin' a diamond, says she's movin' in with her new boyfriend, gonna quit when the show folds, get married, start a family. And get this: I tell this gal Noreen's Dudek's sister—"

"She doesn't believe you."

"Those gals're all nuts about the radio show, don't know why Noreen wouldn't talk up something like that. So then I run over to KRZI—"

"Why?"

"Noreen's next of kin, maybe she wants some of his stuff. Place is dead on Saturday, but I run into the Halprin chick, she says, 'Detective, I been engaged to Jerry over a month, he never mentioned a sister.' So I call up that guy Fried's secretary, ask if she knows anything, Duboice is her name? And get this: she says, 'Detective, Jerry's my boyfriend, we're gonna get married, he doesn't have any sister.' Bottom line is, half these folks never heard of Noreen Dunn, the half that did haven't seen her."

"Get me the picture. I'll have Adane put out an APB and get

the Margate department to keep an eye on Hopper's place. Firearms says the weapon was a thirty-eight revolver."

"Had a snub as a backup once."

"No, this one was a standard."

"Hard to conceal. Kinda weapon folks keep around the house for protection."

"And take out of the house only if they have an object in mind," Victor concluded, grimly.

"Right."

"You know the overtime situation, but the press has been on the DA, so it's seven-twenty-four until we find the Dunn girl."

"S'long as I don't gotta make the rounds in four inch spikes, I'm happy."

Mrs. DiLorenzo called to tell Victor that his door was all fixed, a nice, new steel reinforced one and could he find out if the installers really complained to the animal warden? It wasn't her fault, the guy came in to get the check ("Seven hundred thirty-eight forty-seven, my insurance, they're gonna die!") and it wasn't a real bite. Everybody knows you don't try to pet a constrictor if you just ate a Reuben sandwich for lunch, don't they? And what was she gonna do if the animal warden tried to take Nero away, he was such good protection? Victor kindly refrained from informing his landlady what a gun or poison or even a few strategically placed ice cubes could do to "such good·protection," promised to call off the animal warden and asked her to leave the new key in his mail box.

He hung up and dialed Cat's number.

"Austen residence." Jane.

"Jane, this is Lieutenant Cardenas. Is your mom around?"

"Yes." Pause. Jane was evidently in a literal mood but at least she hadn't hung up.

"May I speak to her please?"

"Mom!" Jane hollered. "It's him."

Cat came on the line and said hello.

"Everything okay over there?"

"Every one of my brothers called today and asked the same thing. You're still at the office all this time?"

"How did you know that?"

"You're using your official voice. Learn anything?"

"Not much," he hedged. "Listen, Cat, can you give me anything more on Noreen Dunn? Even an impression?"

"What can I say? Tom didn't want to talk about her and Jerry avoided questions about his personal life or invented the details. Jerry did seem to make a big deal out of playing Cupid, but it's not like Tom would need a lot of encouragement. She's very beautiful."

"Why would Jerry go out of his way to get them together if he's only going to split them apart, though?" he mused.

"What?"

"She and Jerry had a blow-up Wednesday. Right after that, she walks out on Tom."

"Maybe that's why. To have the fun of splitting them up."

Good answer, he thought.

"It explains why Tom was so anxious to link up with Noreen Thursday night."

"But not why she showed up there in the first place. Are you sure Hopper said he'd caught up with Noreen after the raffle?"

"Yes. And that he told her to take off when he heard the fight inside the club."

"Because he told Sergeant Rice this morning that he never saw her Thursday night."

"Maybe I misunderstood. Or maybe Tom's upset. He loves her and I'm sure he suspects the worst. You can't arrest someone for being in love."

"For obstruction of justice, withholding evidence, you'd better believe I can."

"Isn't Whitney Rocap a suspect any more?"

"I spoke to her today. She said she was worried you might print something about her fight with Dudek, didn't want bad publicity."

"Now that's a lie! She threatened me. And she could have followed us last night and still got to the station before air time."

"Perhaps. But Sherlock Holmes says it's a capital mistake to theorize without data."

"But it's tremendously entertaining. You *do* think, don't you, that Jerry's killer and the person who fired a shot at us last night are one and the same?"

Stan Rice poked his head in. "Oops, sorry, Lieutenant, but firearms just called, they say you wanna do this on a Saturday, it's gonna cost our unit a round at Bud an' Lou's."

Victor laid his palm over the mouthpiece. "You make the owner?"

"Get real. All's I can tell you is it's not registered in New Jersey, prob'ly surplus someone picked up at a flea mart, like the ME says. Lab says the slugs look to be a match, same gun did Dudek hit your place."

"Tell the lab the drinks are on me. Thanks."

Stan backed out.

"What was that all about?" Cat asked.

"Nothing," Victor lied. "Nothing at all."

# CHAPTER
## TWELVE

Victor called Cat at two o'clock Sunday afternoon to tell her that something had come up and he would try to make it to her place for dinner, but not to count on him. Had he found Noreen, Cat asked? Had they made an arrest? Victor's responses were terse and vague and Cat decided that he was not up to the scrutiny of the brothers Fortunati and was using the case as an excuse to back out. A man you've known fewer than three days *and* a cop, she chided herself. What difference does it make whether he comes to dinner or not!

The "something" that had intervened was not Victor's reticence but the corpse of one Alameda "Granma Al" Thurman, discovered two hours earlier by her friend Mrs. Malba Shallett, who had dropped by to inquire why Granma had missed two consecutive Sunday services at the True Spirit Tabernacle.

Instincts benumbed by so recent an encounter with the Holy Spirit, Mrs. Shallett was not alerted by the unlocked door, the suffocating silence, the odor of decay and very nearly tripped over the inert, bloated, vaguely female thing on the bedroom floor.

The horrified Mrs. Shallett stumbled into the street, ran six blocks (at a respectable pace) and collapsed on an icy curb where she was discovered by a couple of conventioneer's wives from Minnesota searching for husbands who had last been seen sightseeing along the Pacific Avenue stroll.

Victor examined the crime scene, conferred with the two city detectives assigned to the case, endured the ME's levity, and turned the matter over to Sergeant Rice. Stan's calm, easy-going manner and dimpled, boyish smile immediately soothed the hysterical Mrs. Shallett, the flustered midwestern ladies, the covey of neighborhood cronies wringing their hands at the police barricade.

Victor watched with a rueful smile as Stan romanced them all, knew that in another fifteen minutes, he would be in someone's kitchen, drinking tea, munching store-bought cookies and in an hour, he would have the name of everyone who had passed Mrs. Thurman's door in the last year, learn the entire saga of the neighborhood while dispensing advice on personal safety, admiring the pictures of grandchildren. Such was Stan's gift.

At four-fifteen, the forensics team departed. Stan was reveling in the admiration of the neighborhood ladies and the prospect of a good autopsy in the morning. Victor checked in with the city detective assigned to the Dudek case, Carbone ("We found the lot attendant, he left Bel-Ave at ten"), took a call from the county DA who informed Victor that the media were hounding him for a press conference, would Victor take it, called Tom Hopper who said he had heard nothing from Noreen, checked in with the Margate department, which confirmed that Noreen had not been spotted entering or leaving Hopper's place, asked Adane to check into the possibility of getting a tap on Rocap's phone, Hopper's phone, then drove home, showered, changed, bought a dozen roses and drove to Cat's.

All of Cat's immediate family were assembled for Freddy's belated birthday: Carlo and Annamarie; Vinnie and his dour wife, Lorraine, with their three sons, Vinnie, Jr., Jason and Johnny (eighteen, sixteen, thirteen); Marco and his wife, Nancy, who was a photographer and Annamarie's younger sister; their two kids, Marco, Jr. and Andrea; Dominic in his clerical garb; the dapper

Joey and Joey's pregnant, ex-showgirl wife Sherrie, who was twelve years his junior, divorced and the mother of a ten-year-old girl.

Lorraine resented those slender thighs, the rose petal complexion, suspected Sherrie would be back in her size four jeans a week after delivery. "Did my husband wait on me hand and foot when I was carrying the boys?" Lorraine griped to her sisters-in-law. "She can't come in here and peel a cucumber?"

"Sherrie offered to help; I told her to take it easy," Cat replied, counting ten. Why was everything getting on her nerves all afternoon?

"That *puttan'* wife of Joey's don' even cook."

Cat gritted her teeth and stalked off to the dining room. Lorraine took advantage of her absence to expostulate upon Freddy's disgraceful infatuation with Cat's *mulagnan'* friend, which she wouldn't have dared to do had Cat been present. No one criticized either Freddy or Ellice in front of Cat.

Victor arrived at five-thirty. He was greeted by Cat's mother, who was not the broad, somewhat provincial grandmother he had expected, but a small, trim woman with curly auburn hair and Cat's capricious brown eyes.

Cat heard "*He's here*" from the foyer, the swift cessation of her brothers' banter, then a sequence of greetings that at least *sounded* civil. She beat it to the kitchen and pretended to be busy. Sherrie waddled in, her round, aquamarine eyes sparkling. "Cat, he's *gorgeous!* And he brought your mother *flowers!*" Sherrie, like Jane, was a devotee of italicism.

Jenny Fortunati strode into the kitchen, Victor at her heels, "Anna, *nuora*, get me something to put these in. My own sons, they don't bring me flowers," she beamed.

Cat wiped her hands on her apron, took it off. She was wearing ivory wool slacks, a violet sweater, her chestnut hair loose, brushing her shoulders. "I'm glad you could make it," she murmured, introduced him to her sisters-in-law, then drew him off to the living room. "It's like this," she said in a low voice. "The women get KP, the men get the shop talk out of the way. I'll stick around if you're uncomfortable. They won't talk about the Dudek case in front of me."

"I'm fine."

"You want a drink?"

"Soft drink, maybe. Ginger ale?"

"You can duck into the den, watch *The Hustler* with Freddy and Ellice."

"You think I can't hold my own with your brothers? I've worked tougher rooms."

"If you don't want to be hassled about the investigation, talk to Dominic."

"What does Dominic like to talk about?"

"Ballet."

Cat made the introduction and went off to get his Canada Dry. When she returned, Dominic was explaining to Victor how he'd had to drop off the seminary track team because wind sprints were ruining his turnout. Victor listened with characteristic solemnity and without a trace of derision. Many times, Dominic's brothers had ridiculed him mercilessly for taking up ballet. Still, when the neighborhood boys had taken to tormenting him on the way to his classes, the Fortunatis felt obligated to beat up several of those with whom they were otherwise on good terms.

The dining room accommodated only the adults. The eight cousins sat at card tables in the center hall. Dominic said a blessing that was brief and to the point, Joey started pouring the wine and Cat began to relax when Freddy launched into an account of a round of strip poker he had lost to Ellice, got as far as the phrase, "—and me, I'm down to my jock—" when Carlo pitched a hunk of bread at him to shut him up.

"Freddy, the kids, for God's sake!" Nancy laughed.

The bread missed and knocked over a dish of butter mints on the breakfront. Mats scrambled to repair the damage, popped a few in his mouth and declared, "Uncle Carlo, we're not 'llowed to throw food, 'cause some people don't have none," then informed his Aunt Nancy that Uncle Dominic had said God was a bad word and asked his Uncle Freddy, "What's a jock?"

"See what you started, Freddy," Nancy giggled. She had dark hair threaded with grey and a mischievous dimple at the corner of her mouth. When Annamarie had offered to fix up her sister with one of her fiancé's brothers, the rollicking Nancy had expressed an unaccountable preference for the serious Marco.

"I'll explain it to you, Matty," offered ten-year-old Andrea. "In school they make us have health."

"What health?" demanded her father. "We never had health."

"No, we got our sex education sitting next to Danny Furina in bio lab, remember Cat?" Freddy teased.

Victor saw Cat's cheeks go vermilion, wondered who the hell Danny Furina was.

"Danny Furina, I ran into him last month, the dumb fu—" The eight children fell silent, expectantly. "'Furfant'" Carlo amended. "He asked about you, Alley Cat."

"Can we change the subject?" Cat suggested.

Cat's mother, seated on Victor's left, inquired, "So Victor, you Cath'lic?"

A gnocchi descended whole, thudded to Cat's stomach.

"Yes, Ma'am."

"'Ma'am,' that's for old ladies, you call me Jennie. Some people," she conceded, generously, "they're not Cath'lic, that's okay."

"Who's not?" Dominic demanded. "What people?"

Everyone laughed and the conversation relaxed. Marco complimented Victor on a lecture he had given at the Academy, where Marco was an instructor; Joey asked how Philip Long was working out. Carlo bragged about his twenty-four-year-old twins, Carla, in medical school and Michael, in the Air Force. Vinnie, not to be outdone, boasted Vinnie, Jr.'s, SATs, Jason's straight As, griped about Johnny's obsession with "that damn rap crap."

"Lighten up," Freddy cautioned.

"Call that music." Vinnie shoveled rigatoni onto his plate. He turned to Ellice. "You people really like that kinda music?"

Cat tensed.

"By 'you people,' I assume you mean we Ph.D.s," Ellice drawled imperturbably. "Actually, I prefer Tony Bennett. Just like you people."

"We saw him in Vegas," piped in Sherrie, oblivious to the conversation's underlying hostility. "Or maybe it was Al Martino, the one who was in that old movie *The Godfather*."

"Or maybe it was Vic Damone," Cat suggested. "The one who was married to Diahann Carroll."

Freddy laughed so hard he choked and Carlo ordered his wife to "Give him the fuckin' Heimlich," which provoked an eddy of giggles at the children's table.

The food came in courses: some kind of eggplant antipasto, gnocchi and rigatoni, chicken roasted with whole garlic and white wine, sausages baked over lentils, sautéed cabbage and steamed spinach (neither of which the children would taste), a cucumber-walnut-orange salad dressed with tart red wine.

The food kept coming long after Victor had the will or inclination to eat. He recalled his eighth Christmas Eve, the night before his debut as an alter boy, gorging himself on *mojo isleno*, *zarauela*, crisp-fried *plantanos* and a treacly confection called *yemas* that his Mexican grandmother made once a year. Victor had gotten so miserably sick that Juanito Ortiz had to take his place at Christmas Mass and Padre Vargas had actually come to the house to lecture Victor on the sin of gluttony.

When the women rose from the table to shuttle dishes from the kitchen, Victor got to his feet as well, the courtesy his parents had drummed into him in childhood reflexive now. Cat's brothers said nothing until Victor declined their invitation to watch some of the Eagles game while the women cleared the table for dessert, opting instead to lay out cups and saucers with Jennie. "You tryin' to make us look bad, or what?" Carlo kidded, but Cat's mother patted Victor's arm and told him he was a "nice boy."

In the kitchen, Cat wrapped leftovers, Annamarie scouted for candles, Lorraine and Nancy eased a two-by-three sheet cake out of the refrigerator.

"He's a doll." Annamarie nudged Cat.

Cat counted dessert plates, silently.

"Sexy, too," Nancy giggled. "Even if he is the serious type. They're fun where it counts, lemme tell you."

"Where'd Sherrie go?" Cat asked.

"Upstairs." Lorraine swiped a fingerful of icing. "Lying down. Showgirls. All they think about is that body, every little ache and pain—"

"I've never heard Sherrie complain once," Cat said. "Most of the complaining I've heard—"

"What Joey gets for marrying some—"

"Joey thinks the world of Sherrie and it's really none of your business, is it!" Cat stormed past Victor and her mother, up the stairs. This afternoon was unsalvageable. Victor was going to think her family was demented and run for cover.

"Families," Jennie shrugged. "Whaddaya gonna do?"

Cat found Sherrie in the bathroom, vomiting fiercely. "Sherrie, are you sick?"

Sherrie flushed the toilet with shaking hands.

Cat rinsed a washcloth in cold water, pressed it to Sherrie's throat. "Let me get Joey."

"No, it's just delayed morning sickness." Sherrie leaned over the sink, rinsed her mouth with water. "Let Joey have a good time with his family. How often can they all get together like this?"

Too often, thought Cat, who felt a twinge of guilt for twitting Sherrie at the dinner table. Lorraine had been crude and verbal, but hadn't they all thought pretty much the same when Joey'd eloped? Hadn't she? "You come lie down," Cat insisted.

Sherrie sat on Cat's bed, worked off her shoes. "You know, I think that Victor's real cute. He likes you, too, I can tell. Who cares if you've only known each other a few days? Joey and I got married a month after we met, remember?"

Cat would never forget it.

"You have to tell yourself you deserve to be happy, Cat. Lennie—that's my ex—he used to tell me I was dumb, not good for anything. He beat me up, too. I didn't have the nerve to do anything about it, until he went after Meryl, then I got the guts to divorce him. I had to get a restraining order, but he got to me one day while Meryl was in school and, well, he put me in the hospital. See that little cut under my jaw?" Sherrie arched her slender neck. "He tried to cut me, and he did other things and my face was swollen out to here and I was a mess. I called the cops and Joey came to the hospital. He got someone to take care of Meryl and came to court with me and made sure the DA had a case that would get Lennie put away. It was Joey who wanted to get married right away, I wanted to wait, and we eloped because I was still bruised in the face and had a cast on my arm. That's why we didn't have any pictures."

Joey had told nothing of this to his family, only said he'd met Sherrie working on a case. Cat understood now why Sherrie and Ellice had hit it off so well.

"So Joey's gonna adopt Meryl if he can, and I said I'd convert and we could get married in the church, but Joey says we'll do whatever makes me happy. He even says it's okay if I wanted to make the rounds again after the baby is born."

Something clicked. "Sherrie . . . Are you still friendly with any of the girls you worked with in Atlantic City?"

"Sure. I still take class a couple times a week, when I feel up to it. I run into a lot of them."

"Did you know a dancer named Noreen Dunn?"

"Tall, short dark hair, real pretty? We took a few master classes together a couple years back, and I think I saw her in the last revue they did over the Showboat."

"Do you know anything about her?"

"Not really. She was kinda shy, didn't hang out after class. She kinda reminded me of like I was after I divorced Lennie, like you don't wanna get too close to anyone."

"Did she ever look beat up?"

"Nope. Sometimes it doesn't show."

"Did you ever see her with a boyfriend? Or family?"

"I never saw her with anyone. But I think she had family because one time?" Sherrie pursed her childish mouth, "I went

131

backstage to see some of my friends who were in that revue "Cinemafestique"? And she was on the pay phone, saying something like, 'What do you care if I see her or not? I'm *her* daughter.' Just like that. 'I'm *her* daughter.' Why?"

"Well, it's sort of confidential."

"I won't tell. Except Joey. I tell Joey everything."

"Noreen Dunn was engaged to Tom Hopper. You know, the radio guy who worked with Jerry Dudek? I wanted to talk to her for my article, but she's dropped out of sight and Tom's getting worried. I just wondered if you knew of someone she was close to, someone she might be staying with?"

"You don't think she's dead, do you?" Sherrie's eyes widened dramatically. "Maybe somebody's trying to send a message to Tom Hopper, you know, first his partner gets bumped off, then his girlfriend gets snatched!"

Married to a cop for five years, Sherrie's view of criminal behavior continued to be derived from television.

Cat smiled. "I don't think it's anything like that."

"Mom!" Jane hollered up the stairs. "It's time to surprise Uncle Freddy with the *cake!*"

Sherrie patted her stomach, shook her head. "Look, I'm supposed to have brunch with Ingrid Alonzo tomorrow. She's choreographing a show down here, and I think she knew Noreen. I'll pump her for information."

"Thanks," Cat said. "Now you rest."

The family had reassembled in the dining room, was halfway through the "Happy Birthday's" when Cat entered. "I thought you guys forgot about me," Freddy exclaimed, in mock surprise.

"We jus' kep' it a secret," Mats explained. "It's okay to keep good secrets. They said so in school."

The phone rang. Cat took it in the kitchen.

"So how come you're keepin' it under wraps, you gettin' shot at again!" Ritchie's elated squeal needled her eardrum. "You're over some guy's place, it was the cop investigating the Dudek hit, in his apartment, you're there and you get shot at! Again! I'm lovin' it!"

"You'd never let me get away with such redundancies," Cat observed, noncommittally.

"Big brother must have some clout, keepin' the whole business outta the papers. Not one line in the morning's *Press*. So why'd they pull in Whitney Rocap yesterday, she a suspect?"

"How should I know?"

"Don't play dumb with me."

"You do that better solo."

"Why would Rocap whack Dudek? I heard they were tight."

"Maybe too tight."

"What's that supposed to mean?"

"Patience. I'm going to call Ron Spivak today or tomorrow and then I'll be able to put two and two together."

"Just don't come up with zero. Dudek's funeral's tomorrow. Check it out, but try not to get into the line of fire again, okay, 'cause I don't have anyone else I can put on this."

"Don't worry, Ritchie. This Cat's got nine lives and I'm only down two or three."

The family ate their cake and began their exits. Jennie, toting her roses ("You're a nice boy, you come around some more," she told Victor), Lorraine bearing a grocery bag filled with leftovers, ("It's just her an' the two kids and that girl, why should it go to waste?"), and Sherrie with her uneaten slice of cake wrapped in a paper napkin, ("I'll get the dope and give you a ring," she promised Cat). Carlo left last, grabbed Jane and Mats for a good-bye kiss, pressed something into their hands.

"I told you not to give them money," Cat insisted.

"Eyes in the back of her friggin' head." Carlo gave Cat a rough kiss, beat it before she made the kids give the money back.

Freddy halfheartedly offered to help her clean up and hustled Ellice off for a drive when Cat refused.

"Was it awful?" she asked Victor. He stacked dishes in the dishwasher while she rinsed.

"What?"

"Dinner. They can be a little hard to take."

"I've seen worse. I like your mother."

Cat smiled. "When I was little, it was nice, having so many people around. Holidays were great. But now I feel a little smothered. They don't like my being on my own."

"They want you to marry again?"

Cat studied a wine glass. "I guess."

"So who's Danny Furina?"

Cat blinked. "Just some guy Freddy and I went to school with. Freddy and I were in the same grade."

"Like your lawyer Delareto is 'just some guy' and Kevin Somebody and the guy who runs with you is 'just some guy'?"

"Yup." Was he jealous?

"Who was on the phone?"

"Am I being interrogated, Lieutenant?"

"Yup."

Cat handed him a platter. "Ritchie Landis. He heard about Friday night, wanted all the gory details."

Victor frowned. "Whoever was supposed to keep a lid on that dropped the ball."

"Ritchie finds out things."

"So what did he want? Reminding you you've got a deadline?"

"Don't you, Lieutenant? I'm sure the press has been pressuring Kurt Raab, and he's probably looking for someone discreet and photogenic to throw to the media wolves. So you want to give a hard-working reporter something for the record?"

"No." Then, after a moment, "I want us—what's between us—to remain off the record."

Cat glanced at him, studied the parenthesis of black mustache, the right angle of the jaw. He made it sound like they would last beyond the Dudek case. *Fratelli* Fortunati hadn't scared him off. "Have you found Noreen Dunn?"

"Who wants to know, you or Landis?"

"If you're going to be selfish, two can play at that game."

Victor said nothing.

"Do you think she skipped town?" Cat wondered aloud.

"Where did she bank? I mean, if she withdrew a lot of money before the shooting, maybe she's been planning it all along?"

"I do have a news flash, come to think of it. That's already occurred to me."

"Don't be condescending. What about phone calls?"

Victor smiled ruefully. "Okay. Tom called Dad, Tom called Philly—"

"Philly One Oh Four? From home, not from work?"

Victor nodded.

Cat snatched a paper towel, dried her hands, thoughtfully. "So maybe Tom was negotiating with One Oh Four and maybe Jerry was excluded . . ."

"Tom didn't give KRZI notice."

"Their contracts aren't up until the first of the year. He's got time. Remember the tape, when I asked him about Philly One Oh Four? I was there. It threw him."

"You think he was planning to go it alone?"

Cat nibbled her lower lip, absently. "Well, if I were in Tom's place, I would be wondering how long an act like that could play. I don't think there would be financial concerns, but there might be other ones."

"Such as?"

"Whatever the Six A.M. Circus can't give him. Credibility. Stability. Permanence. With a partner like Jerry, Tom must have felt like he was always this far from getting sued or kicked off the air. This has been the first job he's held for any length of time since college. Now that he's proven to himself that he can stick with something, thinking about settling down, maybe he wants something more secure. Of course," she added, "you don't dissolve a partnership by killing off the other half."

"Either one of them ever mention Ancora?" Victor asked, casually.

"Only on the air and in the context of a joke. Why?"

"No reason."

"That's mean!"

Victor leaned his hip against the counter, crossed his arms over his chest. "Well, we can't give everything to the press. I've told you far too much already."

Cat changed the subject. "What about the funeral? Do you think Noreen might show up?"

"You're not going."

"Are you?"

"I've got a court appearance in Mays Landing tomorrow. And Cat, I mean it, I don't want you anywhere around—"

"Would you like some more coffee? It's no trouble."

"Your family's right. You shouldn't be on your own. You can't be trusted." He unrolled his sleeves, dug his cuff links out of his pocket. "Look, I've got to go do some homework for my court date tomorrow. When will Freddy and Ellice be back?"

"I think they were going to a movie. Now don't frown! I'll lock the doors and I've got the PD on automatic dial and I have a gun."

"Indeed?"

"Marco taught me how to shoot when I was sixteen. I'm not bad."

"Put my number on automatic dial, too."

"I'll have to bump somebody. The phone—could you pick it up for me?"

Victor reached for the ringing phone, said, "Austen residence," heard the hiss of an expletive, a click.

"Wrong number?"

"What would you say to a tap on your phone? You could block out personal calls, Danny and Steve and Kevin."

"Absolutely not."

"What kind of gun?"

"What? Oh, a Taurus. Nine millimeter."

Victor cocked an eyebrow. "You keep it loaded?"

"Don't be silly. It's locked in a case near my nightstand and the ammunition is in a canister in that cabinet."

"*Dios mio*," Victor rubbed his eyelids, wearily. "I'll hang around until Freddy brings Ellice home."

"You will not. Who was on the phone, anyway?"

"Heavy breather."

"Oh." Cat's shoulder undulated in a sensual shrug. "Him."

There was an arch to her upper lip that could be prim one moment, then insolent, inviting. Victor slipped an arm around her waist, heard footsteps and withdrew it, biting his tongue.

Jane strode into the kitchen, yanked opened the refrigerator door, grabbed two slices of cheese product and peeled away the plastic. "Mats is *sleeping* on the floor," she announced. "Is *he* staying over again?"

"No," Victor replied. "Actually, I was just asking your mother's permission to invite you to accompany me to Victoria's Ice Cream Parlor Friday after school."

Jane's eyes narrowed, skeptically. "What *for?*"

"For the pleasure of your company."

"What about Mats and Mom?"

"It would be just the two of us."

"Like a *date?*"

"Exactly like one." He could feel Cat's sides quivering with laughter.

Jane envisioned herself being escorted from school, whisked off in Victor's sleek Jaguar, calculated the effect upon the Popular Girls. "I gotta go call Meryl!"

Victor turned to Cat. "You want me to carry Mats up?"

"I can do it."

They heard Jane squeal, "a *date*" and "a *Jaguar*" into the living room phone.

"How does Jane get to school?" Victor asked, casually.

"She gets the bus right down there at Morningside and Beach." Cat cut through the dining room, retrieved Victor's coat from the stair closet. "Why?"

"Do you walk down with her?"

"I've been informed that only total dweebs are accompanied to the bus stop by their mothers."

"What about Mats, is he in nursery school?"

"Three days a week."

"And you drive him there and pick him up?"

Cat's dark eyes flashed defiantly. "If this is some low tactic to scare me into staying home, not going to the funeral—"

"I don't want you to go there or anywhere else. It's not safe—"

"Don't you point your finger at me like that, Lieutenant. Who do you think you're talking to, one of your subordinates?"

Victor's jaw relaxed. He wished he had known her when they were kids; he'd bet she had been more than a match for those brothers of hers.

"Don't worry about me. Don't *worry* about me." She kissed the tip of her index finger, pressed it to his mouth. "Nothing's going to happen."

# CHAPTER

## THIRTEEN

Monday morning, Cat remembered that the back door key hadn't turned up. She let herself out the front, mentally backing up to the last time she'd used it. Thursday morning, the day of Jerry's murder, she'd tucked it into her bra for her morning run, then stuck it back on her key chain. Hadn't she? Or maybe thrown it on her bed. Cat tossed the matter to the back of her mind, finished up her six miles, sprinted in and out of the shower, put on a black knit dress, dark stockings, comfortable pumps, checked under the bed, in her jewelry case, no key, forgot about it for good.

Ellice was giving Jane and Mats breakfast, yawning. Cat wondered how late she and Freddy had stayed out. "You going in today?"

"Advanced English, but I don't have to be there 'til ten. What about you?"

"Funeral," Cat mouthed over Jane's head, drank her coffee at the counter while she made two peanut butter sans jelly sandwiches, quartered them and bagged them with apples, box juices, a cheese stick, Tastycakes. "I can come back after I drop Mats off if you want a ride to the high school."

"I got a lift. I'll be back before Jane gets home."

"So will I," Cat replied. She penned J. *Cassandra*, A. on one bag, tucked it into Jane's book bag, combed her daughter's hair and offered to walk her to the bus stop.

"Only total *dweebs* get walked to the bus!" Jane reminded her mother.

"I forgot." But Cat watched from the dining room window until the bus pulled up and Jane got on.

Cat threw a load of laundry in the washer, made the beds, dumped dishes in the sink, drove Mats to nursery school and stopped at a diner for a second cup of coffee and some raisin toast. She eavesdropped on two truckers debating which video had been the funniest on *Eye See Something*, which Cat deduced was a television show, though she couldn't remember ever having watched it. "The one where the kid pops the golf ball right in the old man's nuts, I thought I's gonna die!" bawled Trucker Number One. "Yeah, but how many times you see someone sets his hair on fire with the birthday candles?" countered his companion. Cat wondered if there was a seed of a story here; probably not.

Wylie's Funeral Home was a prominent structure on Route 9, red brick and white pillars, a cluster of south Jersey's ubiquitous holly garnishing the subdued grey and white sign. Cat parked in the rear and made her way to the parlor where Jerry lay in state. She was only the fourth arrival, matched up the three names on the register with the three faces accurately, though she knew none of them.

Wistful music was piped into the room. Barry Fried's voice echoed the phrase "respec'ful kinda music" in Cat's head and she came very near to giggling aloud. She ducked into a chair in the last row, pressed her lips together and waited for the impulse to pass.

The room began to fill with a flashy, quite young set who gave Cat the absurd sensation of being underdressed. Cat doubted that any had known Jerry well, suspected they'd just turned out for a morbid thrill.

Deanna Halprin glided in on Barry Fried's arm, wearing what looked like a black silk tuxedo. A few reporters from *Newsline90*, a writer from *The Press* whose name Cat couldn't remember, though they had been introduced a few months before. Tom Hopper ambled in alone, looking dazed and haggard. He caught Cat's eye and took a step in her direction, but Fried jumped up and yelled, "Yo, Tommy, over here!" Tom shrugged and slumped into a chair between Fried and his date.

Little Miss Du Bois-pronounced-Duboice took a chair in the row reserved for family and began to weep. Whitney Rocap tripped over the threshold, regained her footing, shot Cat a venomous glance. She resembled a blurred photograph of her soignée self; the signature flip was awry, the hazel-green eyes bloodshot, the brown suit wrinkled.

Cat let her gaze slide away from Whitney. It settled on a young black male with an enviable complexion, seductive dark eyes and the defensive posture of a cop. Cat decided he was Major Crimes, turned her face away and sank deeper into her chair.

By ten, the room was SRO. A priest stepped forward to recite a few prayers and deliver a vague eulogy that was many adjectives short of commendation. Cat felt for the man. The Catholic Church had been one of Jerry's favorite targets. There had even been a papal parody titled "The Holy Roman Umpire" that had drawn a protest from the archdiocese of Philadelphia (though Cat had found it rather funny).

Cat decided to check the names on the register. She sneaked through the archway, careful not to attract the attention of the young detective who was eyeing the KRZI gang in front. She began copying names into her notebook; her elbow was roughly jostled, and "Excuse me, Miss" clouded in whiskey, muttered into her ear. She glanced over her shoulder to see an elderly man, broad, square shoulders, grey hair, watery blue eyes, peer into the parlor and scan the crowd. Whoever he's looking for, he's not having any luck, Cat decided. He reminded her of someone and she impulsively jotted: *heavyset, poorly dressed, sixties, eyes: grey-blue, hair: salt-pepper.*

The heavy gaze settled on an oblivious Tom Hopper. "That's him," he said, softly.

"I beg your pardon?"

"The other one . . ."

"Jerry's partner? Yes, that's him."

The service was winding down. Cat headed for the parking lot, wondered if there was any point in going on to the cemetery. Noreen hadn't shown up here; the cemetery was a long shot. Maybe she should just go home. Ritchie's paying you top dollar, she reminded herself. Would Ron Spivak just go home?

She heard the "boop-boop-boop" of a few dozen car locks being disengaged. A hand clawed at her coat sleeve, yanked her about-face.

"Do you have it?" hissed a bleary-eyed Whitney Rocap. "That bastard stashed them with you, didn't he?"

"Stashed what?" Cat tugged her arm free.

"Don't play dumb. How much? I was set to sign over the Beemer, you want that?"

"I want you out of my face."

"You mess with me, I'll kill you—"

Tom Hopper appeared at Whitney's side, deflected the swipe aimed at Cat's face.

"She's been drinking," Cat said, shakily.

"I know where you live, bitch!"

"Get her out of here, there's a cop over there," Cat pleaded, glancing nervously at the *NewsLine90* crew that was setting up at the front entrance.

"Whitney, come ride with me, you can't drive," Tom urged.

Whitney threw him off. "Go to hell." She made her way between the cars jockeying for position in the funeral procession.

"Are you all right?" Tom asked.

"Go keep an eye on her, she shouldn't be behind the wheel. I'll catch up with you later. And thanks," Cat said.

Cat wound up at the end of the caravan behind a rusting beige Chevy driven by the heavy-set stranger who had collided with her in the funeral parlor, and eyed Tom Hopper so strangely. Cat made a mental note of his license plate number, wished she had time to phone Freddy and ask him to run the plates for her.

The procession approached a traffic circle, veered south. The Chevy turned north. Instinctively, Cat followed. The Chevy turned onto the Garden State Parkway, northbound. Cat scrambled for a token, tossed it into the toll basket, checked her gas gauge. "What am I doing?" she muttered aloud. Fifteen minutes up the parkways, he hit the Atlantic City Expressway, continued inland. Cat began to panic. Why didn't I stick with Jerry's funeral? Should I get off and turn back? No, wait. He's turning off. What exit is this? Blue Anchor. What's in Blue Anchor, it's in the middle of nowhere, there's nothing for miles except—

("Either of them ever mention Ancora?")

Cat had lost the Chevy, but it didn't matter. When she pulled into the hospital's visitors' lot, there it was, parked, its driver heading up a walk toward a rectangular yellow building.

Cat got out, locked her door. The network of concrete walks was deserted, not many cars in the lot. She strolled over to the Chevy, fingered the passenger door, flipped the handle, idly. It's unlocked and no one's around, Cat informed herself.

The glove compartment was likewise unlocked. The car was registered to a Harry Rankin, the address an RD in the center of Cape May county, some crossroads community called Erma. Cat shoved the plastic billfold back into the compartment, dislodging a dull, metal object. A revolver. A thirty-eight. It looked like the service weapon Carlo used to carry years ago. Cat dug an old Kleenex from her back pocket, lifted the gun gingerly by the barrel, checked the chambers. Three rounds. Three empty.

Two shots Thursday night. One, Friday.

Cat lay the gun back in the compartment very slowly.

You've gone this far, she reminded herself.

Cat got out of the car, approached the yellow building, entered a dim, square lobby: brown linoleum floor, orange plastic chairs, glassed-in reception desk, pay phone, outdated magazines on an end table. Beside the double doors that closed off a long corridor, a woman in a blue smock was talking to the man from the funeral. "No, I know she was here Wednesday some time after you left. You can ask the switchboard if she's called, I wouldn't know. Why don't you take a chair, Mr. D, the orderly is bringing Mrs. D down."

Cat backed up to the pay phone, pumped some change into it, dialed her own number. It rang four times and the answering machine kicked in. Cat pressed her ear to the phone, watching the man out of the corner of her eye.

*She* was here Wednesday. Mr. D. Could "she" be Noreen? Did "D" stand for Dudek? Nobody gets that lucky, Cat told herself.

A young male attendant backed through the double doors, guided a wheelchair up to Mr. D. The occupant was a small, pale woman with vacant blue eyes, a porcelain complexion, thick brunette braid falling over one shoulder. Eyebrows were painted over plucked-bare flesh, a happy pink daubed onto the weary mouth. Cat put her somewhere in her fifties.

The man nodded to the attendant, bent over the wheelchair. "Love, see what I bought you?" He produced a small, gold candy box from the pocket of his threadbare coat.

"Will Chipper come today?" she asked, hopefully.

"Not today, love."

"Norie?"

The man swallowed. "I don't know . . ."

"I saw Norie. She knows. That damn brat told her. They took my radio. You make them give it back."

"I'll talk to them," the man soothed, wheeled her toward a solarium behind the reception desk.

Cat hung up the phone. She couldn't follow without looking conspicuous and she couldn't hang around the lobby either. She decided to retreat to her car and think.

A man named Rankin, but called "Mr. D." Conclusion? "D" borrowed Rankin's car. So who's gun was it, then? And Mrs. D, talking about Chipper and Norie and the brat. Well, Norie had to be Noreen. Had she really seen Noreen the day before Jerry's murder? Could the brat be Jerry? And who was Chipper?

Cat checked her watch. The funeral had to be over, and she

couldn't lag around here and wait for Mr. D to come out. Work with what you have. A man with a gun in his glove compartment shows up at Jerry's funeral, then drives to Ancora to visit his invalid wife. Time to play fill in the blanks, and for that she'd need help, Ron Spivak first, then check in with Sherrie.

Cat walked in her door around one-fifteen, heard her answering machine beeping quietly. She kicked off her pumps, hunted up some cold pasta and a Diet Pepsi, carried it to the living room and pushed the ANSWER button on the console. Beep. Ritchie: "So where are you, I'm goin' crazy here, I heard Rocap popped you at the funeral—" Cat fast-forwarded to the next beep. Victor: "Cat, if you're there, and you'd better be, call me as soon as you can. It's eleven-thirty." Beep. Ritchie: "How come you didn't show up at the cemetery—" Fast-forward. Beep. Sherrie: "Cat, it's me, I just got in, give me a call this afternoon, I found something out."

Cat dialed Sherrie's number.

"Hello?"

"Did I wake you, Sherrie? You sound tired."

"I'm okay. I'm stuffed."

"How was your brunch?"

"Great. We went to the Downbeach Deli. I'm surprised I could eat anything at all. Ingrid wants me to help her work out a variety number they're gonna put in the *Christmas Magic Show*."

"That's nice. Did you ask about Noreen?"

"Oh, yeah! And you'll never guess!"

"No, I don't suppose I will."

"Well, Ingrid says a long time ago, maybe a couple years, she's driving up to Philly with Noreen and another girl and they pick up Tom and Jerry's show, the one they used to do from Camden? And Noreen says, 'Oh, God, that's Jerry' and they ask her where she knows him from and she says, 'He's my brother' like she's not real happy about it. She means Jerry *Dudek*. They thought she was putting them on, but Ingrid says when she thinks back, something in the way Noreen said it, it could have been the truth."

"It is. She is his sister."

"Serious? Anyway, back then, Noreen was going out with Danny Alonzo, Ingrid's kid brother, he was a dancer, too. They're practically engaged. And here's where it gets weird. Jerry and Tom move into the area, Jerry even gets an apartment in the same building as Noreen, he and Danny run into each other a few times. Well, Ingrid doesn't know what happened next, but it seemed like Jerry did something or said something to split up Danny and Noreen. Something so bad Danny wouldn't even tell Ingrid what it was. He took a job down Paradise Island and he's been there ever since. Noreen wouldn't talk about it to Ingrid, but apparently she tried to contact Danny a couple times; he wouldn't talk to her."

"And Ingrid has no idea why they broke up?"

"Not a clue, except that Jerry was involved. I guess Jerry made it up to her by introducing her to Tom Hopper."

"I guess." Cat made a mental note of the name Danny Alonzo, wondered if Noreen could have fled to Paradise Island.

"Anyway, Ingrid hasn't any idea who Noreen could be staying with unless it's her folks. Maybe you should ask someone who knows Jerry's family background."

"I will. Listen, you've been a great help, Sherrie, I really mean it." Cat said good-bye, hung up, laid aside her pasta and reached for her address book. Ron Spivak lived only seven blocks west, in a townhouse on Ocean City's bay side. Cat considered dropping by, decided he might not be ready to go public with the reconstructed nose.

"Ullo?"

"Ron, is that you? It's Cat Austen. I got saddled with the Tom and Jerry piece, remember?"

"Yeah. I spogue to Tob earlier—dode worry, I'be nod cudding idto your agshun, it's your piece, he just wadded to know how I wads feelig. How's the story goig?"

"Cosi, cosi. I need some background. Are you up to going through some of it?"

"Did you ged their redsumes?"

"Too sketchy. I wanted some family history."

"Lemme ged my nodes. I haven't had tibe to pud it onto a disg."

Cat heard adenoidal mutterings, then, "Cad?"

"Yes, I'm still here."

"Ogay, Hobber. He's god bunny."

Tom's god bunny, Cat thought wildly. Oh! *Got money!* Tom's got money. "I know Jerry kidded him about being rich."

"Well, he ids. Gradfadder's an ex-state sedator frob North Carolida. That's Tobas Hobber, sedior. Number two's dad, he's a CEO wid a big tobago cobady."

Cat took a swig of her Pepsi, reached for a pad and pencil.

"Dad's been barried three tibes. Barried sob girl nabed Agnes Sobethig, 'bout thirdy-five years ago, quiggie Bexican barriage, lasted a few years. I really had to dig for thad one, 'cause they wend to a lod of trouble to hush id ub, god hib an annulmend."

"Oh yeah?"

"Thad ain' all. They had a kid, Dad geds cusdody."

"You mean . . . Tom?"

"Yub. The Hobber heir, they're nod gonna gib id to sob teenage gold digger he barries. Paid her obb. Then Dad barried a psychiatrig nurdse nabed Irene Dowling, fixes id so she adobs Tob, raises him like her owd. They were real tide. She dies whed he wads in college."

Maybe that's why Tom's been so rootless, Cat thought.

"Eddyway, Tob geds sob bajor bunny whed heed's thirdy-five. Rilly big bugs."

*Really big bucks,* Cat scribbled.

"Ad yeards ago, Dad barried a third tibe. Brianne Eulalie Lejeune. Heed's sigsty, sheed's tweddy-seved."

"Bay-Decebber," Cat blurted, without thinking.

Ron didn't pick up on it, though. "College, jobs, thads on hids redsume, you god thad. Now, Jerry was tuv. Hids nabe's not Dudek, it's Dudvornicek." Ron spelled it.

*Mr. D,* Cat wrote, underlined.

"Jerry chaged it whed he was ateen."

A teen, Cat wondered? Or eighteen? She opted for the latter.

"Thads why hids diploba, ID all says Dudek. So I go to the Bureau of Stads, cheg out Dudvorniceks, come ub wid one in Cabe May couty. So I cheg phone, voder reg, proberdy tax rolls, nothig. So I go bag to Stads, I go bag five, ten, fifdeen yeards, find a record of a divordse, Jerzy and a Noreen Dudvornicek, so I figure I'll go bag furder, ged a line on the bird certificad, the barriage license. I had lunge wid Jerry, tried to pumb him, he stonewalls me, I thig aboud asking Tob to worg on him, thed I ged the call for the Nucci interview and, well, you know."

The Nose. Cat thought, if Mr. D was Dudvornicek and he didn't have a phone, or vote or pay property taxes, it's likely he had to borrow a car, right? Likely, or just wishful thinking? Don't guess.

"Eddway, I figure Jerzy Dudvornicek and Jerry Dudek, they godda be fadder and sond, right?"

"So it would seem."

"Baby Jerry's illegal or sobthig, you odda cheg oud the barriage licenses, Jerry was tweddy-seved, right? See iv the barriage was before or avder and—waid, there's by bell."

Cat tapped her pencil against the pad, impatiently, her ear to the receiver.

Slam! "Hey!" Crash! And a panicked, "Elb! Elb!"

# CHAPTER

## FOURTEEN

Later, the reconstructive surgeon would weep at what had been done to his handiwork, but when Cat crept through the wide-open door two minutes before the squad car arrived, she found Ron alive, though unconscious, his pepper-maced eyes swollen shut.

It had been quick and efficient. Files pried open with the crowbar that had disassembled Ron's face, the PC screen wiped blank, desk drawers upended. Cat dared not touch anything. The cops found her kneeling beside Ron, holding his hand.

Cat gave a brief statement to the first officer, rapidly calculating how far knowledge of her latest escapade would reach. The polite sergeant didn't recognize her name, but she knew his superior often played ball with Joey, and his superior's superior had gone through the Academy with Vinnie. "We were working on a story together, we were on the phone," Cat hedged, praying he wouldn't ask what story, make the connection to the Dudek case, call Victor.

"Look, if there's not anything else, could I follow the ambulance to the hospital?" Cat asked.

From the ER, Cat called the high school, left a message for

Ellice to meet Jane at the bus stop, then sank into a cracked vinyl chair, waited for someone to tell her how Ron was doing, wondered whether she should call Ritchie, Victor.

She had met Ron only once, spoken to him a few times on the phone. Such slight acquaintance did not obligate her to hang around, she knew; Ron probably would not have done the same for her unless there was a story to be had, but she stayed and the angel of all good Samaritans paid up.

Idling outside the X-ray department ("By doze," the semi-conscious Ron could be heard moaning. "By doze!"), Cat was rudely shunted aside by two orderlies barreling into a cubicle with a gurney. Cat got a glimpse of a dark, cropped head, and a pale, slender arm before the curtain was whisked shut.

"No ID . . . overdose . . . get a pressure!"

Noreen.

Cat heard nothing over her own heartbeat. *What do I do now? Somebody tell me what to do, Ritchie, Tom, Victor.* She leaned her forehead against the wall, sick with exhilaration. No ID. Nobody knows who she is, nobody but me. *Don't count on being told what to do. Use your head.*

An ER doctor dashed in, poked his head out to lash out at a nurse because there were no beds in intensive care, ordered another to report the Jane Doe overdose to the local police, disappeared behind the curtain once more.

Noreen was wheeled into the corridor, left stabilized and unattended while a bed was sought. An IV was taped to her arm, her lips were waxen, her breathing audible. A student nurse approached, checked her pulse, arranged a blanket over her.

"Excuse me," Cat spoke up. "I know her."

"Yeah? Lemme get my supervisor." She scuttled off.

Cat crept up to Noreen, whispered her name.

The head lolled. The grey-blue eyes fluttered. "Hmmm . . ."

"Noreen, can you hear what I'm saying?"

". . . can't go on . . ."

"You've got to, Noreen. Think of Tom, think of your father—"

A bitter expletive cut Cat off. The translucent lids lifted. The gaze Noreen turned on Cat was horrible to see. The lids dropped.

A stout nurse in green scrubs strode up, clipboard in hand. "Did you bring in the Jane Doe?"

"No, I just know her."

"Name?" The nurse produced a pen.

"Mine or hers?" put Cat on the receiving end of a "don't-mess-with-me-I'm-at-the-end-of-my-shift" glare. She hadn't meant to be funny. "Her name is Noreen Dunn."

"With an 'E'?"

"No."

"Husband? Next of kin?"

"I don't know," Cat fibbed.

"Address?"

Should she give Tom's address? "Somewhere in Margate, I think."

"Friends or relatives you're aware of?"

The late Jerry Dudek. "None that I know of. We've only met a few times. Can you tell me, is she really sick?"

The nurse clicked her ball-point. "You know what an overdose of acetaminophen can do to the liver?"

"No."

"She could die." The woman strode off.

Cat sank into the cracked chair, felt her legs shaking. It was just supposed to be a dumb interview, maybe fifteen hundred words, two thousand tops. She was out of her depth. Cat turned to the pay phone and dialed Victor's office.

"Yeah!" Not Victor.

"Stan, is that you? It's Cat Austen."

"Lieutenant's not in yet. Heard I owe him fifty."

"I negotiated for twenty-five percent. Want a kickback?"

"You shoulda held out for half. You're too easy, Cat."

"Stan, are you working on the Dudek case?"

"Nope, I got pulled, put on the old lady turned up yesterday."

"You don't know if they found the gun?"

"No gun and no Dunn. Same weapon, though, did Dudek did the lieutenant's apartment. All we need's a suspect."

"I have it."

"What, the gun?"

"Suspect. Noreen Dunn was just rushed into the ER over here at Shore Memorial."

"What're you doing over Shore Memorial? You okay?"

Cat explained about Ron Spivak.

"Honey, you stay put, I'll get through to the lieutenant, and be right—"

"I can't. If I don't pick up Mats in fifteen minutes, they'll call DYFS on me. Victor knows where to find me."

She hung up and hoisted the white pages against her hip, thrashed through the Ds. Somewhere down county, Ron had said, no phone. But nobody *really* had no phone, did they? No Dudvornicek, one Dudick but no Dudeks and far too many Dunns. Damn. What about the name on the car registration? Rankin. Cat combed the Rs. There! H. Rankin, Erma. She dialed the number, heard the click of an answering machine: "You have reached the Holly Acres Campground and Mobile Home Park. No one is in the office at this time, please leave a brief message at the beep."

Cat hung up, looked up Holly Acres Campground in the yellow pages, scribbled the address on the corner of the page, ripped it off.

She dialed Tom Hopper's home phone, his machine kicked in. "Tom, it's Cat Austen, if you're there, please, please pick up!"

"Cat!" Tom sounded like he had sprinted for the phone. "Where have you been? I thought you'd be at the cemetery; I tried to call you, your line's tied up."

"It's a long story. Thanks for getting Rocap off me, I owe you. Look, I don't have much time, so listen: Noreen's just been admitted to Shore Memorial Hospital, she OD'd." *She could die,* Cat almost added; didn't. She remembered Carlo's face when he had told her about Chris, realized for the first time what it must have taken for him to say those words.

"Is she okay? Is she conscious? Did you talk to her?"

"She's in and out, I only saw her for a second—"

"Look, if you're there, wait—"

"I can't, I have to go. But, Tom, I have to tell you that the police'll be called in for sure. Her relationship to Jerry's no secret and they'll certainly consider her a suspect, but she won't be the only one if they can track down her father—"

"Father? What do you mean, her father?"

A patrolman appeared at Cat's elbow, cleared his throat, conspicuously. "I have to go now," Cat said pointedly, and hung up.

"Mrs. Austen?" He was not from the Ocean City force.

"Yes."

"You brought in the Dunn girl?"

"No, actually, I came in with a friend of mine who'd been injured. I was waiting around when they brought her in."

"You know there's an APB out on her?"

"So I would suspect. I already called Major Crimes."

"Yeah, so did we; lieutenant's on his way over. Look, can you tell me anything, she talk, mention the name of the father?"

How had they found out about Dudvornicek already? "Noreen's—"

"No," he interrupted. "I mean her baby's father."


Freddy and Ellice were standing on the porch when Cat pulled her car into the drive. She saw Ellice's drawn face, Freddy's arm locked around her waist. *Jane. God, no.* Cat unbuckled Mats' seatbelt, bundled him into her arms, hustled up the front steps.

Jane came out, her caramel braid dangling over one shoulder. "*Mom!*" she cried, elated. "We got *burglarized!*"

Freddy met Cat halfway, took Mats. "Cops just left, everything's cool. Where the hell were you?"

Ellice extended her palm. "Your back door key."

Cat put her arm around Jane, kissed the top of her head, tugged her braid, affectionately. "Go do your homework, sweetie."

"What's burglarized?" Mats wanted to know.

Cat took the key, followed Ellice and Freddy into the house, closed the door. Locked it.

"Let's go check out the fridge," Freddy suggested to Mats.

Cat waited until they were in the kitchen. "Okay. Tell me."

"He was in the house when I got home, must've let himself in the back, went through the upstairs, 'cause there's stuff thrown all around your room. Mine, too. He was in the kitchen when I came in the front door. I heard drawers banging, thought it was you, I called out and then I heard the back door slam. So I went in there, which Freddy informed me was a stupid thing to do because the guy—the 'perp' as it were—could still have been in the house."

"You see him?" Or her. ("*I know where you live, bitch.*")

Ellice shook her head. "I ran around the front, but he probably cut through the backyard, came out on North. I didn't see a car. When I went to lock the back door, I saw your key in the outside lock; he must've spooked and forgot it. I called the cops and called Freddy and went to meet Jane at the bus."

"They dust for prints?"

"The back door. They'll come back and do the house, if you want."

Cat drew her key ring out of her pocket, fastened the key in place.

"They want you to check real good, let them know if any valuables are missing."

Cat nodded, walked upstairs to her bedroom. Her bureau drawers had been pulled open, the floor was littered with underwear, hose, sweaters. VHS tapes dumped out of their jackets. No jewelry missing. In her closet, opened purses lay on the floor, a shoe box of old photos overturned. Cat sat on the bed, thought. She picked up the phone and dialed KRZI.

"NewsLineNinety, KRZI. Miss Dubois speaking."

"This is Mrs. Austen. Why isn't Miss Halprin at the desk? She looked well enough at the funeral."

"She's auditioning."

"For what?"

"Whitney Rocap's old weather job."

"Is Miss Rocap there by any chance?"

"No, she's not due in until tonight. If she's sober. She was pretty spooky at the cemetery; there was a lunch afterwards, she never showed. You wanna leave a message?"

"No, thanks. Oh, by the way, do you remember when I dropped my keys the other day, you brought them out to me?"

"Yeah, I think so."

"Where exactly did you find them?"

"They were on the floor, outside Tom's office. I ast the guy in the control room if they were his and he said no, so I ast Whitney to look them over an' she said maybe they were yours, so I ran them out."

"I don't remember seeing her there."

"I think she just ran in to get her check. Friday's payday."

"I see . . ."

"Lissen, Mrs. Austen, if you need any help on your story, anything you need to know about Jerry, I'm the one to ask. Could you just make sure you say I was his fiancée? I mean, the girl in the obit department over *The Press* wouldn't put it in and I don't know why not."

Cat promised and hung up, went downstairs. Freddy left Mats immersing Oreos in a mug of caffe latte, drew Cat aside. "I'm not gonna call Carlo if you don't want—"

"I don't. I can handle this."

"Look, I gotta clock in in half an hour, I get off at midnight. I could come by, sleep over."

Cat gave him a wry look.

Freddy grinned. "Hey, it was worth a shot. But serious, maybe you guys oughta stay the night at Mom's."

"I can handle this, I said. I'll call you on your dinner break. And thanks for coming, you're a Sicilian prince."

"I'm gonna go say good-bye to Ellice."

"Send Mats in here if the farewells get above a PG-Thirteen."

When Freddy left, Cat checked her tiny office. What was left of her notes, the tape of the Tom and Jerry interview, were in a locked drawer. The burglar had overlooked the inconspicuous pantry door. Stupidly overlooked it. Or irrationally. Or drunkenly. Cut the adverbs, Austen.

"He get into your stuff?" Ellice came up behind her.

Cat shook her head. "Went right by him. Nothing valuable's gone upstairs. You okay?"

"This is nothin'. I been through worse than this. Cops think it's vandals, you know, off season, isolated neighborhood, kids cuttin' seventh period study hall, out for kicks."

"No." Cat told her about Ron Spivak, Noreen. "Somebody wants something I've got. Or something they think I've got. All I've got to do is figure out what it is. Oh, and you can forget about the weather girl gig, Deanna Halprin's got the inside track."

"She got smarts?"

"She's twenty-two."

"Ouch. Blonde?"

"Hair down to here." Cat patted her hip.

"Sheeit."


Stan Rice was pacing jumpily outside Noreen's hospital room when Victor arrived. "Look, they won't let you in yet, they're givin' her some kinda antidote, say her liver's shot. Bird watchers found her in the woods off Route Nine, down county. County hospital's got a triage situation, methane gas leak, so they shipped her up here."

"How'd you get a line on her? I thought you were working the Thurman case?"

"I was. I am. Look Lieutenant, you're not gonna like it."

"I already don't like it."

"Cat Austen. She called me."

Anger constricted Victor's mouth. "Where is she?"

"She took off before I got here. I talked to the ER supervisor, she said Cat came in with some guy—"Stan tugged a notepad out of his breast pocket, read, "Spivak, Ronald. Him, they shipped to Philly. Someone took a crowbar to his face."

"Spivak?" Why did that name sound familiar?

"Right." Stan spelled it. "Ocean City cops say Cat was on the phone with him, conversation breaks off, she hears him let out a yell, calls the cops, runs over there herself, he lives a couple blocks away. Spivak's unconscious, place is all torn up, Cat follows him to the ER, she's waiting around, Dunn girl is rushed in. No ID, but Cat made her and called me—that is, you."

"Spivak. That was the guy who was supposed to do the feature on Tom and Jerry. He dropped it, Cat picked it up."

"Her place is five minutes over the bridge. I'll stick around with Dunn if you want to run over, Lieutenant. Whoever worked over that Spivak—I don't wanna think about him getting to Cat."

Cat and Ellice were sitting on Cat's bed. Cat was methodically thumbing rounds into a clip. "Just hold it in your hand a few minutes to get used to it."

"I never held a gun. Wished for one once."

Cat took the gun back, jammed the clip into place. "Now look, this little doohickey on the side, you push it up, that's the safety— here, I'll put one round in the chamber."

"Doohickey. Is that police jargon?"

"Joey calls his gun his 'rod' and the rest of them refer to it as their 'piece,' but all of the women officers I've talked to just call it their weapon. You think I could put together three, four hundred words on that?"

"Whoever thinks a faultless piece to see, Thinks what ne'er was, nor is, nor e'er shall be.' Pope."

"*The* Pope or Alexander Pope?"

"Al. Maybe you should take it with you."

Cat shook her head. "You just keep the kids safe, I'll take care of myself. Look here, just push the lever to the center position, now it's on 'fire.' But leave the safety on unless you mean business, and keep it on you. I don't want the kids to get it."

"I feel like that gal in *Aliens*."

"I loved that movie." Cat bent over, yanked her attaché from under her bed. "I could give it up, Ellice. I could tell Ritchie I've had it and he could get someone else."

"I know all about that." Ellice cradled the gun in her palm. "I know all about gettin' scared off and running away and trying to play it safe. After a while, safe is as bad as dead. Worse."

"I don't want Jane to be like that."

"You do what you gotta do," Ellice said. "And I'll blow away the first thing comes through the front door."

"Ellice," Cat's voice had a mischievous lilt. "You sound almost Sicilian."

Route 9 cut through the rural heart of Cape May county, its capillaries sprouting east and west through hamlets with hick names like Goshen and Dennis, Grassy Sound and Green Creek (pronounced "crick"), an honest-to-God Miami Beach.

The state house in Trenton didn't put a high priority on efficient transit within the southern third of the state; roads shot here toward the Atlantic, there toward the Delaware, many signless, many curbless, many prefixed "Sea" and nowhere near it.

The fitful geography of the county vexed even Cat's keen instincts. She didn't even realize she had entered Erma until her headlights hit a white rectangle with red lettering, HOLLY ACRES. She veered onto a narrow gravel path barely a car width across. The path snaked around a batch of modest mobile homes, deadended in a marsh. The first trailer was a dingy brown affair with H. RANKIN, MGR., painted on a post in front.

Cat backed onto a tuft of dead grass behind the trailer, took a deep breath, asked herself what could possibly happen to her in an old, semi-deserted trailer park, didn't wait around for the answer, walked straight up to the manager's door, which was a good two feet off the ground with no step-up, gave a timid knock that bumped the door open a few inches.

"Mr., um, Rankin?" Cat called. "Mr. Dudvornicek? Somebody home?"

Silence.

*Don't go in there. Go ahead. Don't go. Go.*

"Hello?"

*Go.* Cat pushed the door wide, shoved her attaché over her wrist, gripped the door frame and hoisted herself up, in.

The living area was about eight-by-eight, cheap shag carpeting, tan Herculon love seat, two yellow canvas chairs, two tables of laminated pine. No television, radio, newspapers, magazines, stereo, no clock. Cat switched on a chipped plaster lamp; started. An impressive paperback library was piled on a makeshift bookcase: biographies, classics, plays, poetry, essays.

A four-by-four kitchenette, a powder room with a cramped shower stall, a narrow sleeping area separated from the kitchen only by a drawn curtain. Two bunks, a suitcase, unzipped, and thrown open, a denim backpack, leather dancer's tote lay on the upper.

"You're breaking the law," Cat reminded herself.

She peeked into the suitcase. Women's clothes, stylish, not expensive. She lifted a pair of jeans, held them to her waist. The narrow legs extended a few inches beyond her insteps, the hips two inches shy. Someone tall, quite slim. Noreen. Cat threw them back, saw a manila folder protruding from beneath a cosmetics case, "Birth Certs" penned on the tab. Empty.

Cat froze.

A car door creaked open, thudded shut, somewhere outside, near. Cat backed into the living room. Heavy footsteps shuffled outside the front door, a broad palm slapped it open.

Cat stepped back. No way out. *Rush him! When he gets one foot on the threshold, shove him off balance and run for it!*

The man from the funeral parlor, the psychiatric hospital. Dudvornicek. Jerry's, Noreen's father. The blue eyes raised, fixed on Cat, the stare watery, dull.

"I knocked," Cat offered, faintly. "The door was open."

"You looking for Norie?"

"Are you Mr. Dudvornicek?"

"You know my name?"

"You are, aren't you?"

The forehead creases smiled, wearily. "I thought I had made myself no longer a person."

"You've done a fairly good job," Cat agreed. "But no one can become a non-person entirely until he's dead." Ellice had said that.

"'There are worse things waiting for men than death.' A poet said that. Sit down, Miss."

Cat lowered herself gingerly onto one of the canvas chairs, wondered where the gun was. Dudvornicek took the love seat. "Where's Mr. Rankin?" she asked.

"After the season, he goes to Florida. I can fix things, he lets me live here. Summer, I make a tent down by that field." He sighed, heavily. "So, you are the police?"

"No, sir, I'm a writer. I was working for—" she decided he wouldn't recognize the name of her magazine. "I was writing a story about Jerry and his radio show."

"I know you now. You were at the funeral."

"And I was the one who was there when Jerry was shot. I'm sure Noreen must have told you about that," she suggested.

"I do not see Noreen for years." The accent was Eastern European, the construction not entirely comfortable with any tense other than the present. "She visits her mother sometimes. She's a good girl, just like my own. Sometimes, it's hard to forgive . . ."

Forgive what, Cat wondered? And what did he mean *just like* his own? "But you have seen Noreen. She's been staying here."

The shaggy head bobbed, mournfully. "She came last week. I know she has been to see her mother. We promised before God never to speak of it, but when she tells me why she has to know . . ." He lurched off the sofa. "I have a drink somewhere." He made his way to the kitchenette, returned with a half-filled bottle of Jack Daniels, two plastic tumblers, poured, handed a drink to Cat.

Cat accepted, sipped warily. Don't get drunk, you're onto something here. Noreen went to her mother to find out something the Dudvorniceks had promised never to reveal. Something Jerry had told her? Victor had said Jerry and Noreen had words the day before the shooting. Then she went to her mother. What was Noreen so desperate to know? What was it that only that en-feebled woman could reveal? "How long has Mrs. Dudvornicek been ill?" she blurted, then panicked.

But he didn't ask Cat how she knew. "All her life, I suppose," he sighed. "She is a beautiful woman, more beautiful than Noreen. She married very young, a wicked man, divorces him and runs away. She is terrified he will find her, take away the child she is carrying. I tell her that if we get married, the law says it will be my child." He drank. "I loved her, you see . . ."

"The child was Noreen."

He nodded. "We promise each other never to speak the name of the father. I am Noreen's father now. My wife isn't in love with me, but we are content. Then Jerry is born."

So that would mean that Jerry was Noreen's half brother. Cat scribbled in a notebook, the tumbler gripped between her knees.

"Jerry, he is born bad. All the time, the teachers, the princi-pal, the other parents are calling, Jerry did this, Jerry did that. He has the power to make people notice him, to make people laugh, but his is cruel. He lies, steals. You know Shakespeare, Miss?"

"Austen. Mrs. Austen." *Shakespeare?* "Some."

"A great writer she is. JaneAusten." He paused. "Shakespeare. Titus Audronicus. There is a character called Aaron. A villain. Tor-ment to others gives him pleasure. That is Jerry."

*A better high than sex,* Tom had said.

"To plague his family is the best of all." He upended the glass, poured the remains of the bottle in, drank. "He destroys us."

His tone sent a chill along Cat's neurons. "How?"

"We are not rich. I provide. A home, clothes, dancing lessons for Noreen. She is a gentle girl, many friends. Jerry is not so well-liked. People notice him, but they do not like what they see."

"He was jealous of Noreen," Cat interpreted.

The grey head nodded. "He decides he wants her all to himself."

Cat swallowed a trickle of nausea. "I don't understand."

"All to himself," Dudvornicek repeated, thickly. "They write a paper for school. Their family. Jerry writes about his father who

161

has sex with his own daughter. The teacher shows it to the principal. Authorities come to the house. They talk to Noreen. They say she is abused, and think it is me. I go before a judge and that is when it comes out that Noreen is not my natural daughter. She says we have lied to her. I go to jail."

"Noreen didn't tell them that it was Jerry who was . . ."

Dudvornicek shook his head. "Worse. She draws closer to Jerry. It is what he wanted, planned. This was fifteen, sixteen years ago. My wife wants a divorce. She is afraid to lose her children. In time, Jerry grows tired of the trouble he creates. Noreen goes away to a dancing school. My wife has depression, is that the word? Needs to be in hospital. Jerry is alone."

"What became of him? And Noreen?"

"Money goes for private hospital for my wife. When it is gone, she must go to the state hospital. There is no money for Jerry's college. He is angry, changes his name and after high school, moves away. Noreen goes to work on the stage. I know she goes to see her mother sometimes. When I had a phone, we spoke. Not often. Once, twice a year maybe." Dudvornicek contemplated the bottom of his glass. "Some months ago, I hear that Jerry had been to see his mother. He brings her a radio as a present, says he is on the radio now. I do not listen to the radio, but I see no harm in it, he is her son, after all. You see how I live. How could I know what he had done?"

Tension compressed Cat's rib cage. She was close now, up against the truth. "What had he done?"

"The worst of things. He found out the truth and told Noreen. That is why she went to her mother last week. To me. We had to tell her . . . I should have killed him years ago. Drowned him like a cat."

"Did you loan Noreen your car Thursday night?"

"It is not until she comes back and tells me Jerry is dead I think to look for my gun."

"It was gone?"

"Yes. I am afraid to ask, afraid for her. For two days, she cannot eat, sleep. Many times she goes out, comes back. Sunday, she is very quiet. I ask her if she would like to come with me to visit her mother. They let you stay longer on Sundays."

"Did she?"

"No. She told me to give her mother a kiss. When I come back from hospital, she is gone. Does not come back."

Horror rammed Cat's solar plexus. He didn't know. "It was Noreen you were looking for, at the funeral."

"She is not there, she has not been to her mother . . ."

Cat rose, sat beside Dudvornicek, patted his massive hand, awkwardly. "Noreen's in the hospital. In Somers Point. She took pills."

Inebriation blunted his shock. "Pills?"

"She's very sick." Should she mention the pregnancy? "The police think that she killed Jerry."

"Jerry." The words were slurring badly. "I should have killed him. Up here," he rapped his forehead with his knuckles, "I have done it. Many times."

Cat shuddered; she was acutely aware that she had told no one where she was going, that she was in an isolated trailer park, unarmed, sitting beside a drunken man with murder on his mind. *Nice going, Lois Lane.*

Alcohol was her ally, though. Dudvornicek tried to rise, lurched sideways, fell back onto the couch. "She didn't kill Jerry . . . it was the other . . ." The grey head lolled against her shoulder. The tumbler slipped from his grasp. He emitted something like a sob and closed his eyes.

# CHAPTER

## FIFTEEN

Cat lay a finger against Dudvornicek's pulse, took a thin blanket from one of the bunks and threw it over his shoulders. Fled.

Hypotheses cut into her attention span as she sped up the parkway. Think. *You've had six cops in the family, you can figure this out.* Wednesday, Jerry and Noreen fight, he tells her something she is so desperate to confirm she runs up to Ancora, then visits the father she'd cut out of her life. Stepfather. Fast-forward. What had Jerry said about his new agenda. Kinky sex. Family intrigue? A boutique owner's affair hardly qualified. Porno flick, maybe. Noreen took the notes. Kiddie pageant. *A DJ who's—*

Noreen pregnant.

*—sleeping with his sister.*

*("He decides he wants her all to himself.")*

A brown form loomed in the headlights; Cat hammered the brake, saw a young doe's mournful gaze. Cat idled, waiting for the animal to back onto the median, dart off. A DJ sleeping with his sister. Noreen pregnant by Jerry. Jerry threatens to tell Tom. Noreen kills him.

Victor's car was parked in front of her house. Cat pulled into the driveway, turned off the ignition, sat in the car a few minutes. May as well get it over with, she told herself.

Mats flew to her the moment she entered, his face alight with information. "Mommy, Victor's here!"

"I know, baby." Cat threw her jacket on a chair, tossed her attaché over it. "I'm home!"

Jane appeared from the den. *"Victor's* here."

Oh, so now it was "Victor," not "he."

"An' he said 'hell' three times!" Mats was ecstatic. 'Hell' was one of those tantalizing expletives Mats was permitted to utter only in communicating direct quotes or inquiring after a definition. The day that Zack Libertini had said, "Fuck you, lady" to Teacher Dorothy had been the highlight of Mats' fall semester, one which he dutifully related to each member of the family in turn. The H word of course, compared wanly with the F, but Cat suspected that Victor's multiple utterances had significantly enhanced its appeal.

"He said 'where the *hell* is she,' 'when the *hell* will she be back' and 'why the *hell* didn't she call.' "

Victor emerged from the kitchen, Ellice a half step behind. "You want some coffee?" Ellice asked, her hands semaphoring danger.

"When I get down." Cat swung Mats into her arms. "Let me put the kids to bed first."

"You promised to *read* to us," Jane reminded her.

"Did I?" Cat often wondered if Jane was implanting these "promises" in her mother's addled memory.

Cat got the children's teeth brushed, tucked Mats into his bed and sat with Jane on her lap. They read *The Pain and the Great One,* Cat and Jane sharing the roles. Mats was asleep before they were done.

Ellice was waiting at the foot of the stairs when Cat descended. "He is *mad!*" she whispered.

Cat winced. "Irreversibly?"

"That's for you to figure out, honey. I'm outta here." She eased Cat's Taurus from her waistband with two fingers. "You can put a smile on that man's face, I'll give you fifty, double if you get a laugh. Does that man ever laugh?"

"I don't know."

Victor was sitting at the kitchen table, stood automatically when Cat entered. She studied the dark, irritated gaze, the mouth pursed in a scowl. Mischief needled her. She turned away to pour a mug of coffee, jerked her head up. "Did you hear that?"

"What?" Victor's eyes panned the room, immediately alert.

"You don't hear it?"

"I'll check outside."

"No," Cat shook her head. "It sounds like . . ." She deepened her voice, laid in a Cuban accent, "Luceee, you've got some 'splainin' to dooo!"

The mustache jerked violently, settled in an angry arch, but the gaze thawed a couple degrees.

Cat set down her mug with an impatient shrug. "Ellice will give me a hundred dollars if I can make you laugh. But it's got to be the real thing, you know?"

"How long have you got?"

"Midnight, I think."

"You're not gonna make it."

Cat slipped into the booth. "Mats said you said 'hell' three times." She held the Taurus over a place mat, released the clip.

"You know Ellice had that thing drawn when she answered the door?"

"She's great, isn't she?"

Victor shook his head. "I should have been more circumspect about the language."

"Well, a few measly 'hells' are no match for Carlo, I can tell you that. The first was 'where the hell did she go,' right?"

"Right."

"You know about Ron Spivak?"

"And the break-in here," Victor nodded grimly. "And Noreen."

"Well, I decided to try to locate Jerzy Dudvornicek."

"Come again?"

Cat sighed, cupped her cheeks in her hands, realized that her hands were icy. She chafed them against her mug.

"You look tired, Cat."

"I've been going since six this morning."

"I thought we agreed you were to stay home."

Cat raised her chin. "I agreed to no such thing. I suppose that detective of yours went on to the cemetery?"

"Detective Long, you mean?"

Cat's eyes sparkled. "*That* was Philip Long? The one who worked vice with Joey? He *is* pretty!" Her rippling laugh snagged on a note of weariness.

"Long said you and Ms. Rocap had words after the funeral. Said Hopper practically had to pry the two of you apart."

Cat related her version.

"After the grave-site service, there was a luncheon over at KRZI, started breaking up around one-thirty, one forty-five."

"KRZI's five minutes over the bridge from Ron's place."

Victor frowned. "Maced. He didn't see anything. Two year-round tenants in his condo, off season, forget about coming up with witnesses." He paused. "Ellice said there were a couple of hang-ups on your machine."

"Someone wanted to make sure I wasn't home."

"Or that you were."

Cat stared into her coffee. "Noreen couldn't have attacked Ron. Whitney was too drunk. Tom was home when I called him from the hospital."

"Tom could have made it to Margate, Whitney could have sobered up and don't change the subject. Who is this what's-his-name?"

"Would you like some more coffee?"

"No thanks."

"A drink?"

"No."

"Valium?"

"Cat."

"Dudvornicek's Jerry's father."

Victor's silences were ominous. Cat writhed, uncomfortably. Why couldn't he just yell, like Carlo?

"And that would make him Noreen's father, also."

"Stepfather," Cat corrected. "He married Noreen's mother when she was pregnant. There was an allegation of abuse that got him thrown in jail when Noreen was a teenager. Jerry spread the lie, apparently, then changed his name when he got sick of being associated with the scandal. That's why his ID says Dudek."

"How did you track down this Dudvornicek?"

"He was at the funeral. He looked—I don't know—out of place. When everyone queued up for the cemetery, he split off and headed up the parkway. I followed. A hunch," Cat sighed. "I suppose you don't believe in intuition."

Victor rubbed his chin, absently. "Where did he go?"

"Ancora. It's cold in here. Are you cold?"

"Don't change the subject, querida. I distinctly remember telling you that Ancora showed up on Tom's phone log."

"You only implied, actually, but thanks for the confirmation, Lieutenant. Dudvornicek's wife—it's ex-wife, because they got a divorce, though he's still devoted to her—is a patient. She's Jerry's and Noreen's mother."

"Did you know who he was when you followed him?"

"No. I told you, it was just a hunch."

"Then how did you find out?"

"Well . . . To begin with, he didn't lock his car."

Victor propped his elbows on the table, pressed his palms together. "So if," his tone was cautionary, "one happened to enter his unlocked car, one might discover his identity by examining the registration."

"The car was registered to a man named Rankin. But an attendant inside referred to him as 'Mr. D.' When I got home, I called Ron Spivak and his information put me on track."

"So who's Rankin?"

"He owns a trailer park. Dudvornicek minds the store while Rankin winters in Florida. Loans Dudvornicek an old car." She paused. "The gun was his, though. Dudvornicek's."

"What gun?"

"The one I sort of found in the glove compartment."

Victor's brows lowered, gravely. "You're on thin ice here, Cat."

"Well, then, you get a search warrant and—"

"Based on information you obtained by breaking into this guy's car? Not likely."

"Well, if you want to be *technical*."

"*Dios me salve*," Victor muttered. "Okay, go on."

Cat recounted the scene between Dudvornicek and his wife, her references to Chipper, Norie and the brat, then related the information Sherrie had obtained from her choreographer friend, repeated the phone conversation with Ron Spivak, the rush to the hospital, the encounter with Noreen. "When I got home, Ellice was here with Freddy. Apparently someone got in through the back door with that key I thought I'd misplaced."

"The key you were missing Saturday morning?"

Cat nodded, repeated her conversation with Miss Du Bois. "Friday morning, I wasn't up to a run, so the last time I know I had it was Thursday morning. Noreen *could* have taken it Thursday night. Or someone at the station could have, Friday morning. Rocap said, 'I know where you live' when she took a swipe at me today. I should have taken her literally, I suppose."

"Damn it, Cat, you have no business being so careless!"

" 'I am sure care's an enemy to life.' *Twelfth Night*, I think."

"I give up."

"I've always suspected you suits at the prosecutors office have no staying power."

"I'd be happy to give you the opportunity to test that theory."

Cat blushed, shook her head.

"Subject tabled for future agenda. Okay, where's Dudvornicek?"

"A trailer park down Route Nine in the middle of nowhere."

"And you did all of this detective work today?"

"Yes. Why? You want to arrest me?"

"I ought to hire you."

Cat smiled, rolled her head to ease the tension in her neck.

Victor grabbed a sheet of paper from a pad beside Cat's wall phone and began to write. "This guy Noreen used to date, the dancer. Your sister-in-law said Jerry broke them up?"

"That was her friend's impression."

"So that Jerry could set her up with Tom? Cement the working relationship?"

"Or maybe to have the fun of breaking them up, like he did with the Alonzo boy." Cat reached for a canister in a high cabinet, removed a small box, dropped in the clip.

"I spoke to Noreen's doctor," Victor said. "He thinks she'll be lucky to make it, probably lose the baby."

The canister trembled in Cat's hand. She shoved it onto the shelf, slammed the cabinet door. Her mind flashed to the race to the hospital, a week to the day after Chris had been killed. "Not the baby!" she had prayed, Freddy clutching her hand until Jackie Wing pried him away, hustled him off to the waiting room. The leaden awakening an hour later; the emptiness.

Cat pressed her palms to her eyes. You're not going to cry, she ordered herself.

Victor's arms were around her. "What is it, love?"

Cat shook her head. "Nothing. I'm tired, that's all." She pulled away from him abruptly. "Let's go sit in the living room."

Cat pried off her sneakers, curled up on the sofa, stuffed a cushion under her head. "I take this place for granted. Maybe I shouldn't be so careless . . ."

Victor threw a striped green afghan over her, sat on the floor, stroked her hair. "I'm a good listener, Cat. A cop has to be."

Cat lay quietly for a moment. "I was pregnant when Chris died. I lost the baby a week later. He never knew."

"Did you want more children?"

Cat smiled wistfully. "When we started out, it was going to be six. After two pregnancies, the six became four. I think the third would have been it."

Marisol had wanted three children.

"I felt so sorry for Dudvornicek. I guess he could be the killer, since we're tallying suspects. There was no love lost between him and Jerry, but the way he's living now, I mean I don't think he'd care enough to make the effort. And they had no contact at all. I'm not sure he'd know how to find Jerry to kill him." Cat tossed her head impatiently. "Whitney's threats, Noreen's suicide attempt, Jerry's estrangement from his parents, the shooting at your place, the break-in here, something has to tie it all together, make sense of it all. It's like a collage with no theme."

"I like the analogy. The murderer is the theme."

Cat shook her head. "No, that's the 'who.' We want the 'what' and the 'why.' "

"What's this 'we,' Austen?"

"Of course, blackmail can't be ruled out," Cat mused, ignoring him. "Jerry said something about a TV personality and a porn flick, and what with the anchor slot and all, I don't think Rocap would want to see Whitney Does Walla Walla turning up on the video shelves. And everything she's done implies she thinks Jerry let me in on something."

"Well, he wasn't stashing it in his apartment. We combed the place. No safety deposit box, either. We're looking into self-storage places."

"Check the PC disks?"

"Games. Junk."

"And not much money in the bank?"

"Spent it."

"Bills?"

"Some credit cards with thousand dollar limits, more than his share of speeding tickets. If he had anything on Whitney, anybody, he buried it pretty well."

"What about notes, a notebook, calendar, diary, letters?"

"You may not believe this, but it actually occurred to us to look."

Cat punched his shoulder, playfully. Victor caught her fist, kissed it. Cat shrugged the afghan into place, let her mind run back over the past few hours. "Shakespeare," she declared, finally. She got up and strode over to the wall of books.

"He's got an alibi." The capricious turn of her mind eluded him, fascinated him.

Cat's lids lowered, wryly, unconsciously sensual. "*Titus Andronicus.*"

Victor leaned back against the arm of the sofa. "A very minor play, but I have the distinct recollection of several parents banding together and attempting to have it removed from the high school curriculum when I was a junior."

"Really?"

"Lust, adultery, betrayal, decapitation, mutilation, rape, insanity, murder, cannibalism—have I left anything out?"

Cat yanked a thick volume from a lower shelf. "That about covers it, if memory serves. Mr. Dudvornicek is a reader. He said Jerry was like—here, listen to this—like this character Aaron. 'Even now I curse the day' . . . hmmm . . . 'Wherein I did not some notorious ill as kill a man or else devise his death; Ravish a maid or plot the way to do it; Set deadly enmity between two friends,' and so on and so on, and then he goes on here: 'I have done a thousand dreadful things, As willingly as one would kill a fly; And nothing grieves me heartily indeed, But that I cannot do ten thousand more.' " Cat slapped the book closed. "There! What do you think?"

"I think the sequence of your thoughts would make a fascinating reel of film. I also think Dudvornicek's evaluation of his son is pretty near the mark."

Cat hugged the book to her breast, reflectively. "Jerry may have been blackmailing Whitney, but I doubt that he could fill an apartment with those expensive toys on her salary alone. There had to be others. He wouldn't have stopped with one; it was too much fun for him. A better high than sex."

"Don't you believe it."

Cat shoved the book into place. "Tom said that. That Jerry thrived on animosity. He really must have found his niche in shock radio," she added, thoughtfully. "The *Six A.M. Circus* was the perfect forum for someone who liked it down and dirty. I wonder how far he'd go if the forum were threatened . . ."

"What do you mean?"

Cat's mouth puckered in what Victor found to be a particularly inviting frown. "Tom's an only child, raised by his father's second wife. When she died, it seemed to shake him up; he starts to drift, first because he's got no roots, then Jerry starts dragging him from station to station. Noreen's the first serious attachment he's forged since his stepmother died. Why did Jerry fix on Tom, I wonder? Good instincts, possibly. A sense that together they had something marketable."

"So he hustles them down to KRZI to gain entree to the Philly market and uses his pretty sister to cement the relationship?"

Cat slid back onto the couch. "Everybody underrates the straight man. I don't think Jerry did. I think he came to understand how well Tom's sort of droll satire complemented his outrageousness. Separate, Tom's still a talented guy with a good resume and an inheritance three years off. Jerry's a hustler and something of a freak who can't even save his paycheck. So okay, Jerry does introduce Noreen to Tom to cement things. But what if it backfired? Because now, Tom wants to settle down and go respectable, take that solo offer from Philly One Oh Four. Jerry finds out—"

"How?"

"Somehow," Cat said, impatiently. "And he tells Noreen to get Tom to stick with the act or else."

"Or else what?"

"Or else he'll tell Tom whatever he told the other boyfriend. That he and his sister had been sexual . . . you know. Partners. Maybe that's what they had words about the day before Jerry got killed."

"It works," Victor admitted. "In its fashion."

"It gives Noreen motive and opportunity because she could easily have obtained access to Dudvornicek's gun—a thirty-eight, incidentally—and brought it to CV's with her Thursday night. I checked the chamb—"

Victor yanked her onto the carpet beside him.

"It practically jumped into my hand."

Victor kissed her on the mouth.

Cat nudged his lips away. "Is this how you conduct all your investigations, Lieutenant?"

"Always." He kissed the line of her jaw. "You know, when this business is turned over to the DA tomorrow, I could take a few vacation days, the two of us could hop a plane to San Juan—"

"I don't know what sort of murder witnesses you've been interrogating, Lieutenant, but running off with a total—relative—stranger isn't in the cards for this one."

"Reshuffle the deck."

"Victor, I barely got through one semi-romantic dinner without getting shot—"

"Semi, was it?"

"Victor," Cat said gravely, "when I began to get a grip on things again, I worked out this great plan for how everything was going to be for the rest of my life."

"Life needs to be thrown a curve once in a while. Shaken up. Surprised."

"I don't like surprises."

"You've just never met the right one."

"That's what they all say."

Victor grinned, rose to his feet. "I'm serious about San Juan, *querida*. You sleep on it. And I'll go home and figure out how to explain to the DA why I need a warrant to search Dudvornicek's trailer—"

"Actually, it's Rankin's trailer, and the car is registered to him, too, but the gun's Dudvornicek's—"

"Enough." Victor shrugged on his coat. "Adane writes a mean affidavit, but how she's going to translate 'Mrs. Austen broke into the suspect's father's employer's car and trailer—' "

"He didn't throw me out, did he?"

"*Dios mio.*" Victor leaned down and kissed her hastily, remembered that the kids were safe in bed, kissed her again. "Make sure you lock both doors. '—Suspect's father's employer's car and trailer and extracted an admission from an inebriated man that his gun had been fired.' "

"I should think Mr. Raab would be grateful for the information."

"He's a stickler for the legalities."

Cat shrugged off the legalities. "Tell him my theory about Jerry using Noreen to keep Tom from breaking up the act. That should be worth fifteen minutes of his time before I have to file my story."

"Until I file mine, you work from your phone. I'll call you tomorrow."

"When?"

"Never mind. Whenever it is, you'd better be here."

"I hear an 'or else,' Lieutenant."

"Good. Then we understand one another."

"I understand that you're not one hundred percent certain that Noreen did it, or it wouldn't matter where I went tomorrow."

Victor looked at her, soberly. "One day, I'll tell you about those years I spent undercover. I'm alive today because I conditioned myself not to be a hundred percent certain of anything." He kissed her again, pulled the door closed after him and waited on the porch until he heard her throw the locks.

Cat retreated to the couch, drew the afghan around herself. A month ago, two weeks ago, she would have been more than willing to take the 'or else' to heart and back away. But . . . without Victor's staff or resources, nothing but the head on her shoulders and a bit of intuition and nerve and persistence, look how much she'd turned up. Maybe she actually had a knack for this. Maybe that life plan could stand a few alterations.

Cat leaned her head against a cushion and let her thoughts mingle. *Victor's not one hundred percent on Noreen. Why? Because there's an outside chance that one of Jerry's blackmail victims was the killer.*

Break-in. Trying to find something he—or she—believes Jerry passed on to her. Papers, letters, pictures, tapes, software, where would Jerry keep something like that? Not in his apartment or the office, too risky. Ditto a safety deposit box and public storage.

Cat focused her empathetic neurons on the matter. If, she projected, I were unregenerate slime and a blackmailer, where would I keep the goods? Where . . . ?

Or *who?*

Jerry didn't trust people, he used them.

Used Whitney, Noreen, Tom.

Someone else, someone who had demonstrated loyalty. Devotion.

And then Cat knew. And then she fell asleep.

# CHAPTER
## SIXTEEN

The ocean's surface was as jagged and immobile as chipped slate. Shards of reflected sunlight caused Cat to squint, lower her gaze to the buckling boards. "'Fortune favors the brave,'" she panted to herself, the whispered syllables keeping pace with her stride. "'The riders in a race do not stop short when they reach the goal.' Ol-i-ver Wen-dell Holmes."

She sidestepped a pair of teenage surfers emerging from the Seven-Eleven, got a whiff of wetsuit rubber, coffee, waved to the high school track coach as he sprinted by with his wife.

Sleep had not blunted Cat's conviction that she was right, but it had taken the edge off her audacity. She couldn't afford to take the sort of risks she had taken last night, the morning light told her. She had her children to consider. They needed her.

A wave to the trim woman in designer sweats who charged past without so much as a nod. A wave to the substitute teacher who gave Ellice an occasional lift to work. A few short years and they wouldn't need her. They'd leave home, leave Mom, who taught them not to take risks. Play it safe.

The wide, commercial strip of Ocean City's boardwalk narrowed; shops boarded for the winter continued for a couple blocks more, a few hotels, then, private homes, their landscaped yards backing up to the sea wall adjacent to the boards.

" 'Courage is the price life extracts for granting peace,' " Cat panted, turning toward home. "Amelia Earhart. Did they ever find her body, I wonder?"

Cat hit the back steps two at a time, took the key tucked in her glove, unlocked the back door, kicked off her shoes, poured out juice and cereal and set it on the table. "Breakfast time, guys!"

While the children ate, she showered and changed into slacks and a sweater, came downstairs and asked Ellice if she could baby-sit Mats for an hour or so, walked Jane to the bus stop, maintaining a discreet distance lest Jane be marked for a dweeb, walked back to her driveway, got into her car and headed across the bridge to Somers Point and KRZI.

Sondra Du Bois was flattered that Mrs. Austen was coming to her for information at last. All the police had done was ask a few routine questions, then hole up with Deanna and Tom and Mr. Fried, like she wasn't even important.

Cat got right to the point. "Did Jerry have mail sent to this address?"

The girl flushed maroon. "You mean like fan mail and stuff?"

"No," Cat replied, gently. "I mean personal mail, correspondence that wasn't work-related."

Sondra swallowed, audibly.

"He had it sent care of your place, didn't he?"

The girl lowered her voice to a whisper, though the corridor was empty. "At the place he lived, they just have those mail slot things at the front desk and he said, like, anybody could get into his mail that way."

He did have mail sent there, though, according to Victor. Bills, bank statements, the public stuff. "If he wanted privacy, why didn't he just rent a post office box?" Cat asked.

"Jerry?" exclaimed his loving fiancee. "He's as cheap as the day is long!"

Cheap. "Then I guess he used your phone as well? For long distance." Cat spoke with certainty and it worked.

The freckles darkened against the flushed cheeks. "I know he woulda paid me back. Jerry was hitting the station up for a big raise when they signed the new contracts in January and Mr. Fried said the new station owner said to okay whatever they wanted."

"It was all set then?"

"Uh huh."

"I guess Tom decided to take a pass on the Philly offer."

Du Bois examined her typewriter keys.

"Tom didn't tell Jerry about Philly One Oh Four. I know that for a fact." Cat knew no such thing.

Du Bois caved, nonetheless. "The guy from Philly called and left a message for Tom and I didn't think it was fair for him to be going behind Jerry's back like that."

"I don't suppose you mentioned this to the police."

"They didn't ask."

"Did they ask you about Jerry's papers or phone calls?"

Miss Du Bois shook her russet head, indignantly. "They just ast what went on here at the station and did Jerry have fights with anyone and how could they get in touch with Deanna, like she was more important, so why should I go out of my way?"

"I think you were the most important person in Jerry's life," Cat soothed. "He didn't trust Deanna with his personal belongings, did he?"

"You mean like that box and the bank book and stuff? He said in January we were gonna make it a joint account."

Cat could hear her pulse hammering in her eardrums. *Go slowly,* she told herself. "A nest egg," she said, thickly. "Do you have any idea how much was in it?"

"No, I just left it in the file. I don't think Jerry would want me to pry; he trusted me."

Cat swallowed. "Sometimes a reporter can get a better picture of someone through his personal effects. Papers, correspondence, that sort of thing. Would you mind if I went through the things Jerry kept at your place?"

Cat had managed the deferential tone one directed toward

next of kin and felt a twinge of discomfort that the girl was so easily taken in. Jerry had chosen his ally well.

"Look, my place is about four blocks from here, on South Bridge Road. Champagne Manor. Apartment Nine." Sondra reached under her desk for her purse. "I don't get off for lunch until twelve-fifteen, so why don't you let yourself in and look at whatever your want?" She held up a ring of keys by a pink rabbit's foot. "There's a file cabinet in the coat closet. Jerry's stuff is in a folder and there's a box on the top shelf that was his, too, all taped up."

"You never opened it?"

"Jerry said not to."

Jerry's dead, Cat wanted to say; instead she just took the keys and prayed no one would try to sell this poor, gullible girl the Longport Bridge.


Champagne Manor was a brick longhouse with a flat, white roof and white numbered doors at twenty foot intervals. One front window per apartment, one parking space. Cat parked in the one with a 9 painted in the center and let herself into the unit.

The living-dining area was carpeted in pale green, matching fiberglass curtains at the windows, two decades old and badly frayed. The furniture was upholstered in a cotton jungle print. Tables were glass ovals on pitted chrome, a glass étagere securing a paperweight collection, a stack of fashion magazines on the floor, one of Jerry's publicity stills in a frame that had cost money.

The coat closet had sliding pine doors. Inside, Cat saw a spring coat, a denim jacket, two cardigans, a metal file cabinet and, on the shelf above, a wool hat, two umbrellas and a brown cardboard box, secured with packaging tape.

Cat threw aside her jacket and purse, pulled open a file drawer. "Jerry's Stuff" was filed under J. Cat pulled out a thick folder and sat on the floor. A couple letters. A copy of Noreen's birth certificate, Noreen Maria Dudvornicek, born to Jerzy and Agnes Noreen Dudvornicek, nee Dunn.

("... find a record of a divorce," Ron had said. "Jerzy and a Noreen Dudvornicek.")

"Not *a* Noreen, Cat realized. *A.* Noreen. Why was this starting to ring a bell?

Bank statements!

There were more than a dozen of them, dispatched from a Delaware savings and loan to JD Productions, Inc, care of a Somers Point PO box. Monthly deposits, twenty-five hundred each. Cat tore a sheet of paper from her notepad, scribbled down the bank's phone number, the account number, wondered if she could pass herself off over the phone as a secretary from "JD Productions." A few black-and-white photos of a woman who resembled Noreen: Mrs. Dudvornicek, when she was younger, happier. Nothing else.

Cat jammed the folder back into place, walked her fingers to the Ps where she correctly guessed Miss Du Bois had filed the phone bills. Long distance calls were a few 1-900 numbers and periodic calls to Raleigh, North Carolina, the most recent being a week before Jerry's death. Cat wrote the number down, stuffed it into her pocket and got to her feet.

She tugged the cardboard box from the shelf, knelt and hacked at the layers of tape with the apartment key. Under some shredded newspaper were a stack of manila envelopes, several audiocassettes, a dozen labeled video cassettes, CD disks. Cat opened one of the envelopes, spilled out several eight-by-ten glossies. A prominent attorney embracing a blonde, her back to the camera. (His businesswoman wife was a frequently-photographed brunette.) A Mercedes sedan with personalized plates and the logo of an obscure motel reflected on the car's highly polished trunk. A memo to Tom that Philly 104 had called. And an Eyes Only to Tom from Barry Fried saying he'd spoken to Philly, was Tom going to sign the new contract "or what?" A Xeroxed obit from *The Press*, Christopher Michael Austen, 36, the grainy press photo above it. Cat had a flashback to Jerry brandishing that toy gun, firing at his temple, realized it had been a deliberate attempt to rattle her. A copy of her grades from that last semester of college, right before she had dropped out. He couldn't even submit to an interview with a small-scale freelancer without digging around for some dirt that might give him the upper hand.

Cat picked up one of the videocassettes. It was addressed to the managing editor of *The Press*. Cat checked the other labels: editors, a couple TV program directors, a New York shock jock who did some late night public access cable. She scuttled over to the TV and shoved a cassette into the VCR, turned on the set, pushed the PLAY button. Fast-forward, fast-forward. A much younger, less blonde Whitney Rocap and an anonymous man were going for the gold in sexual gymnastics.

Cat rewound the tape, shoved it into the jacket. She put everything back except the videos; those she locked in the trunk of her car, then drove back to KRZI and returned Miss Du Bois' keys, was reminded that 'Du Bois' had an upper case D *and* B.

"Tommy just came in, I think he's talking to Mr. Fried about taking some time off; he looks sick. Do you want to wait around for him?"

"No thanks, I can call if I need anything more from him."

Cat headed home. Okay, so Jerry was a blackmailer. Now Jerry's a dead blackmailer. Who? *Find the 'why' and you'll nail the 'who,'* her instincts told her.


Ellice and Mats were playing CandyLand. Mats couldn't understand why Uncle Freddy was always saying Ellice was so great at games when she lost at CandyLand every time. There she was, stuck in the Molasses Swamp again and he was three spaces from the Gingerbread House. Hah!

Cat checked her watch. Eleven-fifteen. A little voice suggested she call Victor, but Cat swatted it away and offered the players lunch at McDonald's. "Ellice, you shouldn't l-e-t h-i-m w-i-n."

Ellice grinned. "Not like there's any money riding on it."

"Anybody call?"

"Nope."

"I just need to make two phone calls and I'm done for today."


Lewiston Savings and Loan bought the "Miss Cates from JD Productions, Inc.," told her that her boss had twenty-five thousand, was he still planning to turn it into CD's? "Can I get back to you on that?" Cat parried, hung up and tried the Raleigh number that had shown up on the long distance bill.

"Hopper residence." "Residence" was uttered with equal emphasis on the first and third syllables, the cadence genteel Dixie.

*Hopper. Of course! Tom was from North Carolina.*

"Is this Mrs. Hopper?" Cat asked. *Why would Jerry have made secret calls to Tom's father?*

"No, ma'am, this is the housekeeper. May I ask who's callin'?"

"My name is Mrs. Austen. I'm calling long distance from New Jersey. Is Mrs. Hopper at home?"

"One moment, ma'am."

The second voice had the same sway, but was more youthful, assured. "Mrs. Austen, this is Brianne Hopper. How can I help you?"

"I'm a friend of Tom's." *Keep talking,* Cat ordered herself. "I've been, uh, working on a magazine article about Tom and his partner."

"Oh, Lordy, wasn't that the creepiest thing? It really shook my Tommy up an' he didn't even know this guy Jerry, even though they spoke on the phone. Chipper sounded real shook up when he called, and my Tommy wanted him to come home for a spell, but I think Chipper wanted to be there for the funeral."

"Chipper?" Cat repeated, faintly.

"Oh, Tommy's always called him that, you know like when they say chip off the old block? Chipper's an only child."

"I understand . . ."

"Did y'all want a quote or something? I mean, my Tommy's been kinda under the weather; he can't come to the phone."

"No, I was just doing a background check and I'd like to ask you a few questions if I may."

"I guess it's okay."

"I hope this doesn't offend you, but I was wondering if you knew Tom's—Chipper's mother?"

"Oh, why honey, that was before I was born, practically! Can you believe it, Chipper's older'n I am. An' Tommy doesn't like to talk about his other marriages much."

"There were two."

"Yeah. One when he was young and wild, the family got that one annulled. She was a teenager, pretty as a picture and crazy as a loon, Tommy said once. That's why they split up, she was nuts. Then he married Irene Dowling, and that lasted about eighteen years."

Cat's stomach was slowly constricting. "I was wondering . . . do you happen to know what her maiden name was? Mr. Hopper's first wife?"

"Oh, lemme see . . . it started with a D, too."

"Dunn?" Cat suggested.

"That's right. Aggie Dunn."

Agnes Noreen Dunn Dudvornicek. *Tom's mother!*

"Do you happen to know the last time your husband spoke to—Chipper—before his partner's death?"

"Oh, Lordy, it musta been that morning he called Chipper early, tried to catch him before work. He was taking the plane to New York, said he could stop over in Atlantic City and meet Chipper for lunch. But he didn't get to talk to Chip and he got so upset with that girl, he had to take a heart pill and the doctor wouldn't let him fly after all."

"What girl?"

"I don't know, Chipper's girlfriend, maybe. Tommy shooed me outta the room an' I heard him yellin' something about that guy Jerry an' a pair of con artists and then it got real quiet for about ten minutes an' when I went back in, Tommy'd hung up an' he was just sitting there on the bed, like he'd seen a ghost."

"Or talked to one," Cat murmured.

"Huh?"

"Nothing."

"Say, would you like a picture or something? My Tommy's got a real cute one of him and Chipper when Chip was a teenager, won that target shooting trophy at the club. Chip's wearin' one of those little hats with the ear flaps an' all."

Cat cleared her throat. "A gun club?"

"Uh huh. Chip's a crack shot."

"I'll let you know about the picture." Cat stuttered. "I really appreciate your time, Mrs. Hopper." Cat promised to give their love to Chipper and hung up.

She dialed Victor's office. Adane told her that the lieutenant had signed out for the morning, would Cat like to leave a message? Cat said no, hung up, got a drink of water and went downstairs to take Mats and Ellice to lunch.

While Cat had been rummaging through the box in Miss Du Bois' apartment, Mrs. Dudvornicek's psychiatrist was explaining to Victor why he could allow an interview only in the presence of a social worker. The employee in question was a Miss Carolann Rose who was determined to impress the handsome lieutenant with her efficiency. She spoke to the patient gently for several minutes before introducing Victor.

"You're not Chipper," the woman stated, bluntly.

Victor took it for a comment upon his appearance, then recalled Cat's information: Chipper was a proper name.

"No, Chipper couldn't come today," he replied, gently.

"Chipper never comes," the woman pouted. "You look like the man who married us, Chipper's dad and me. He had a face like yours."

"Where were you married?"

"In Taxco. That's Mexico. I was sixteen and he was almost thirty. His family didn't like it, they said I was just after his money. That wasn't it."

"I believe you," Victor soothed.

"Chipper was born there. Then he brought me back to Carolina and they put me in a hospital. Said I tried to hurt Chipper. I never tried to hurt Chipper." The dull eyes brightened in agitation. Miss Rose caught Victor's eye and shook her head.

"Where is Chipper now?"

"Inside the radio!" The woman seemed exasperated with Victor's stupidity. "Jerry argued and wheedled, but I never told him, neither did Mr. D. He said he'd figure it out and he did!" The woman cackled at the thought of Jerry's malicious ingenuity. "He brought me the radio to prove it. They're right in there, together!"

"Jerry and Chipper?"

"Of course Jerry and Chipper!"

"Does Chipper have another name, Mrs. Dudvornicek?"

"Of course Chipper's got another name! Who would name their baby Chipper? It's Tommy, like his Dad. Thomas Hopper, the third."

# CHAPTER
## SEVENTEEN

Cat showed Mats how to make vampire fangs by dipping two shoestring fries into ketchup, tucking them under her lip, over her incisors. Mats thought there was nothing his mother couldn't do.

"Ellice, do you remember *Titus Andronicus?*"

Ellice took the last bite of her triple cheeseburger. "We did a scene from it, junior year, advanced lit. I was Tamora and this white kid named Hughie, ears stuck out to here and couldn't have weighed ninety pounds, he was Aaron. You should've heard him say, 'Oft I have digged up dead men from their graves and set them upright at their dear friends doors,' in his squeaky, Mickey Mouse voice. The kid who was directing the scene wanted to do the part where Lavinia gets r-a-p-e-d by the two brothers, and they do you-know-what so she can't rat them out. Vice principal shot that down."

"Lavinia . . ." Cat murmured, thinking of Ellice.

"What's the matter, honey?"

"From now on, I'm going to be perfectly happy to be Ritchie's entertainment girl. Too much snooping around, you start to suffer from, what was that line from Wallace Stevens? The something of seeing things too well?"

"Fatality. 'The fatality of seeing things too well.' "

"Oh, yeah. I forgot."


"It's a common delusion," the social worker told Victor as she walked him out. "A face on the television, a voice on the radio, they can get fixed on it. Of course, we try to monitor what they see and hear." She sneaked a glance at Victor's left hand. "Mrs. Dudvornicek's son—"

"Jerry Dudek?"

"Yes. He brought her a radio as a present, oh, over a year ago. It was the first time we knew she had a son living. Mr. D. never mentioned him. He—Jerry—never came again after that one visit."

"He must have told her to tune into the show."

"Apparently. Of course, we don't allow radios to be played before eight A.M., and then, the signal doesn't always carry well."

"Does she know he's dead?"

"On, no. We told her the radio was broken and took it away. Doctor will decide when she's ready to be told."

"What about the daughter? Did she ever visit?"

Miss Rose shrugged. "Every few months or so. She'd call. It seemed like she didn't want to run into the father, but that's none of my business."

"When was she here last?"

"I believe it was Wednesday. One of the nurses said the daughter looked like she had been crying, and that Mrs. D was upset that evening. They had to sedate her."

"What about the husband?"

Miss Rose smiled. "Oh, Mr. D's the exception. Four or five times a week at least, and always with a little present. She's a lucky woman."

"I beg your pardon?"

"To have someone who loves her like that. He still sees her the way she must have been in better times. Maybe what he sees is only in his head, maybe it always has been," she sighed. "It must be wonderful to have someone so devoted to you."

Victor looked at her with appreciation. She was quite young, maybe twenty-four or so, plain, but with a pair of lovely brown eyes. Like Cat's. Victor's mind superimposed Cat's face over the social worker's earnest gaze.

"Lieutenant?"

Victor focused on Miss Rose.

"You looked strange. Anything wrong?"

"No, Miss Rose. Thank you for the observation."


"The affidavits are a little tricky sir, because the mobile home and the car both belong to Mr. Rankin."

"Emphasize probable cause and don't go to Judge Harkness unless you want a point by point on the Fourth Amendment."

"Councilman Blackwright called to remind you about the neighborhood watch meeting."

"Can't make it. Send Rice."

"Mr. Raab has scheduled a press conference regarding the Dudek matter for four. He wants you to be there."

Victor turned into Shore Memorial's parking lot. "I thought he was going to hold on that."

"The press has been rather insistent."

"Okay. Get on the warrants. I'll be back around one."

"Oh. And Mrs. Austen called."

"Did she leave a message?"

"No, sir."

"When was this?"

"A few minutes ago."

Victor thanked Adane, hung up and dialed Cat's number. The phone rang, rang, rang, rang; the answering machine kicked in. Damn.

A police officer was stationed outside Noreen's hospital room. She rose when Victor approached. "Look," she began, a little defensively, "I let the father in. I didn't think it would do any harm."

"It's okay. This way, I don't have to send someone to pick him up."

Noreen Dunn was reclining on the bed, her face the color of parchment, the eyes red-rimmed, their whites pale yellow. Dudvornicek sat in a chair beside her bed.

"Miss Dunn, I'm Lieutenant Cardenas."

Noreen nodded, weakly.

"I've just been to see your mother."

Dudvornicek eyed him icily; the massive hands clenched.

Victor ignored the tacit threat. "Miss Dunn, you have the right to have an attorney present. Is there someone you would like me to call?"

"I did it," she said, softly. "I killed Jerry."

Victor pulled a chair up to her bed, beside her glowering father. (Stepfather, he reminded himself.) "Your rights were explained to you when you were placed under arrest?"

Noreen nodded.

"You can refuse to talk to me. I could call the public defender's office, but I understood that Tom Hopper might hire private counsel for you."

Tears blurred the blue and yellow eyes. "I don't need his help. I killed Jerry."

Victor hesitated. But the doctor had told him the day before, "Don't expect her to see her day in court," so he decided to proceed, take the heat from the DA later. "You shot your brother?"

"Yes."

"Why?"

"It doesn't matter."

"From a legal standpoint, it matters very much."

"I killed Jerry." She winced, shifted uncomfortably in her bed. "Why would I say I did if I didn't?"

"To protect someone you love."

"You can't prove that."

"Perhaps not," Victor replied gently. "I can only put myself in your place and imagine what I would do."

"Some things can't be imagined."

"Or ought not to be," Victor amended. He turned to Dudvornicek. "Jerry and his mother had been estranged. He left home as soon as he legally could. Yet within the last year or so, he moves back to the area, visits her, brings her a present. A radio. As if he wanted her to pick up his show, impress her with his success."

"Success," the man spat. "At making trouble he was a success."

"Your wife may have sensed that. In any case, she still doesn't feel kindly toward him. In fact, she seems to have transferred her maternal feelings to Tom Hopper, even refers to him as her son. Her social worker says it's a common delusion."

Noreen turned her face away.

"And you never straightened her out," Victor added, quietly.

After a long, forlorn silence, Dudvornicek replied, "No. It is no delusion. When my wife is very young, she is married to Tom's father. He is a rich man and could have what he liked, and she is a very beautiful girl. Wait, I show you." Dudvornicek hiked up his threadbare overcoat, tugged his wallet out of his pocket. He handed Victor a creased black-and-white of a pale, dark-haired beauty with a face that could stop a heart in mid-beat.

Victor gazed at the photo for several seconds. "Your wife is a very beautiful woman, Mr. Dudvornicek."

The grey head nodded. He took back the photo and gazed at it, wistfully. "He is much older, and she is easy to influence. They run away to Mexico. Tom is born there. The family convinces Hopper to get an annulment; they say that she is a danger to the child. He keeps the boy. She runs away, does not take a penny from him."

"Why not?"

"So that he could not claim the child she was carrying."

"Noreen."

Dudvornicek nodded.

"And at the time of your arrest, Jerry and Noreen learned that you weren't her natural father."

"Yes."

"You had no idea Jerry intended to locate Noreen's father?"

"When I heard he left home, I was glad for my wife and girl. Good riddance. I did not know about his radio show."

"You must have seen him in the local papers, television."

"No. Newspapers are rubbish. I have no television. I have books. I read books."

Victor turned to Noreen, cleared his throat. "Jerry initiated a sexual relationship with you when you were teenagers?"

"I was fourteen, he was twelve."

"This was with your consent?"

"Not at first. I was afraid to tell. Then I found out Dad wasn't my real father; he and Mom had lied all those years. Jerry made me feel like I couldn't trust anyone but him."

"I see."

"I didn't care enough even to try to find out who my real father was, but it made Jerry crazy that something like that had been kept a secret. Then my dance scholarship came through and I had a chance to get out. Jerry didn't want me to go away, he—" her voice choked. "He said I'd be sorry for the rest of my life if I left him. The next thing I heard, he had left home himself."

"He found out who his mother's first husband had been and hooked up with the man's son, got him to move up here and introduced the two of you."

Noreen nodded. "In high school, he got rid of any boy who was interested in me. There was even a guy I worked with . . . Jerry came back to the area, moved into my building and then Danny was gone. I knew Jerry had gotten to him, got rid of him, so I didn't trust it at first when he introduced me to Tom. I kept wondering, 'what's he getting out of this?' But Tom was so nice, I let myself believe Jerry had reached a point where he didn't need to hurt anyone anymore; he got rid of it all on the air, you know what I mean? And he was famous now, too, so there were women, and he didn't need me for . . . I thought he introduced me to Tom because he wanted me to be happy, too."

"Until last week."

"Yes. We were going to tell Tom's family about our engagement over Thanksgiving, they didn't even know about me. Tom was going to break it to Jerry then, too, that he was leaving the act." She winced, shifted her position. "Then Wednesday morning, real early, he called. Tom's father. I told him Tom just left and thought I may as well introduce myself, and when he asked how Tom and I met, and I said I was Jerry's sister, he went insane. He said Jerry and I were a pair of con artists and then he said, 'Did you say Noreen Dunn?' and I said 'Yes' and his whole tone changed and he asked me how old I was and about my parents and he got all choked up and hung up on me. So I called Jerry at the station because it sounded like he'd been squeezing money out of Tom's dad somehow. He came by from work and told me everything. He had Tom's birth certificate and Mom's old marriage license from Mexico and the second one from her marriage to my—to Dad." She squeezed Dudvornicek's hand.

Victor stared out the window until he could trust himself to look at her again. "Jerry was blackmailing Tom's father?"

Noreen nodded. "He found out Mr. Hopper's second wife had been passed off as Tom's mother, brushed off his first marriage as a brief fling. Tom never had any reason to doubt it."

"Wednesday morning, Jerry told you that you and Tom were siblings. How long had he known?"

"It was," Noreen choked on the words, turned her face away. "It was why he put us together. To have the fun of . . ."

"I see." Victor bit his lip, prayed his revulsion did not show. "And if you hadn't accidentally spoken to Hopper's father last Wednesday, how long was Jerry going to keep this to himself?"

"Until the honeymoon. But then Jerry found out Tom was thinking about leaving KRZI. I don't know how he found out. Tom didn't have to sign with Philly until December seventeenth, a week before we planned to get married, Jerry said I had until then to talk Tom into staying with the Circus. If I did it, he'd keep everything he knew to himself."

"And once the contracts were signed, you would what? Disappear?"

"Jerry didn't care. He said we could go ahead with the wedding. I told him about the—the baby, and he laughed. He *laughed.*" She wrung the sheets in her slender hands. "I'm a coward and Jerry knows it. It didn't matter to him if I ran, because he still had the information. I knew he'd use it somewhere down the line. Unless he was stopped."

"Wednesday you visited your mother and father to confirm Jerry's story. Then you ran out on Tom the next morning, hid out with your father. But you turned up at CV's Thursday night."

"It was so crowded. I was afraid if I shot him in the club, I might hit someone else. Then Tom saw me, so I ran off. I hid under the Boardwalk ramp and thought I'd wait until Jerry came out."

"Wait another hour or two in the cold?"

Noreen said nothing.

"Hopper said he caught up with you outside the club, heard some commotion and told you to take off."

Noreen swallowed. "I shot Jerry, I tell you! I made sure Dad drank enough to put him out and I took the car and the gun and went to the club and killed Jerry."

"Where were you standing when you shot him?"

"Under the ramp, I said. I saw Mrs. Austen leave the club, and a minute later, Jerry came running after her. They stood arguing in the parking lot across the street and I just shot him."

"How many times did you fire?"

"Once, I think."

"Not twice?"

"Maybe twice," Noreen faltered. "Once or twice. Look, I'll sign a confession—"

Victor turned to Dudvornicek. "Noreen told you she killed Jerry?"

"She told me Jerry was dead."

"You realized your gun was missing?"

"Yes."

"You didn't report it to the police?"

"It came back."

194

"When?"

Dudvornicek glanced furtively at Noreen.

Victor sighed. "It won't work, Miss Dunn. There are too many discrepancies." He looked at her, earnestly. "I will find out the truth."

Noreen sank back against the pillows, closed her eyes. "I meant to kill Jerry," she said, softly. "And when I got a look at Mrs. Austen's notebook, I realized I didn't have much time before Jerry started telling the whole world what he knew."

"Why would he do that?"

"Fun. Because it was fun for him." She turned her mournful, blue-grey gaze on Victor. "You really don't believe that someone could be capable of such malice, do you?"

"I'm beginning to." Still, seasoned cop that he was, it was hard. "You and Hopper did meet outside the club Thursday night."

Noreen nodded. "I told him everything, told him the information on Mother's old marriage license. He called his dad from a pay phone on the boards. I can't forget the look on his face . . ."

"Go on."

"He took the gun from me and told me to go back to my dad's and call him from a pay phone the next day. I drove around a long time before I went back to Dad's. I heard the news bulletin on the car radio."

"When did you next talk to Tom?"

"Friday morning. I called him at the station. He told me to lie low while he figured out what to do. He was worried about that reporter, Spivak. I was more worried about Mrs. Austen. Jerry'd made sure she knew I was his sister, and told her about the engagement. But Tom said she was a lightweight and he could scare her off if she got too nosy."

"When did you see Tom next?"

"Sunday." A tear rolled down her cheek. "I saw what killing Jerry had done to him. Tom wouldn't even swat at a mosquito, can you believe that? And Jerry made him a murderer. He's probably laughing from the grave." She sobbed, clutched her waist in pain. "He gave me the gun back then, said he'd put a scare into Mrs. Austen and he didn't need it, the gun, to take care of the other one. Spivak. But he wasn't—wasn't thinking straight enough anymore and there was no future for us anyway, so I thought if I died, everyone would believe I killed Jerry and Tom would be free and clear. Tom told me to hang on, he would take care of everything—"

"How did he know you were planning to attempt suicide?"

"He didn't."

"You said you thought about dying and he told you to hang on."

"Last night. They let him in to see me last night."

"And he told you to hang on because he was going to take care of everything?"

"Yes."

"Take care of what? Whom?"

"You know, Spivak. And Mrs. Austen."

From mid-October to mid-May, Morningside Drive's twenty summer homes were shut up for the winter, its curbs and driveways devoid of cars, save for the Ufflanders' twin Mercedes, the Misses Nixon's thirty-year-old Chevy and Cat's Maxima.

Occasionally, a car would pull up along Beach Road, the driver cut through the dunes for a solitary stroll. But the white Merc was parked right in Cat's driveway, its driver sitting motionless behind the wheel.

Cat sighed, resignedly, cruised past her house, rounded the corner onto Beach Road, braked when her driveway was out of sight.

"What're we doin', Mom?"

Cat turned to Ellice. "Listen. I'm getting out and going over to the house. I want you to take the car, get to a phone and call Victor." Cat scribbled his numbers on a piece of junk mail. "Tell him to come over right away."

"What's up? Who's car was that?"

"I think it's Tom Hopper. He's been—upset—since Jerry's death. I told him if he wanted to talk, he should come by. I just don't want him to upset Mats, okay?"

"You're a lousy liar."

"Look, I'm not going to do anything stupid or d-a-n-g-e-r-o-u-s. Just take Mats with you and call Victor. Trust me." Cat got out of the car, leaned into the back seat. "Mats, you stay with Ellice, baby. She's gonna run an errand for me."

Cat waited for Ellice to drive off, then walked around the corner and tapped on the window of Tom's car.

He turned his harrowed gaze on her and Cat realized she had made a big mistake.

Tom got out. His blue eyes (so like Noreen's, now that Cat thought of it) were overly bright, the whites bloodshot, the face slack from sleeplessness. Cat realized how little equipped Tom had been to deal with the aftermath of Jerry's murder, how far the Six A.M. Circus had accustomed him to license without consequences.

"You shouldn't have shot at me Friday night, I was with a cop."

"I only wanted to scare you."

"You did a good job."

"Not good enough. I didn't scare you off."

"You broke into Ron's apartment—"

"He'd gotten the birth records. Sandy Du Bois told me he'd had lunch with Jerry a couple weeks ago. How do I know he wasn't in on it with Jerry?"

"Ron's just a thorough reporter, that's all. Look, Tom, you must know it's only a matter of time before the police put this all together—"

"Without Spivak's stuff, the stuff Jerry told you at the club, they've got no case—"

"Ron could tell them—"

"He never saw me through the mace."

"Deanna overheard—"

JANE RUBINO

"Deanna's got the brain power of cement."

"Mrs. Dudvornicek—"

"My mother—" Tom rubbed his forehead with a shaking hand, "is not competent."

"Well, I guess that just leaves me."

"I guess so." He grabbed Cat's elbow. "Let's do this inside."

"No."

He drew a small pistol from his coat pocket. "Inside."

"Fine."

Tom yanked her up the steps, shoved her over the threshold, ordered her to lock the door. Cat thought of her Taurus, the ammunition in a canister in the kitchen, thought of her kitchen knives. Could she get to one, drive it into flesh? Into Tom?

"Let's move toward the back of the house."

"That's not the gun that killed Jerry."

"No. Got this from the doorman at my building. No paperwork, no waiting."

"They know where the murder weapon is."

"It's November. People wear gloves."

*Not today,* Cat thought, looking at his bare hands. Not afraid of leaving prints, and that wasn't a good sign. It meant he was careless or desperate, dangerous.

She walked into the kitchen. "I already called the police, you know," she lied.

"When? An hour and a half ago, you were going through Sandy's apartment. I saw you leave KRZI, I got her to tell me everything, the dumb kid. Then you called my dad's wife, she calls me at the station, worried she said too much. So I came over here and saw you driving away, decided to wait it out. I figure with a kid in school you won't be gone too long."

"Too bad you left my key last time you were here."

"I was improvising; I got panicky."

(*"I know where you live, bitch."*)

"Whitney managed to make off with it at the station, you got it from her at the funeral."

"She was too drunk to know what she was saying, and too

198

drunk to know it was gone. What'd he have on her anyway?"

"Porno."

"No kidding. Any good?"

Cat shrugged.

"Yeah, well doin' Spivak spooked me," Tom said, thought-fully. "And I didn't expect your roomie to walk in on me; I ran. Hasn't been easy to get you or this place alone, Cat; I've been try-ing for days."

Cat informed God that if she lived through this, she would never gripe about large, meddlesome families again. She glanced at the clock, calculated how long she had until Jane's school bus drove up. Glanced at the knives on the kitchen counter, at Tom. No, she couldn't do it. She had time. *Try to hold out until Ellice gets to a phone.* "Your Mercedes," Cat said to Tom. "Now that's a really nice car . . ."

Victor was headed over the causeway into Ocean City, tailgating. Red brake lights flashed and Victor slammed the pedal, avoided a rear-ender by half an inch. Traffic was backing up. He heard the irritating, "dang, dang, dang" of the drawbridge bell, saw the red and white barriers lower. "Damn it! Goddammit!"

His car phone trilled. "Cat?"

"No, it's me, Ellice. Cat told me to call you."

"Where is she?"

"Home. I'm in a phone booth at the North End Market. Mats is with me—"

"Ellice, answer me: is she alone or with someone?"

"Tom Hopper. She said—"

"Just the two of them?"

"Yes. Should I go back there?"

"No! Stay where you are. Call nine one one and tell them to get a unit over there; tell them Hopper may be armed. Do it now!"

Victor revved his engine, impatiently, saw the two masts idle through the raised bridge, cursed all recreational sailors. *I'm gonna kill her*, Victor thought, his eyes fixed on the lowering bridge. *If she comes out of this alive, I'll kill her myself!*

"You did good, Cat. I thought you were just some lightweight freelancer, but you put it all together, in four days, what I go thirty-two years and don't find out." Tom was pacing, his erratic gestures flicking the gun to and fro. "We made jokes about incest on the air. And then there was our Chang and Eng routine."

"I preferred KMEN, cable news for the primal male."

"Too arcane. You gotta remember your audience, Jerry always says. Said." The gun began to tremble. Tom cradled the barrel with his free hand. Cat watched him, thought about Chris.

"I was wondering Cat, about the tapes you made at the station?"

"That pantry over there. It's my office."

"I missed it. Kinda like the purloined letter. Your notebooks in there, too?"

Cat nodded.

"Get them."

Cat rose, drew out her keys, unlocked the door.

"Nice house, by the way."

"It was an inheritance."

"No kidding? Still, taxes must be a bitch." Tom snatched the cassette Cat handed him, threw it in the microwave, nuked it.

The phone rang.

"Don't answer it."

The smoke detector got a whiff of scorched plastic; shrieked.

"I have to. People know I'm home."

The phone rang again; again. Soon her answering machine would kick in. *Please*, Cat thought. *Please.*

"All right." Tom shot the smoke detector dead quiet. "Pick it up."

Cat grabbed the receiver from the wall phone. "Hello?"

"Cat, I heard a shot, are you all right?"

"I'm fine, Freddy. It's my brother, Freddy," she told Tom.

"Get rid of him."

"What did you want Freddy?" Cat asked Victor. These days, when Freddy did call, it was a quick "How are things?" and then "Ellice around?"

"Where are you? Downstairs?"

"Yes, I think so."

"He's armed?"

"Of course."

"I want you to stay calm."

"Oh, all right."

"I said get rid of him!" Tom hissed. The gun flicked toward the phone.

"Are you in the front of the house?"

"No."

"Kitchen?"

"Uh huh. Look, I have to get off now."

"Keep him in the kitchen."

"We can but try." It was Sherlock Holmes' motto. Cat had heard that Victor was a fan of Conan Doyle. She hung up.

"You got a brother?" Tom asked.

"Six."

"Any of them ever do it to you?"

"Oh, no," Cat replied, weakly.

"Mother and father?"

"Just my mother living."

"Real thing?"

Cat nodded.

Tom clutched the revolver to his breast, his eyes clouding. "I'm in love with Noreen. What am I supposed to do about that? Sell my story to some hack TV producer? Sit in the pen, watch myself on the tube bein' played by the kid who was John Boy Walton?"

Cat swallowed. "I don't know."

"I'm not sorry for what I did to Jerry. I just didn't think there would be so much clean-up after, you know what I mean? I mean, at the Six A.M. Circus, we always . . ."

"Got away with murder," Cat said, softly.

"Can't be done. But I can get off . . ."

"Tom!"

He had tilted the gun, angling the barrel toward his chest. His index finger slid toward the trigger.

Cat sprang. She grabbed for the barrel, twisting it away from Tom's heart, the short cylinder slippery in her wet palms. *If you let go, it's over.* Her fingers crawled along the barrel, wedged beneath Tom's grasp, trying to break his hold. Tom yanked hard and the gun jerked, rotated; Cat truly did not know whose finger was on the trigger when it fired.

Still, for the result, she had only herself to blame. Hanging those cast iron skillets on the wall had been all her idea; Chris hadn't been crazy about it, but Cat thought it contrasted nicely with the textured white of the walls, and it was certainly handy. The bullet made a loud PANG against the largest one (hardly a dent, though, they didn't make cookware like *that* anymore!) and ricocheted into a lower rib on Cat's right side.

Cat stood erect for a moment. Tom hadn't sucker-punched her, had he? That hardly seemed fair. A door slammed. Or perhaps it was being thrown open. She had told Jane about that, it would scratch the trim, but of course Jane was still in school.

"Cat, Jesus, I'm sorry! I'm sorry!"

Tom eased her to the floor so she wouldn't fall. Cat thought that was very considerate of him under the circumstances and would have told him so if it hadn't hurt so much to breathe.

Someone was shouting obscenities and Cat would have sworn it was Victor, but Victor never raised his voice, never swore. Shoes crowded her floor, clumsy black shoes. Cat had told Carlo once that cops ought to wear Reeboks or Nikes and he had laughed and told her brothers and they had laughed except for Freddy who said actually it made some sense when you come to think of it. Anyway, thank God they had opted for the checkerboard linoleum. If they had gone for that expensive mosaic tile, she would never have been able to get the blood out of all that grout.

And that was Cat's last conscious thought before she decided that a little nap would be just the thing.

# CHAPTER
## EIGHTEEN

Chanting; chanting. Cat's lids lifted a drowsy half-inch; ten spare fingers were working over the jade and silver rosary Cat had given her mother last Christmas. A head leaned in, said something; the hair was dark, thinning and wire rims circled the eyes.

"Dominic?" Her parched tongue adhered to her palate. "You didn't give me last rites or anything, did you?" she asked, thickly.

"I didn't."

" 'Cause I only get one shot at that, right? I'm saving it." Cat's Catholicism, if not entirely lapsed, was sagging considerably. "Mama . . . how many rosaries you got me down for?"

Dominic grinned at his mother. "I'll go tell the others she's coming out of it."

Cat's eyes followed, stopped at a dark figure silhouetted against the window. The figure turned and she made out dark eyes, a scowling mustache, white face.

She became aware of something planted on her ribs; she groped at the covers, trying to shove it off so she could breathe. There was an IV taped to her left hand.

A firm, comfortably warm grasp circled her wrists. "It's the surgical dressing, Cat. Try not to touch it."

"Victor?"

"Right here."

". . . Isn't the recovery room . . ."

"Private room. Carlo insisted."

"Is . . . Tom okay?"

"We'll take care of Tom."

Anger slowed his monotone, punctuated each syllable.

"It wasn't his fault. Or yours."

Victor leaned over, spoke into her ear. "I love you, Cat."

"Watch it, Cardenas. They wouldn't have moved me out of recovery if they didn't think I was going to make it."

"You mean," Victor whispered in mock panic, "you're going to live?"

Cat's laugh jabbed her ribs, brought tears to her eyes.

"Sorry, love. I'm going to let you get some rest."

"Wait. Could you send Ellice in? And could I talk to her alone?"

Mrs. Fortunati rose, tucked the rosary into a pocket, shrugged. Anyone who had been shot by a frying pan was entitled to be indulged in her little whims.

Ellice crept in, drew a chair up to Cat's bedside. "I'm startin' a pool on how long you'll be in here." Her voice was shaky. "You can have in for ten bucks."

"What's it running?"

"Fifteen to twenty days."

"I'll be out in a week. You can take the ten from my wallet." Cat shifted, uncomfortably. "It doesn't feel like I thought it would. Getting shot."

"Too much TV. It's distorting our sensory reference. I read an article."

"Ellice, I need a favor. A big one."

"Shoot. Sorry, poor choice of word."

Cat smiled, faintly. "Chris's sister, Charlotte and Freddy, they're the kids' godparents, but we never got around to putting anything in the wills about legal guardians, you know? And Charlotte, well, she writes for travel magazines, she's all over the world and you know how you always put things off, like you have all the time in the world?" Cat inhaled; it hurt. "What I'm not saying so well is that if anything happens to me, I'd like you to be the one who takes care of the kids. Steve Delareto could write something up."

"Honey," Ellice took Cat's hand, gently. "You're on drugs. They put drugs in that IV."

A tear slid down Cat's temple. "I'm serious, Ellice. There's a little money put away for their educations and my family would help out."

"You name me legal guardian, they'll freak out."

"Don't be silly. Why you're just like part of the—" Cat seized her ribs; the giddy spasms erupted into giggles, pain.

Ellice shook her head, wryly. "You've got nine lives and a couple to spare. But anything happens, I'll take care of Jane and Mats like they're my own blood." She leaned down, whispered, " 'Member all those TV sitcoms, white folks adopting these orphaned black kids? Wouldn't it be a hoot, though?"

"Ouch!" Cat clung to her smarting ribs. "Stop!"

Ellice rose. "Let me bring the kids in now, okay? They need to see you."

Mats had to be told not to jump on his mother. Jane hung in the doorway, keeping her distance from the horrible possibility that her mother might be dying.

"I'm not going to die," Cat told them immediately. "But I have to stay here awhile. Ellice will take care of you and see that you get to school, and she'll bring you here to visit."

Two tears crept down Jane's cheeks. Cat held out her arms and Jane ran to her; Cat held her close, not caring that it hurt.

"Is the bullet still in you?" Mats wanted to know.

"No, sweetie, the doctor took it out."

"Where'd they put it?"

"They might have to give it to the police."

"It's *evidence*," Jane sniffled, knowingly.

Mats was crestfallen. A real used bullet would have made an impressive Show'n Tell.

"Mom's gotta rest now." Ellice drew Jane away from Cat.

"Can I stay home from school tomorrow?" Jane asked.

"No."

Jane's drawn face relaxed. Cat understood. The child had missed more than a week of school when Chris died and Cat had suffered the miscarriage. Dispensation would have meant that her mother might be dying and they just weren't telling her. But as long as she wasn't, there was something to be said for the social advantages of having a mother who had been shot. Why, Mom was practically a *hero*. At school, Jane would be treated like practically a celebrity. And wouldn't the Popular Girls be just green!

Ellice had strategically added three days onto Cat's estimate of her hospital stay, hit it right on target, ten days, and won ninety dollars.

Those ten days were an exercise in forbearance for the hospital staff. Cat had agreed with the restriction to immediate family only, but Wednesday morning, her breakfast was interrupted by a high-pitched plea, "I'm her cousin! I'm her cousin!" and Ritchie cannon-balled into the room. "You got shot! By Tommy Hopper! An' my dad wanted me to go into real estate! I'm lovin' it! I'm lovin' it!"

Barry Fried crept past the guards who were ejecting Ritchie. "Is it true? Are you gonna be okay? I mean, I'm as speechless as a bug in a vacuum cleaner. Whaddamy gonna do for my six to ten slot? It's shot to hell, you'll should excuse the expression. They keep Tommy in state, maybe I could run a hook-up from the pen, whaddaya think?"

Ellice was nearly turned away, but Cat insisted that Ellice was her sister and Ellice added, "Some of us southern Eye-talians are very dark-complected."

Sherrie entertained Cat with tales of her showgirl days. "Did I ever tell you my Julio Iglesias story, that New Year's in Miami? You oughta write this one down." Moreover, Sherrie produced a chiffon negligee, which Cat gamely donned, but her rather dour surgeon fumbled and stuttered so that Cat reverted to her plaid flannels.

Jackie Wing sneaked in on her break with a half pound box of Teuscher truffles and the two of them guiltily ate them all. Stan Rice brought Cat two dozen red roses and asked her if she knew the nurse named Jackie, the brunette with the almond eyes. Steve Delareto brought violets and tried unsuccessfully to talk Cat out of her decision to name Ellice the children's guardian; Annie brought newspapers and gossip; Mama brought trays of cookies for the entire nursing staff; Lorraine brought a squat, frowning cactus that bore an uncanny resemblance to its giver.

Carlo sneaked in one night after dinner with an Italian hoagie and a six pack of Diet Pepsi. "Babe," he said, jamming a quarter of the sandwich into his mouth. "It's the damnedest thing. This guy, Victor, he had a great record on the force, I checked him out, but there's something else I couldn't place about the guy, know what I mean? From the time I saw him in the ER. Then I started thinking, right around the time me an' Annie got married, I get called out to this shooting, 'round Rhode Island Avenue, little bodega, mom and pop place, you know? Pop took one in the chest; didn't make it. He had a teen-age son, couple little girls, Puerto Ricans, real nice family. So I kinda come around once in a while, see that she gets through the trial okay, thinkin' she might need some help to keep the kid off the streets, but no, he's a straight-A and the girls, they were cute kids. Couple years later, they sold the place, moved inland. So here's the thing. I think their name was Cardenas. And then, I'm thinkin', nah, it can't be the same family. Anyway, it's been about twenty-five, twenty-six years. Victor ever tell you anything about his folks?"

Cat sipped a Diet Pepsi, said nothing.


Victor felt uncomfortably conspicuous, standing in the main hallway of the middle school. Concentration gave an ominous caste to his expression; the youngsters headed for the bus lines looked askance at the scowling mustache, the gold shield clipped to his belt, and skirted him, warily.

"Victor!"

Jane's long, thin legs trembled visibly beneath her short denim skirt, the brown eyes were wide with trepidation. A covey of girlfriends hung back, waiting.

Victor removed the sunshades, smiled gently, and produced from behind his back a corsage of yellow rosebuds. "You haven't forgotten our date, linda? We did say Friday afternoon, didn't we?"

"Is Mom okay?"

"Excellent. We can call the hospital from my car phone if you would like to hear it for yourself."

The covey huddled, whispered.

Victor leaned down and pinned the corsage to the lapel of Jane's winter jacket. "Please allow me to carry your book bag." He offered Jane his arm.

Jane took it, beaming.

The "Windsor Castle" was billed as five scoops of ice cream, caramel sauce, whipped cream, a sprinkling of crushed toffee, crowned with slivers of white chocolate and diced maraschino cherries. Victor watched Jane tackle it with amused awe.

"Ellice an' Uncle Freddy are taking us for pizza tonight."

Victor sipped black coffee. "When I was a teenager," he said, slowly, "my father was killed."

Jane ran the spoon around the bowl, scooping up caramel.

"I have two sisters. Younger. Everybody said I was the oldest, I had to be the man of the family, be brave. But I was just a kid and it was hard."

Jane spooned a trench in the mound of whipped cream.

"I felt angry a lot because the other guys had fathers and I didn't. Sometimes I cried."

Jane concentrated on the symmetry of the excavation. "Didn't you feel like a baby?"

Victor shrugged. "I missed him, so it was okay to cry about

that. But sometimes I cried because I got scared something would happen to my mother and then we'd be left all alone."

"Sometimes . . . Mats gets scared like that."

"Then we moved, and my mother got a job. I worried a lot that she'd get hurt or get in an accident going to work. I wanted her to stay home all the time and just take care of us."

Jane nodded, slowly.

"Do you think that was selfish?"

Jane licked the caramel from her spoon. "Maybe a little."

"And then I began to wonder if my mother would get married again. I didn't want anyone coming along trying to take my father's place."

"Maybe if he was kind of nice you could sort of get used to it," Jane advised.

"I suppose," he conceded, repressing a smile. "But then if he went away, too, I could get hurt all over again."

"I think . . . Mats is a little worried about that."

"Well, if Mats should bring it up, you tell him that I'm not going anywhere."


Jackie Wing crept into Cat's room like a thief. "She's pretty lucid today, the DA's sending someone over to get a statement. She asked me to give you this." Jackie tucked a folded sheet of note paper into Cat's hand, scurried out.

Cat unfolded the paper.

*Dear Mrs. Austen,*

*Nurse Wing kindly agreed to get this past the guard. I owe you the truth and I don't believe I will live to tell it to you face to face. If I had courage, I would have killed Jerry years ago. But I am a coward. I brought the gun to CV's and made sure Tommy saw me because I knew him. I knew he could do it and that once he heard the truth, he wouldn't hesitate. But I didn't realize how far he would go. Please believe that I never meant any harm to come to Mr. Spivak or you or your family.*

*Jerry destroyed me, but maybe it's not too late for Tom if someone would help him. I love him, you see.*

*Nurse Wing says you have a brother who's a priest. Would he come to see me, do you think?*

Noreen Dunn

Dominic came to Cat's room later that night, sat down by her bed. "She's at peace," he said.

"Peace," Cat echoed. "Peace costs too damn much."

Victor had sent flowers, fragrant white lilac, flame-colored roses, red and white carnations. But Cat had not seen him since she woke from surgery and he had told her that he loved her.

Perhaps she had been mistaken. A middle-aged widow with two kids, a meddlesome family and a knack for getting into trouble. She had been a witness in a murder case, that's all, and now that it was turned over to the DA, he would go back to his life and she would resume hers, that safe, sane life that had been two years under construction. Why did it seem so dull all of a sudden? Maybe security was overrated. Maybe it did cost too damn much.

Cat was scheduled to be released the day after Thanksgiving. Jackie Wing worked an early shift on the holiday so that she could get off at three and have dinner with her son. "So maybe he's got the holiday off, he'll come by during the day for a change." She slipped a thermometer into Cat's mouth.

"Moo?"

"What? Who? That guy, the detective. You know, tall, dark and a little too serious for me?" The thermometer beeped and Jackie withdrew it. "Normal."

"You mean Lieutenant Cardenas?" Cat asked.

"Uh huh. What is it with him?"

"He was here?"

"*Was* here. Cat, he's been here every night since you were admitted." She fit a blood pressure cuff onto Cat's left arm. "You must be a sound sleeper; what're they giving you?"

"Halcion, I think."

"Well, that'll do it. He's been coming in around eleven every night, just sits in that chair. Mary Morales says it gives her the creeps. Just sits a couple hours and leaves. One-sixty over one-twenty, it's up there a little. They'll start bringing in breakfast in a couple minutes, you need anything?"

"No . . . no."

"Well, Happy Thanksgiving."


The first night had been hard. He looked at Cat, her eyes closed, her hair black against the white pillow and saw Marisol, Marisol's face, growing whiter, thinner, until he believed it would dissolve altogether, only her frail impression left upon the sheets.

"Forgive me, *querido*," she had pleaded, her voice down to a whisper. "I never gave you our children. I thought there would be time. Always waiting for the right time, that's no way to live. Promise me you won't live like that. Promise me you'll be happy."

"*Te prometo*," Victor had lied.

Life had not ended. The will to survive had betrayed him and then one day the pain was gone and the laughter with it, and because he owed it to Marisol, he tried to get on with his life.

And there had been the cheery casino nurse and the libidinous bartender and the addled caterer and even a twenty-two-year-old student teacher who "just happened to drop by" during his last visit to his mother. No sooner had this prim, Catholic *latina* taken a chair than Victor's mother scuttled off on some forgotten errand. "*Veinte dos años, mamacita, por Dios!*" he had exploded when the girl finally departed.

And then there was Cat.

Victor knew the address. The house was a compact brick home on a narrow lot on Richmond Avenue. There were bright green shutters, a small, concrete porch enclosed in white wrought iron, a plaster of Paris Madonna hovering over the birdbath on the lawn.

Mrs. Fortunati came to the door, wearing an apron and wielding a slotted spoon. "I'm cooking," she greeted, not at all surprised to have him drop in. "You come in have something to eat."

She led him into her kitchen, a fragrant green and white refuge with bold afternoon sunlight pouring through the west windows. She resumed her task, plopping lumps of soft dough into hot oil. "You like *zeppole?*"

"Yes." The aroma was seductive, hot and sugary.

"Cat, she likes 'em, they don't feed you so good in the hospital." She lifted a golden lump from the oil, drained it on brown paper, dropped it into a bag of sugar and shook it. She set it on a plate in front of Victor.

"Reminds me of *bunuelos.*"

Jennie poured Victor a cup of coffee, turned off the electric skillet and sat opposite him. "Cat, she came home from the hospital today."

"I know."

"Victor, you wanna lissen to an old lady?"

"No, but I'll listen to you."

Jennie laughed. "I got married, I'm a young girl in my teens. My Carlo, he sees me, he talks to my father, I like the idea, we got married, that's how we did it then. We were married forty years, may he rest in peace." She crossed herself. "And when you love someone and they die, some of that hurt, it's never gonna go away. But you get to a point where you gotta say 'I'm gonna live' or 'I'm gonna die.' You wanna die, die and get it over with. You're gonna live, you get on with it. Now Cat, she had a bad time; Chris, he was a good man." She crossed herself. "But she's trying to get on with it. So what about you, Victor?"

Victor was silent for a long time. "Those family dinners, you do that every single Sunday?"

Jennie laughed, slapped his hand.

"It happened too fast with Cat," Victor said, soberly. "I wasn't ready for anyone and neither was she."

"Victor, I'm gonna give you two pieces of advice my mama gave me, a smart woman, rest in peace." She crossed herself.

"One: sometimes the best things don't wait until you're ready, they just come, ready or not."

"And what's the second?"

"When you fall in love, you're gonna be stupid, it's only natural. You just gotta try not to be more stupid than you can help."

Truer words were never spoken, he decided. Smart women must run in the family.

It was a little before five when Victor pulled into Cat's driveway. Ellice answered the door. "Hey, stranger."

"How're the kids?"

"You really got Jane's head turned around, I give you a lot of credit, Lieutenant. You here for a reason?"

"I came to see Cat."

"She hasn't been hard to find the past ten days."

"Don't give me a hard time, okay Ellice?"

"She's not here."

"She just got out of the hospital today."

"Would I lie to a cop?"

"Where is she, then?"

Ellice hesitated. "Try the beach. She went for a walk."

Victor turned; Ellice caught his arm. "Cat's the only real friend I got. You turn out to be a jerk, I'll slit your throat from ear to ear."

"Sicilians," Victor observed. "They do get into your blood, don't they?"

Ellice smiled, ruefully, jerked her chin eastward. "Cut through the dune path and make a right. She can't have gone far."

Victor bounded down the steps, crossed the street, followed the narrow path through the dunes.

The beach was cold and deserted. A brisk wind prodded white crests onto the surface of the black ocean.

Thirty yards to the right, Cat was perched on a long, rusting pipe, two feet in diameter, a remnant of the city's latest attempt to pump sand onto its eroded beaches. Victor approached, sat beside her.

Cat glanced at him, looked back at the sky. "So, case closed?"

"No."

Cat crossed her arms over her chest. "If you had evidence that Jerry Dudek had been blackmailing someone and it was pretty racy stuff but completely unrelated to the crime, would you do the right thing and give it to the police or do the nice thing and give it to the victim?"

"The right thing."

"Oh."

"But I might be prepared to make allowances for someone who chose to do the nice thing." Then, casually. "You're shivering. Why don't we go in, check out the six o'clock news, see how Whitney Rocap's making out?"

"She makes out just fine," Cat replied, calmly.

Victor leaned close, put an arm around her. "Was it deliciously, scandalously erotic?"

Cat cocked her chin. "Off the record?"

Victor crossed his heart.

"More like acrobatic. And somewhat shy on plot. Looked like they were making it up as they rolled along."

"Well, there's something to be said for that." He nudged her face toward his, kissed her mouth.

Cat realized with a shock that his kisses were welcome, that something else was falling away, something real and cherished, but unresurrectable. "When I was born," she said, slowly, "it was quite a shock, you can imagine. After six boys. It was a difficult birth and Mama was pretty doped up, they were heavy into anesthesia then, God bless them, and when Pop told her she'd had a girl, she kept saying '*allegrezza, allegrezza*' over and over. It means happiness. Joy. It was all she could say. Of course, it was the drugs they were giving her and Pop knew that, but he was something else, my dad, and he went and put it on the birth certificate. Allegrezza Caterina Fortunati. Carlo and some of the boys from the old neighborhood took to calling me 'Alley Cat' because I had a knack for getting into scrapes, but now it's just plain old Cat."

And Victor laughed.

## A PLAGUE OF KINFOLKS   Celestine Sibley

**"One of the South's natural wonders."**
*—Pat Conroy*

A pair of distant relatives appeal to Kate Mulcay's Southern hospitality...until Kate realizes their extended visit coincides with an elaborate con game and the grisly murder of one of her neighbors.

*Also available,*
**DIRE HAPPENINGS AT SCRATCH ANKLE**

## THE HOLY INNOCENTS
### Kate Sedley

The peddler-cum-sleuth Roger the Chapman comes upon the village of Totnes—a town that's being terrorized by a marauding band of outlaws suspected of murdering two local children.

*Also available,*
**THE WEAVER'S TALE**
**THE PLYMOUTH CLOAK**
**DEATH AND THE CHAPMAN**